THE SHADOW PROPHECY

THE DARK CARNIVAL
BOOK FIVE

TRUDI JAYE

WWW.TRUDIJAYEWRITES.COM

The Shadow Prophecy is published by Star Media

Published 24 March 2017 by Star Media Ltd
Copyright © 2017 by Star Media Ltd
All rights reserved.

Cover design: PCTC Design

Hi, my name's Trudi Jaye, and I've got a secret...

A secret society, that is.

Especially designed for people like you who love reading my books, the Trudi Jaye Secret Society is a place filled with magic, laughter, and most of all… free stories.

Everyone who joins the society is given access to an ancient tome full of the stories, novellas, bonus epilogues, and deleted scenes from all the different Trudi Jaye series.

Called **The Shadow Archives,** you can access it by heading to my website and joining the secret society…

Join Trudi Jaye's Secret Society… if you dare!

www.trudijayewrites.com/shadow-archives

With thanks to my Mum.

CHAPTER 1

*C*elestine knew she was in trouble.

The morning sun was starting to heat up the rocks where she had fallen, and it would only get hotter as the day wore on. Reaching out with shaking fingers, she tried to touch her swollen ankle, just above the brown sandal. A bright burst of pain shot out from her foot, right up her leg; she jerked back, bumping against the rocks behind her. Her hand landed against the rough surface, and yet more stinging pain launched its way up her arms. The world started to spin, and her vision blurred.

Panting, she lay still for what seemed like hours until the pain ebbed away and the landscape settled back into place. Celestine tried to pull herself to sitting, but her long skirts were tangled and twisted around her legs; she couldn't drag herself up without moving her ankle, and she was afraid she might pass out if she did that again.

She cursed. When she got home, she vowed she was going to change into pants. It was just that skirts were so much lighter and cooler in the summer months. It also fit nicely with her image as the Carnival's fortune-teller.

Celestine looked down at her hands and sighed. The thin cotton gloves covering them were ripped, and blood pulsed out over the material. Her palms stung from the rather large gash on her right hand, and the smaller grazes on the left. Much good they were going to do her now. She eased the gloves off, wincing as she caught the edge of the wound.

She gently ran a finger over a graze, trying to find the little pieces of rock and dirt so she could pull them out. She had long elegant fingers, and often used her hands to create an aura of mystery during the readings she gave. Punters remembered her hands more than anything else, and now hers were all cut up. What kind of impression would scabby, grazed hands give?

Celestine snorted to herself. Some fortune-teller she was. She should have looked into her own future and avoided this whole mess from the start. She sighed and laid her hands against her chest. If only it worked that way, she would have led a much simpler life.

Not that it mattered, now anyway. She was going to die out here quite alone.

Panic rose in her chest and Celestine flicked her gaze left and right, as if a solution would pop out from behind one of the trees grouped on the far side of the rocky ravine where she'd been climbing. She was in the middle of nowhere, up some godforsaken mountain with a broken ankle and no way to get home. She'd done a fair bit of climbing over large rocks to get to this point, and there was no way she could get back down again on her own.

Even worse, she hadn't told anyone where she was going.

Even Artemis had disappeared on her. She glanced around, trying to make out her distinctive spotted fur hiding in the terrain. Usually her cat—more like a behemoth given her Savannah heritage—could be trusted to stay by her side when trouble hit. If she could have had her large comforting presence cuddled up next to her right now, she would have felt better. A rogue tear escaped down her cheek, and she angrily wiped it away.

She wasn't a quitter. This wasn't going to get the better of her.

She pulled out her mobile phone again. Zero reception. She shoved it back in the pocket of her leather jacket. At least she'd been wearing the thick leather; it had protected the top half of her body somewhat—except her hands.

Celestine lifted her skirt and looked down at her leg. The ankle was definitely swollen, and the long graze down her leg was starting to really hurt. She'd slipped on shale, then tumbled down over a large boulder and into a dried-up creek bed. Lifting one hand to the side of her head, she touched the large lump that was forming, and felt something sticky on her fingertips. She pulled her hand away; congealing blood dripped down from her fingers. For a moment, she felt woozy, and the world swayed around her.

Celestine blinked, trying to get her focus back. Her body felt heavy, and she wanted to just lay her head down and close her eyes. But despite the sick feeling in her stomach, and the way the world was ever so slightly blurry, she knew she had to stay awake.

Just at the edge of the rocks, there were flowers growing in a patch of grass under the trees. It would be lovely to lie in the shade rather than here on the rocks. Several stones were poking into her butt and it was as hard as… well, rock.

Perhaps she could crawl. Rolling over onto her stomach, she tried to come up on all fours. Pain tore up her leg, and she cried out. Waves of agony crashed over her, and she fell back to earth.

CHAPTER 2

*S*am gasped for breath, his lungs burning.

Sweat dripped down his face and his legs felt like jelly, but he pushed himself harder, making his exhausted body run through the pain. In the distance, the early morning sun was breaking over the hills. He narrowed his focus to the rocky landscape directly in front of him, ignoring the dappled light, and concentrated on putting one foot in front of the other.

The hills behind the camp were the perfect running track. The physical activity didn't stop the thoughts in the middle of the night; it didn't stop him remembering what he'd done, or how many people he'd hurt. It didn't stop the blood that flowed past his eyelids when he tried to sleep. But if he ran fast enough, his nightmares faded into the sunlight, and he could at least function during the day.

Sam paused at a lookout point, his hands on his hips and his breath rasping in and out. He leaned forward for a moment, his head hanging down and his hair dangling past his eyes. He'd stopped cutting his hair and shaving a few weeks back, and now his bangs were as long as his shaggy beard. It suited his mood and hid his thoughts from the rest of the Carnival.

Far below, the striped cones of the big top rose out of the grassy field, and tiny ant-sized Carnival folk ran between the newly erected structures. He could hear the shouts from the crew bosses as they harangued and organized the workers. Travel trailers in all shapes and sizes were clustered together on the far side, and the crews were finishing the thrill rides alongside the main strip. The Ferris wheel spun slowly, glinting in the sun.

It was the first stop of the new season, and Sam didn't know what to think yet. When Jack, in his role as joint Ringmaster, had approached him, he'd agreed to tour with the Jolly Knight Carnival as their doctor—it wasn't like he had anything better to do or anywhere else to be. He owed a debt of gratitude to the Carnival folk who'd rescued him from the circus show where he'd been trapped, and he was happy to help out.

Right away Jack had assigned Sam a small trailer that could double as a clinic, almost like he was afraid Sam would change his mind. The tall, engaging Ringmaster had grinned and said it was practically the royal treatment, getting a trailer of his own.

Sam pushed his hair back off his forehead with one hand, shaking off the sweat. He didn't quite know what to make of Jack's laughing comment. His new home was a tiny, rickety space that had shuddered the entire drive down from the Compound.

The Jolly Knight Carnival was very different from anything he'd experienced before. Veronica Snow had ruled the LA show called The Experiment with an iron fist—no velvet glove—and had insisted on complete and utter obedience. Always dressed in perfect designer suits and understated gold jewelry, she'd looked harmless, or at least innocuous, at first glance. It was only after you'd irrevocably joined that you learned her true nature.

Meanwhile the Jolly Knight Carnival had two Ringmasters—the stunning and charismatic Rilla and her new husband, Jack—but they also had a ruling council, the Nine, and they often voted on important decisions. There was an openness to everyone's faces, and a tendency to speak their minds that Sam was still getting used to. Sometimes he just had to escape and be by himself, away from their honesty and frankness. It was too much after the years of solitary anguish he'd experienced at Veronica's hands.

He held his left arm across his chest and put his right one up over his forearm, stretching out the aching muscle. Yesterday, Sam had helped the Thrillmaster Viktor and the rest of the crew with the initial set up. He considered himself fit from his running, but he'd used muscles he never had before, and the weathered Thrill leader had run rings around him.

Veronica had employed a more hierarchical structure that meant the doctor—even a pet one who had to do whatever she said—didn't do any of the manual labour.

He glanced down at the blisters gathering on his hands. Despite the pain, he preferred the Jolly Knight Carnival's methods. He hadn't come from a circus background, he'd just joined The Experiment thinking it would be an adventure— and had spent the long years after he was trapped by Veronica's magic wishing he'd never made *that* decision. Dark memories tried to sneak back into his consciousness, and he clenched his fists, pushing his fingernails into his palms until the pain drove the images away.

As he gazed down at the brightly colored Carnival below, Sam admitted to himself the real reason he'd agreed to stay. If Veronica were going to emerge from whatever rock she was hiding under, it would be to exact revenge on the Jolly Knight Carnival for the death of her brother, Marco. They'd accidentally killed Veronica's beloved sibling in the process of escaping The Experiment, and despite the fact that he'd been begging to be set free from her magic to die a natural death, she wouldn't take his death lightly. He knew she was even now plotting some form of vengeance on those she held responsible.

And when she showed her face, he would be waiting.

An elephant trumpeted in the distance, and he glanced at his watch. It was time to head back down if he was going to make his meeting with Jack and Indigo. He'd promised to help with Jack's absorbing powers. He'd seen similar cases at The Experiment where someone new to a talent had struggled to restrain it. At least his time in that hellhole was going to benefit someone.

At first, he took his time over the loose shale, but the sweat was beginning to dry on his body and sending chills along his spine. He sped up, bending his knees and using the hardened muscles in his legs to keep his balance. He was about half way through the shale when he slipped, his heart pounding in his chest as he slid down the decline, his arms out wide, trying to keep to his feet.

He hit a rock and lost his balance, sprawling toward the ground. His hand reached out to break his fall, and scraped over a rock poking out between the foliage. Blood appeared instantly on his palm, and he swore.

That was what he got for not concentrating on what he was doing.

As he clambered to his feet, movement to his left made him glance up. A wild cat, some form of bobcat, or maybe a spotted panther—if such things existed—jumped down onto the path in front of him. It hissed, and he froze. Without taking his eyes off the wild animal, he moved slowly away

7

from it, trying to escape from what it obviously considered its territory.

The cat moved forward again, graceful yet deadly on all four paws. It hissed again, showing rows of sharp teeth, and Sam automatically put up his hands in a calming gesture. "It's okay. I'm not going to hurt you. I don't want to be in your territory. I'll just get out of your way," he said, trying for the soothing tone of voice he used on his most hysterical patients.

The wild cat halted and watched him intently as he edged away. He was going much farther to the right than he'd been planning for his trip down the hill, and he was going to have to do some rock climbing. But he'd do a bit of climbing any day to avoid a run-in with a wild mountain cat.

As he backed away, the cat remained motionless, tensed as if to strike, watching him with its strange, intelligent green eyes.

Once he'd determined the cat wasn't going to follow him, he let out a breath of relief. Moving carefully forward, he soon came to a ledge. He looked over the small cliff he was about to climb down—it wasn't far, maybe a five or six yards deep—and had a moment of doubt. Maybe he should go back the way he'd come? He glanced back to where the mountain cat had been, only to discover the creature had followed him, and was now standing only three yards away, the snarl back in place.

Grabbing a scraggly tree next to the ledge, Sam lowered himself over the edge. As a teenager, he'd almost lived at the local rock-climbing center, but he'd done nothing while studying or even since. His fingers clutched at the narrow outcroppings, and his feet struggled to find purchase in his running shoes. Going down was much harder than going up —when he was about a foot down the cliff, he realized he always used to abseil down the cliffs.

His entire body was shaking, but he kept going, slowly climbing down. What was the worst that would happen to him if he fell? He'd die. A part of him called out softly that perhaps it would be best if he did just let go.

All the pain and hurt would stop. The nightmares, the blood. It would all be gone.

Even if he didn't die straight away, no one would know to look for him up here. He'd die alone or perhaps with the company of a hungry bobcat. It was nothing more than he deserved.

His fingers tightened on the rocks. Today was not the day he was going to die. He had a mission, a self-appointed task to complete before he could think such thoughts.

He was going to find and kill Veronica Snow if it was the last thing he ever did. In fact he was pretty sure it was going to be the last thing he would ever do.

But that was okay.

It just meant he was going to fight a little harder to survive today.

CHAPTER 3

*S*he must have passed out for a moment or two because suddenly Artemis was there, licking her face.

Reaching up, Celestine gathered her cat to her, the creature's large body offering comfort where before she'd had none. Artemis gave a warning meow, and pulled herself away from Celestine, melting back into the shadows of the trees nearby.

"Come back, Artemis," called Celestine. Tears pushed their way up her throat again, and she struggled to hold them back. She didn't know why it was so important that she didn't cry. It wasn't as if anyone else was around. But she hadn't cried when she'd run away from her home and family; she hadn't cried through all the lonely months when she'd struggled to make her way, or even after she'd arrived at the Jolly Knight Carnival and discovered she would have to hide herself away to survive.

She'd be damned if she would cry now.

This was nothing. A mere blip on the screen. She would

figure a way out of this. As soon as her head stopped hurting, and she could think clearly again.

"Artemis," she called again.

A figure loomed overhead, on top of the very boulder she'd tumbled over. He was silhouetted against the rising sun, so all she could see was a large black outline.

He looked like Death come to gather her up.

But where was his scythe?

"Are you okay?" asked Death.

Celestine shook her head.

"Stay where you are, I'll be right there."

Celestine looked down at her ankle, and the wounds on her hands and leg. It seemed Death didn't know everything, if he thought she could go anywhere.

The landscape blurred even further, and she wondered if this was what death was really like. A gradual blurring of the focus until there was nothing more than whiteness—or perhaps blackness?—everywhere. The good thing was that the pain in her ankle and hands was losing its force. Everything seemed to be moving away, and for some reason she didn't mind. What did it matter anyway? She was alone in the world.

And then Death was there with her. At first she flinched away, her instinctual reaction when someone attempted to touch or hold her.

But then, this was Death, wasn't it? What did it matter if Death touched her?

And so she let his soothing voice calm her. Instead of immediately gathering her up against his chest—as she'd halfway expected—Death crouched down by her ankle.

"Is it just your ankle that's hurt?" he asked.

Celestine frowned. Surely he must know? He was Death. She shook her head. Held up her bleeding hands. Pulled up her skirt to show the gash on her leg, just under her knee.

The grazes over her legs. Tears started to fall as she bowed her head and showed the bloodied lump that had formed in her hair.

Death frowned, and Celestine noticed he was rather attractive, in a shaggy, unshaven kind of way. Not the skull head she'd seen in pictures at all.

"You're bleeding from that head wound. You probably feel a little light headed."

Again she nodded. Talking seemed pointless when you were dealing with Death.

"I'm going to check out your ankle first. I'll try not to hurt you."

Then he touched her leg.

Celestine screamed, and immediately everything around them went still. The world froze, like they were hanging, waiting for the next moment in time to load. Then lights sparkled across her vision, a rainbow of colors that shone as if the gods had created them. It was so beautiful, and every time Celestine saw them, she wanted to stay just here, in this place, forever.

But she never did.

She was always jerked into the next place.

She felt her body shuddering, and for a moment, pain from her ankle warred with the on-coming vision, and she thought it might not happen. Her heart leaped. This was it. The one time when the visions didn't rule her over everything else.

But then she was dragged under, and her hope died.

There was so much thick, oozing blood; it was spreading like a virus, covering the ground. There was someone talking, muttering, laughing in the background. A woman. An older woman, wearing a stained and dirty suit, holding a sleek handgun.

Celestine's heart started racing.

There was a body lying face down on the ground, at the center of that stain. Celestine knew he was dead, but she didn't know who he was, even though his face was directed toward her. The body was lying in a large warehouse space.

A train running past blocked out all sound for a moment, and time stilled. The overhead bulb shuddered with the reflected vibration.

The bulb swayed toward the corners, and Celestine saw that there were others in the room; she recognized the Ringmasters Rilla and Jack. She knew their faces because she went out of her way to avoid them in the Carnival. There was also another younger woman, and the little girl who'd joined the Carnival in the last week or so. She had an idea they were sisters. In the few times they'd met, the little girl had watched Celestine with a knowledge beyond her years.

She'd made a point of staying away from her as well.

All four of them were huddled down together at the edge of the room. Rilla had her arms around the other two younger women. They were all dusty and dirty, indicating they'd been in the large space for a while. Celestine looked around the room, trying to understand where they were. Boxes were piled high around her.

"I've been waiting a long time for this," the woman said. A gunshot rang out in the darkened room, and Celestine jerked.

Across the room, Rilla fell to the ground, a red stain spreading across her shirt.

"No!" yelled Jack.

Another shot sounded, and Jack grunted in pain as he fell forward. He didn't move.

The remaining woman screamed.

"This is what happens when you disobey me, Tilly. When you try to take what is mine away from me," the woman whispered, her voice hard.

Tears welled in the other woman's eyes—she must be Tilly. She held tight to the little girl, who didn't seem as upset. She was staring hard at the older woman holding the gun, her face a mask of determination.

"They didn't deserve to die, Veronica," said Tilly. "None of them did, not even Sam. They didn't kill Marco. I did."

"You all killed him. Every last one of you," said the woman—Veronica—her voice rising to a fevered pitch. The whites of her eyes were almost glowing in the dark room. "I will not rest until every single person in the Carnival pays for what they have done. And you and your sister are going to watch every one of them die."

The gun-toting kidnapper walked forward. "And then, when I kill you both, you will understand how I feel, the pain I must live with every day," she said. "Everything I ever did in my life was for my brother, and you took him from me."

Tilly cowered back, glancing from the crazed woman in front of her, to the little girl in her arms.

As the vision faded away, Celestine looked down at the dead man lying in a pool of his own blood. His bearded face was visible, as was the green hooded sweatshirt he wore. She didn't recognize him, but she could see his face.

She would know him if she saw him again.

CHAPTER 4

*S*am didn't know what had happened.

One minute he'd been checking her ankle, which was swollen and probably sprained, if not broken, and the next, she'd fallen back onto the ground, shuddering and shaking like she was having a seizure. Her eyes were squeezed shut, and she looked like she was in pain. He hoped she hadn't knocked her head again.

He scrambled up to her head, and pulled her eyelid open. Her eyes were fully dilated, only a tiny strip of the most unusual violet-colored iris visible. He vaguely wondered if that discoloration was part of her seizure. Did epileptic fits induce a change in eye color?

Then, just as suddenly as she started, she stopped. Her breathing returned to normal, and her body relaxed into the hard rocky ground. He hovered over her for a moment, waiting to see what happened next.

She opened her eyes. They seemed to glow for a moment in the early morning light, and he blinked.

They were mostly dark blue, but the outer rim of her iris was distinctly violet. He hadn't imagined the color.

"How are you feeling?" he asked.

The woman gazed up at him. "It was you," she whispered. Her gaze went to his chest and then back up to his face. "You're wearing the same green sweatshirt."

"Pardon me?" She was definitely concussed.

"You're not Death. But you're going to die."

Sam moved back slightly. She was hallucinating. "You're not thinking straight. We need to get you down this mountain." Maybe something was going on inside her brain. That knock to the head had seemed okay—head wounds always bled a lot—but you could never tell. He needed to get her to a hospital.

She shook her head. "You're going to die. Alongside Rilla and Jack. I saw it."

Sam stilled. Who was this woman? "What do you know about Rilla and Jack?"

"They're the leaders of the Carnival. I'm part of the sideshow." She gazed up at him with a confused expression on her face. "Are you part of the Carnival? I don't know you."

"I joined recently. I'm a doctor."

In some kind of adrenaline rush, the woman pushed herself up off the ground, and grabbed Sam by the arm. "You're treading a dangerous path. If you don't change it, you're going to die. And so are Jack and Rilla. I saw it. She had you, some woman named Veronica." The words rushed out of her, and then she sighed as if it had taken everything she had to say it. Her eyes closed and she collapsed back into a faint.

Sam only just managed to catch her before her head crashed against the rocks for a third time.

He placed her gently back down and stared at her face.

She was pale, probably from the head wound. Her hair was long, a curly reddish brown, although patches of a lighter golden red shone through when the light caught it.

She was wearing a long skirt, with a black leather jacket and a tight black T-shirt underneath. Her eyes were ringed with a dark kohl, and her nails were polished a blood red.

He didn't understand why, but he felt a strong urge to protect her. To make sure she was safe and secure.

He shook his head. He was a doctor, of course he wanted to heal her. That was what he did. He clenched his hands as a wave of misery crashed over him. At least it was supposed to be what he did.

He crouched down again, and put one hand under her shoulders and the other under her knees. The skirt bunched up around her legs, and he almost tripped on a long section that dangled down, until he hooked it over her legs.

His muscles were already crying out in pain after the run he'd put himself through and the climb down the cliff because of his encounter with the bobcat. He glanced around again. He didn't want to meet it here, especially now he had this woman to look after.

But he was soon distracted by her weight in his arms. She was tall, her long limbs probably almost a match for his own five foot eleven in height. She was perfectly proportioned— as far as he could tell—but she was heavy.

No petite, delicate flower this one.

Trying not to think about his screaming muscles, Sam concentrated on where he put his next foot as he slowly returned down the mountain. The rocky terrain wasn't that easy around this area. He skirted outcrops when he could and had to circumnavigate several large rocks that he would have just jumped down if he'd been on his own. It was taking him much longer than it had to get up. He was going to be very late for his meeting with Jack and Indigo.

She came to a while later, her wide eyes staring up at him. "Death," she said. And then fainted again.

He didn't think she was going to die from any of her

wounds, but the idea made him move a little faster. He slid a few times, but his shoes kept him steady, and the tents of the Carnival were steadily getting closer.

When he was almost to the last section of the mountain, movement in the trees twenty yards or so away caught his eye. A black and yellow cat paced silently alongside them. Sam's heart raced. It was the damn wild cat. It was keeping its distance for now, but who knew when it would decide he was a threat?

All he could do was look forward and keep going. He was gasping for breath, his legs were like jello, and he felt like he was about to collapse. Everything started to look hazy around him, and when he saw two people heading up the main path, he thought at first it was a halucination.

He blinked a few times and his bleary eyes eventually recognized Jack's tall frame. He stopped, his relief so strong he relaxed his arms; the woman's limp body started sliding toward the ground. Adrenaline rushed through his veins and he grabbed at her again, clutching her spare frame tightly against his body.

"She's hurt," he said, his throat feeling raw.

"I'll take her," said Jack as he strode up to Sam, his expression grim. "You look like death warmed over."

CHAPTER 5

*C*elestine gasped, trying to inhale. It was as if someone had taken all the oxygen in the air and replaced it with something she couldn't breathe. Her eyes felt like they were bugging out of her head, and she couldn't see. The vision of Rilla and Jack being shot right in front of her kept repeating in her head. Her fear and terror were a reflection of what the people in the room had been feeling; she knew that. But it didn't help when she was trying to come down off a vision.

A hand touched her forehead, and the vision came into focus again. The blood, the fear, the echo of the gunshot.

The death.

She cried out, trying to make it stop. The hand was removed and the visions receded.

She took another deep breath and managed to calm her thoughts. Looking up, she saw the man from the mountains crouched beside her, his expression concerned. The image of his dead, blood-spattered body lying on the ground superimposed itself in front of the reality. She put one hand up to her mouth, trying to stop herself from throwing up. It

19

didn't work. She leaned over and vomited over the side of the bed she was lying in, little chunks of her breakfast landing on his running shoes. Her body spasmed and shook.

The man crouched in front of her, watching. He moved forward, then pulled himself back as if afraid to touch her again.

"I'm fine. I just get like this sometimes," she whispered once the worst of the shaking had stopped. She wiped vomit from her face.

He nodded and handed her a tissue. "It wasn't an epileptic fit."

She shook her head. "No. Another kind. Triggered by being touched."

"Touched?" His eyes widened in alarm.

"Just on my bare skin." People thought she was eccentric, a little strange, even for circus folk. She didn't mind that label, as long as she didn't have to touch them and have visions of their future.

Movement in the back of the trailer alerted her that someone else was in the room. She felt strangely let down as if he'd lied to her or let someone else in on their secret.

"What happened up there, Celestine?" asked a voice calmly. Jack, their Ringmaster.

Celestine blinked, trying to gather her thoughts. "I went walking." She hesitated. "I took a few risks, I guess. I slipped and fell."

"Did anyone know you went out walking?" The censure in his voice was clear.

She shook her head and then winced. Her head felt like she'd been run over by a bus.

"You have a mild concussion," said the stranger.

"Who are you?" she asked.

"Sam. I'm the new doctor." He smiled, and a dimple

peeked out on one side of his face. It made him seem a lot younger.

"You're lucky Sam came past," said Jack.

Celestine didn't feel lucky. Sam had seen her having a vision, and she'd blurted it out to him. She never did that. Plus, he was a doctor. He might try to fix her. She shuddered at the idea of someone monitoring her actions. Perhaps forcing her to see the future so he could see what happened. She knew exactly what happened.

"Thank you," she said, even as she wished he hadn't been there. She looked around. "Where am I?"

"You're in my trailer, the new Carnival Clinic." Sam followed her gaze around the small room. "It still needs a bit of work."

The camper was run down; the paint was peeling and the material on the sofas was ripped and thin. "I'm sure you'll get it running just fine," she murmured.

"Do you have someone who can keep an eye on you for a while?" asked Sam.

Celestine blinked again. She knew people; she smiled at them and nodded as she set up her fortune telling tent. But would any of them miss her? Would they think to check on her? "No. Not really."

Jack shuffled slightly in the background, and Celestine winced. It was the last thing she wanted to admit in front of her boss. For some reason she thought he might try to fix that situation.

"You'll need to stay here for a while, so I can monitor the concussion. They can be tricky."

A familiar meowing outside the clinic interrupted her reply. Her hand relaxed out of its clenched position—she hadn't even realized she was worried about Artemis. There was an open window at the side of the trailer, and a large spotted shape scrambled through the opening. Artemis landed heavily on the bed, and meowed at Celestine, taking a step toward her. Then she saw Sam and Jack and hissed.

"Get back," said Sam urgently. "It must have followed me back." He grabbed a small wooden chair from beside the table.

Celestine shook her head quickly, putting her hand out to protect her cat from Sam. "Don't hurt her. It's Artemis."

At the same time, Jack moved toward Sam, grabbing the leg of the upheld chair. "It's her cat," he said. "It's fine, just a little wary of strangers."

"That's not a *cat*."

Celestine glared at Sam. "She's a Savannah, a breed that's larger than other cats."

Sam put down the chair, but didn't take his eyes off Artemis. "I saw it on the mountain when I was out running. It made me change direction. I thought I'd gotten into its territory."

Celestine smiled and reached one hand out; Artemis smooched against her. "She was helping me. She pushed you toward me." Artemis took a couple of delicate steps in Celestine's direction and then gently head butted her side, rubbing soft fur to clothes. The touch calmed her and Celestine let out a deep breath, leaning back into the pillow.

"I can't have a cat in the clinic," said Sam. "It's not hygienic."

Celestine frowned, tensing up again. First he wanted her to stay, and now he was saying she couldn't? Pushing herself up onto her elbows, Celestine tried to sit up. Artemis hissed in Sam's direction.

"What are you doing?" said Sam, moving forward, his hands reaching out. "Just lie back."

Celestine instinctively lurched back out of his way and he hesitated, hovering over her.

"I thought you wanted us out of here?" she said, confused.

"I said the cat had to go."

"If the cat goes, I go." She glared up at Sam, and Artemis smooched her face. She smoothed one hand down her soft fur and Artemis started to purr.

Sam sighed. "Fine. The cat stays."

Jack shuffled in the background. "I've said to Indigo that we'll have our meeting after lunch. Is that okay?"

Sam nodded. "I'll keep an eye on Celestine for a little bit longer, but I'll get her back to her trailer by lunchtime."

"Then I'll leave you in Sam's care, Celestine." He nodded to them both, then disappeared out the door.

The trailer suddenly seemed less crowded, as if Jack had more than just his own self inside his body and he'd taken his crowd of followers with him when he'd left. Celestine let out her breath in a rush and lay back against the pillow.

"Just rest easy here for a while. I have a few things that I have to work on in the meantime."

"When can I go back to my trailer?" she asked. "There's a show later. I have to set up my tent."

"Your tent?"

Celestine hesitated. People sometimes reacted strangely to her profession. "I'm a fortune-teller. Madame Fortune."

Sam didn't even blink. "Perhaps you can skip it today? You've got a concussion from that knock to the head."

Celestine shook her head. "I feel fine. I want to do my share." And she wanted to get out of his clinic and away from here. She didn't trust the way she felt around Sam.

"Maybe a couple more hours?" he said. "I can help you put up the tent, if you like."

Artemis purred and rubbed her head against Celestine's cheek. She did feel a little woozy still. "Okay. I'll just rest here for a while."

"Do you want the radio on?"

Celestine shook her head.

Sam stood up and moved away to do something on the other side of the clinic.

She lay there for a while, absently stroking Artemis, wondering how she'd gotten herself into this mess. She felt rather than saw Sam, like a faint buzzing on the edge of her consciousness. It made her feel twitchy and unable to sleep or rest. She wanted to blame the way she was feeling on her concussion, perhaps on the aftereffects of the fall she'd taken. But she knew that it wasn't the reason she was so on edge.

It was that every time she looked at Sam, all she could see was his dead body lying on the floor of a warehouse somewhere. She knew that was what he had coming to him. Maybe not today, and perhaps not even in a week or two weeks. But soon, this lovely, vibrant doctor who had helped her down the side of the mountain was going to die.

And she wasn't going to do a thing about it.

CHAPTER 6

"*I* have to go now," said Sam. He was standing next to Madame Fortune's draped velvet tent at one end of the sideshow section of the Carnival. There were people running back and forth around them, solving last minute problems before the Carnival opened its gates for the evening's show. The sideshow acts were lined up, creating an alleyway, all brightly lit and boasting of the wonders either inside their tents or on show outside.

Celestine's tent was a luxurious dark red with a fabric sign held up by two poles proclaiming her fortune-telling prowess across the front. An enormous eye gazed back at him from the center. Golden tassels accented the corners and entrance, which was pulled back to reveal a darkened interior.

Inside was the circular table he'd carried in from Celestine's trailer, which she'd covered in a black velvet cloth and a red and gold patterned covering. She'd placed a crystal ball in the center and some tarot cards to one side. A gas lamp glowed in the dim interior from a long, narrow side table, picking up the golden highlights in the patterned pillows that adorned the chairs. Next to the lamp, there was a skull, half in shadow, a few green and blue bottles, and a jeweled box. Red and gold beads hung in curved chains down from the side of the tent, adding another layer to the atmosphere.

A shiver ran down his spine. Was she really a fortune-teller?

When he was younger, he would have scoffed and said it wasn't possible. But he'd seen an awful lot since then. The Experiment had been filled with people who had abilities that shouldn't have existed; Veronica herself had had the power to control the people and events around her with chilling precision. The Jolly Knight Carnival also had its own magic—more subtle than Veronica's, perhaps, but just as powerful.

What if Celestine was as real as the rest of them?

She'd told him he was going to die. She'd known Veronica's name, had mentioned Jack and Rilla as well.

What if she was right?

He'd hadn't been worried about her words when they'd been up the mountain. She'd been out of her mind, raving because of the bump to her head. But now, as he stood looking at her fortune-telling tent, he began to wonder.

"Thanks for your help," said Celestine from behind him.

Sam jumped. "Uh... No worries," he said, as he turned.

She was leaning on the crutches he had loaned her from his clinic supplies and had changed into another long flowing skirt and a floaty shirt. Her hair was pulled back under a deep red scarf that was tied at the back of her head, and her dark kohl reapplied to her eyes. She looked distant, unreachable. The world's biggest cat, Artemis, curled in and around her legs. Celestine gazed up at him, a small smile on her lips.

He cleared his throat. "Just try to stay off that leg for a

while. I'm pretty sure it's not broken, but sprains can hurt almost as much."

She nodded. "I will."

Her dark blue eyes seemed to know more than they should, as if they could see into the shadows around him. He caught a glimpse of the violet that ringed the edge of her eyes. Everything about her seemed strange, not quite real or normal.

Nothing new there. He should be used to it—he'd been living outside normal for a long time now.

But all of a sudden he felt the overwhelming urge to get away from those eyes. "I'll be off then. Take care." He spun around and stalked off, managing not to look back and see if she was watching.

He barely even saw the rest of the sideshows as he strode past—he didn't slow down until he was outside the big, silver Airstream that belonged to the Ringmasters. The trailer was an older model, but it was in excellent condition with a shine on it that looked like someone had been out just that morning working on it.

He knocked, opening the door when he heard Jack's voice calling from inside. One thing he was sure of was that he could help Jack control his absorbing talent—he'd seen similar cases in his years with The Experiment. If he focused on something else, on someone else's problems, perhaps he'd regain his equilibrium.

Indigo was already there, a hot coffee in front of her at the small booth table.

"Hi," she said, lifting her cup in salute. "Heard you had an exciting morning."

Sam nodded. "Yeah, sorry about that. I know you have to get back to the Compound." He'd only met the Carnival's archivist for the first time when she'd destroyed the block Veronica had placed inside him, but he already knew he liked her. She was efficient and intelligent, and had worked under enormous pressure to protect not only Missy and the other Carnival folk, but also himself, someone she'd never met before. Outwardly she maintained a sleek and elegant persona, always dressed in perfect matching pencil skirts and delicate shirts like the ones she was wearing this morning. But he knew on the inside, she was more like a giant, over-protective teddy bear.

Indigo shook her head. "Don't worry about it. I'm not heading home till tomorrow."

Jack was at the bench, pouring another couple of coffees. "Milk? Sugar?" he said.

Sam shook his head. "Neither. Just black coffee, please."

"Hard core coffee drinker, eh?"

"It's just what I got used to at The Experiment." His hands curled into a fist. He usually tried to avoid thinking about The Experiment at all, but it felt like he'd thought of nothing else today.

"So how's Celestine?" asked Jack, as he brought the cups over to the booth and sat down.

"She's borrowing some crutches and insisted on doing today's show." He took a sip of his coffee, and his hand shook slightly. "I helped her put her tent up."

"Ah yes, Madame Fortune." Jack's voice was amused.

Sam hesitated, but he had to ask the question burning in his mind. "Is she any good at what she does? Fortune-telling?" He rubbed his palms together nervously.

Jack grinned. "World's worst fortune-teller, apparently. Given the magic we have around us, it's kind of ironic. It drives Rilla nuts, but Celestine is so lovely, we can't throw her out. No one can figure out what Abba was thinking when he took her in and let her start her act."

Sam let out the breath he'd been holding. At least he didn't have to worry about her premonitions of his death.

"What's her story?" Why would the previous Ringmaster not have told anyone more about her?

Jack nodded toward Indigo. "Indie probably knows more than me."

Indigo took a sip of her coffee. "She's been with us for maybe three years, I think." She shrugged. "Arrived one morning, looking like she hadn't eaten in a month, terrified out of her wits, and begging for a place. That enormous cat was at her side, even then."

"Why was she so scared?"

"No one knows. Abba never said and neither did she. He took her in, and despite the fact she can't tell the difference between the future and a potato, the punters love her. She knows how to put on a good show, and keep them entertained." Indigo pushed her glasses back up the bridge of her nose.

"And since then? No one has figured out why she was so scared?" Sam felt unease creeping along his body, making the hairs stand on end.

Indigo shook her head. "She keeps to herself. Wears long sleeves and gloves even in summer, and won't let people touch her." She shrugged. "Not the weirdest person here by a long shot."

Sam absorbed what Indigo had said. What had she been running from? What was her secret? He wanted to get to know Celestine better, to help her. But then he remembered those eyes that seemed to see right into his soul. Did he really want someone else to know how dark it was?

Better to put her out of his mind. He turned to Jack. "So how are the exercises going?" He'd given the Ringmaster some training techniques to help him draw his power forth in small increments. Sam had never seen an ability quite like Jack's. He could absorb the magic all around him and use it for himself. It had been misnamed blocking for a long time before Rilla had realized he wasn't just blocking their power, he was actually drawing it into himself to be used or dispersed again.

Jack cleared his throat. "I feel a little stronger. I can control the absorbing better. But I definitely think we need to keep working on it."

Sam nodded. "I have more that you can try as you go along. It's a process, a step-by-step program that you need to go through to get stronger. You can't skip any of it."

Jack leaned back and sighed, his hands linked around his coffee cup on the table. "I can get back to the same energy pool that helped me fight Hugo,"—he glanced at Sam—"the man who used curse magic to attack us last season. That's a massive step. But it's taking all my energy to hold it in, to break the next step in my absorbing power, so I don't steal everyone's magic. I'm exhausted and it's only the first week of the season." Jack's fingers tightened on the cup.

Indigo leaned forward and put one hand on Jack's arm. "I'm researching it in the Carnival library as well. We must have some record of it somewhere, a way to make it better. I'll find something else to help."

For the first time, Sam noticed the bags under Jack's eyes. "Are you sleeping?" he said.

Jack shrugged. "I'm nervous about sleeping. What if I do something while I'm asleep? My subconscious brain doesn't know I'm not supposed to absorb everything."

"What did you do at the Compound over winter?"

"It was easier there. Except for the Winter Spectacular, we weren't relying on our powers. So if I slipped up, it didn't matter."

"How many slip ups did you have?"

Jack shook his head. "Maybe three or four?"

"That's not so bad." *Not great, either.*

"It is while we're on the circuit. What if I start absorbing just as Missy and Alphonso are doing their act? Or while the rollercoaster is at the most dangerous section?"

"Neither of those examples relies totally on the magic," said Sam. He'd known Alphonso a long time; the old acrobat was talented with or without magic.

"The magic helps everything flow better. We use it to push our boundaries. Missy can do things that she would never attempt on the trapeze without the added power of our Carnival magic. If I take that away from her at the wrong moment, it could be disastrous."

"So we train harder. We keep monitoring your progress. This is just like strengthening muscles. You have to practice, do it as often as you can, and eventually you'll get stronger."

"It's the eventually part I'm worried about. I can't keep up this level of concentration forever." Jack's voice was grim, his eyes bleak.

"Then let's figure out a solution." Sam tapped a pattern on the Formica tabletop, thinking hard. "There are people around us who don't need all their power, all the time. There are certain times when they can let you have some of it, right? What if they let you absorb their magic for an hour between five o'clock and six o'clock every morning? Just before people are getting up, outside of show hours. We tell everyone what's happening, and they know they can't use their magic then."

Jack shook his head. "I don't feel comfortable taking anyone's power like that. I need to learn to control this."

Indigo put one hand on Jack's arm. "You might have to accept help here, Jack. We could have a gathering, make sure everyone is on board with it. And it wouldn't be forever. Just until you've got yourself sorted."

"I'll talk to Rilla," said Jack. His voice brooked no arguments.

"Then let's move on to our other topic," said Sam. "Veronica." His voice was harsh, but he couldn't help it.

Indigo nodded. "I've been researching her as well, trying to find a chink in her armour. There must be something in one of those old books about her powers."

"What have you found so far?" Sam leaned forward, his eyes locked on Indigo like she was a lifeline. Perhaps she was.

But she shrugged one delicate shoulder and made an apologetic face. "Nothing useful so far. Alphonso has been helpful in adding to the information you've already given me about her. Based on what you've both told me, I'm convinced she's not just going to disappear. She has an obsessive-compulsive personality that won't allow her to get over her brother's death, or even take any of the responsibility for it. In her mind, we're squarely to blame."

"To be fair, Zeph and Tilly did start the fires that killed him," said Jack drily. "We were technically to blame."

Sam shook his head. "Marco had wanted to die for a long time, he just couldn't figure out how. He was a shell of a person, artificially kept alive long after he should have died by Veronica's magic. I couldn't help him, none of us could. We were too scared of Veronica." Sam took a breath. He'd tried to defy Veronica and help Marco, but she'd caught him every time. "He wasn't living. He was stuck inside that emaciated body, unable to do anything more than look at the ceiling. Toward the end, he lost his senses. He'd given in to the madness. Veronica couldn't see it. She was keeping him alive like some sort of toy. She used him as an excuse to do the terrible things she did. That *we* did."

"She had a block on you, Sam. You had no choice," said Indigo softly.

"I should have..." Sam shook his head, trying to stop the images rushing through his head. All the people he'd helped Veronica punish. The pain. The blood. "We have to find her and destroy her. It's the only way she's going to stop being a threat to us. I want to search some of her old haunts. See if I can smoke her out into the open."

"That's like poking a stick at a bear—while playing Russian roulette," said Jack, shaking his head. "We'd end up with her even more angry at us."

"She's already as angry as it's possible to be. She's focused all her anger and grief into getting revenge for her brother's death. We *know* that. So let me hunt her down. Indigo can give me a few places to look, and we can get rid of her before she even thinks about making a move on the Carnival. No one gets hurt."

"What do you know about hunting? You're a doctor." Jack shook his head. "No. We're going to do this methodically. We're going to know everything there is to know about Veronica Snow before we're done. And we're going to crush her when we do."

The look in Jack's eyes was enough to convince Sam to pause in his arguments. The Ringmaster looked like he would take on Veronica right then and there. Sam took a calming breath. "Fine."

"We have to figure out a way to mitigate the threat she poses to us." Jack glanced between Indigo and Sam. "I'm relying on you both to find a way to neutralize her."

Sam nodded. Now that his block was gone, there was nothing stopping him from taking care of Veronica. He just had to make sure he was the first person to find her, once Indigo worked out where she was hiding. He could wait a little longer.

"I'll keep searching," said Indigo. "There must be something that will tell us where she is. So far, she's gone to ground rather successfully."

"We'll find her," said Sam. It was a promise.

CHAPTER 7

*C*elestine peered around the end of the rollercoaster sign. There was no one there. It was late; the Carnival's opening night was long-since over and the last of the punters had been ushered out the gates. Everyone else in the Carnival was snoring in their beds, sleeping off the night's activities. Overhead, an almost full moon gave enough light for Celestine to make out shapes in the darkness. Nearer the rides, the muted night-time security lights glowed. Awkwardly, she maneuvered her crutches into position and swung herself toward the rollercoaster. She pulled off her glove and touched the metal of the main thrill ride.

Nothing but good thoughts and happy vibes. Excellent.

She continued along her usual path through the rides, touching each one with her bare hand, and making sure she couldn't feel any bad futures. It was draining work, but she was determined to help in whatever way she could. She'd been horrified when she learned about all the terrible things that had been happening to the Carnival right under her nose. She'd kept herself in a bubble, protected from the rest of the world by cloaking herself from head to toe, and avoiding all possible contact.

No one had come to her because she'd cultivated her reputation of being a fake so well. They didn't think she could actually help.

She was haunted by the thought that she could have saved Abba, if only she'd touched his arm in passing. She would have seen what was coming, clear as day. She knew it. He'd been so good to her, had taken her in when no one else would. She didn't even know why he'd done it. She'd never told him the truth about her powers, that she could see a person's future just by touching them skin to skin. He'd been a good man who'd understood that she was desperate and needed a place to call home.

So now she was determined to make sure the Carnival didn't experience any other mishaps. It was too little, too late —but it was better than nothing.

She finished with the thrill rides and moved over to where Alfie kept the animals. Their enclosures had been set up on the far side of the Carnival, away from all the people. The Beastmaster always insisted that the welfare of the animals came before anything else, including the comfort of the Carnival folk. She swung along on her crutches until she was in front of the first stall. Two horses moved over to her, snuffling at her pockets for the apples they'd become used to getting from her.

"Alfie would probably have a heart attack if he knew I was feeding you as well," she whispered, reaching up one hand to scratch the horse's long nose.

The horse nickered, as if to disagree.

She kept moving, the crutches making her nightly rounds slower than normal. Her arms were sore from where her skin rubbed against the old-fashioned wooden frames and her swollen ankle ached. She slowly passed all the animals, touching as many as she could to make sure they were healthy and hale.

She came to the enclosure of the trio of tamarin monkeys that Alfie had recently been given when their owner died. She paused yet again. Two of the tiny creatures had been seriously ill, and Alfie had carefully nursed them back to health using his considerable talent with animals. One reached out its fingers, and she touched it. She knew immediately that the monkey was pregnant. With twins.

"Oh, congratulations, little one," she whispered. She wondered if Alfie knew. She would have to think of a way to tell him without his realizing it.

She kept walking, gliding her fingers gently over the equipment and concentrating on the whispers of energy she received back. It all seemed normal.

Until she came to the dog enclosure.

They were a mixed group. Alfie couldn't bear the thought of only having one breed of dog, and only being able to rescue one type of animal. She'd heard him describe the circumstances in which he'd acquired every single one of the fourteen dogs that now performed in the show, from the funny little mongrel, Squirrel, to the large Samoyed-German shepherd mix, Sash, and the Great Dane, George.

Her hand touched the edge of kennels, and she was immediately hit with images of the dogs escaping, running and barking excitedly as they chased each other through the Carnival. It wasn't a disaster, but it was certainly something that would cause a problem for Alfie and his team of animal trainers.

She ran her hand along the outside of the kennels until she found it. George had been worrying at the back of his kennel, digging at the wood until it was lose and weak. It wouldn't be long before the large animal would be able to get himself out. She wasn't entirely sure how he managed to get all the other dogs out, but she was pretty sure it had something to do with their act, where George unlocked the kennels behind the back of their trainer in the ring. It got huge laughs from the audience, but it had obviously given George ideas.

Celestine stood for a few moments, contemplating her options. She put her hand out toward George, letting him sniff her hand before she scratched him behind his ear. He pushed against her, wanting more. He was a young dog, probably not even fully grown yet, despite being so large. He had floppy ears and was a beautiful grey-blue color. He was so friendly, she had never felt concerned by his size, but now she realized he had been growing faster than his trainers had given him credit for. He was too big for his bed.

She could leave it. It wasn't a disaster. When all the dogs escaped, they'd figure it out as soon as they got them all back home.

But it would take time and effort that could be better spent elsewhere. She sighed and went around to the back of the kennel, investigating the problem. A couple of boards and a few nails was all that was needed.

Fixing the hole was a start, but she would also need to sort out George's problem. He was too big for this kennel now, and it was causing him anxiety and frustration. She would have to try to let Alfie know somehow.

Celestine let out a frustrated breath of air. It was actually quite difficult to tell people their future without letting them know that was what she was doing. She'd been doing it on and off for the last few months, and while she was getting better, she still found it exasperating. Just telling them would be so much easier.

But people could never keep secrets. She'd learned that early in life. If she told even a single soul, word of her whereabouts would get out. And then her brothers would find her,

37

and her life would go back to the drudgery and constant fear that it had been before.

No.

She would find a way to talk to Alfie about it, without letting him know.

But first she had to fix George's kennel. There was an equipment van that sat alongside the animal enclosures where Alfie stored everything he might need to look after the animals in his care. That was bound to have something useful.

It didn't take long before she found a piece of particle board at about the right size and a glue gun, which would be better than the noise of hammering in nails.

George whined at her while she went to work, but she ignored him. It was for his own good. She was just finishing the last line of glue, when a noise behind her made her freeze.

"What do you think you're doing?" asked a voice.

Celestine let out a breath of air. It was Sam.

She turned slowly, holding the glue gun behind her back. Her mind searched for answers, trying to think of an explanation that would make even a modicum of sense. Nothing appeared. "I... uh..." Nope. Total blank.

Sam was wearing jeans and a shirt, but his feet were bare. His hair looked mussed with sleep. "Why are you here?" His tone was accusatory.

"I was... uh... just visiting George. I couldn't... uh... sleep." Celestine shifted nervously, gripping the glue gun tightly behind her back.

"Why were you messing around with the kennel?" He stepped forward again, trying to peer over her shoulder at what she'd been doing.

"I was saying hi to George. He gets lonely."

"I don't believe you." Sam moved quickly forward and

grabbed at her arm, pulling the glue gun out of her hand. "What's this?" He held it up in front of Celestine's face.

Celestine's brain froze and then unfroze on the truth. "George's kennel is broken. I was just trying to fix it for Alfie." She wanted to hit her forehead with her palm, she was so annoyed at the way she blurted it out. She was normally a lot more subtle than this. Something about Sam made her break all her usual rules.

"You realize that it's three o'clock in the morning, right?" He was standing close to her, his hand still wrapped around her upper arm. It wasn't tight, just a warm presence she could feel through the material of her jacket. He wasn't much more than a shadow in front of her, but she saw his eyes sparkling in the darkness. She wondered what color they were.

"I couldn't sleep. I was taking a walk."

"You know that the Carnival has been targeted by sabotage, right?"

Celestine felt her face start to flush with heat. Who did he think he was? He'd been with the Carnival for five minutes, and he was interrogating her like she was the newbie? "Look, it's fine. I wasn't doing anything. I was just heading back to bed." She tried to get him to break his grip on her arm, but he didn't let go. The crutches made everything awkward, and she struggled to maintain her balance, even as she pulled away from him.

"Let me go, or I'll scream," she said.

"Would you really? I would have thought you'd want as few people to know about your late night escapades as possible." His voice was as hard as she'd ever heard it.

Celestine shivered. "I'm not doing anything wrong! I couldn't sleep and I came out for a walk. End of story." She gave another jerk on her arm, and this time he let her go. She stumbled backwards and almost lost her balance. Sam reached out and steadied her with both hands. Without thinking, she put her bare hand up to help with her balance against his bare arm.

Straight away, everything around them went still, and Celestine cried out. She wasn't ready; she couldn't handle seeing another vision for Sam. She didn't want to see his dead body. But it didn't matter what she wanted. Lights sparkled across her visions, the rainbow of colors from the gods. Celestine sighed, reveled in the moment of happiness before she was thrust into Sam's future.

This time he was alive. Barely. He was tied to a chair, and the same woman who had shot him in her previous vision was looming over him. The rattling sound of a train shunted past, and she stood waiting for the noise to settle down. "So you thought you could take me on, did you, Sam?" She smiled, a strange lopsided affair that sent chills along Celestine's spine.

"Let the others go, Veronica. They've done nothing to you. It was all me, all my idea." Sam spoke through swollen lips; blood leaked out his mouth and down his chin. His eyes were almost completely swollen shut.

"Don't try to be heroic now, Sam. It's too little, too late. You were with me through all those years. You were by my side, helping me to gather power from those people. We decided who lived and who died. You can't escape your fate by one little moment of heroism."

Sam leaned back in the chair. "Why me? Why did you have to do that to me?" he whispered.

Veronica leaned in until her face was barely inches from Sam's. "Because you enjoyed it," she said with a smug smile.

Sam jerked as if he'd been struck. "I never enjoyed it. Not once, in all the time you had me trapped there."

"Then why didn't you leave? The block on you wasn't that strong."

"I didn't know how. I didn't know..." Sam's words trailed off, and a haunted look appeared on his face. "Could I have broken that block on my own?" he asked in a whisper.

"Of course you could have. Your magic is strong. But instead you sat back and wallowed. You wanted to stay with me."

"I didn't know. You never told me."

"You knew. Don't tell me you never knew. It was obvious to me from the moment you entered The Experiment."

"I wish I'd never attended that show."

"It's too late for regrets now, Sam. Far too late." Veronica lifted the gun, and pointed it at Sam's head.

She pulled the trigger.

Celestine jerked back into the real world, her heart racing and sweat dampening her body. Her first instinct was to wipe off the spatters of blood and gore that had exploded from Sam's body as he'd been shot. She'd lifted her hand to do just that before she realized she was safe, on the ground, her head cradled in Sam's lap. There was no blood and Sam was still alive. She let out a breath.

Sam was staring down at her, his expression unreadable. Celestine tried to sit up, but she was too weak, her arms unable to hold her weight. The vision still ricocheted around in her head, the words jumbled together, the images of Sam and Veronica caught up together. She was dizzy and disorientated. "Who's Veronica?" she asked softly. "Why does she hate you so much?"

Sam said nothing for a moment. "She's my former employer. I helped kill her brother."

Celestine nodded. "You need to watch out for her. Promise me that you will be careful, Sam." The image of Veronica pulling the trigger was burned into Celestine's mind.

"She needs to pay for what she did. I can't promise anything."

"Then you're going to die, Sam." Celestine pushed herself up again, and this time it worked. She moved so she was sitting next to Sam on the ground.

"I can't let her get away with it. There are too many people, too many lives at stake."

"That's important to you? All those people?"

"I helped her...." Sam's face was bleak.

"You were forced to help her. That's different." Celestine shut her mouth tightly as soon as she'd said the words. She knew she'd said too much, and she could see Sam had picked up on her mistake straight away.

"How could you possibly know anything about it? I've never mentioned it." Sam's eyes were focused on her like a hawk on a mouse.

Celestine wracked her brains. "Someone must have told me." She swallowed. "The rumor mill around the Carnival is pretty active." It was; she just wasn't friendly enough with anyone to be part of it.

"Jack says you're a fake fortune-teller," he said abruptly.

Celestine blinked. Indignation swirled in her chest and she wanted to tell him she was actually a damn good fortune-teller. She opened her mouth, paused, and then snapped it shut. Remembered where she was and what she was doing here.

"Yeah, that about sums me up," she said softly.

CHAPTER 8

*H*e saw the hesitation, the desire to say something else. He recognized it from his years with Veronica. But he also knew he wasn't going to get her to admit anything in the dark at three o'clock in the morning, just after she'd had some kind of seizure.

"I think we'd better get you back to your place," he said. He stood up and gathered up her crutches, which had fallen when she'd started to shake and shudder.

He put out his hand to help her up, but she shook her head. "I can do it myself," she said.

He stood with his arms crossed over his chest while she struggled to stand up. He let out an exasperated huff of breath as she tried for the third time to stand and stepped in, put his hands under her arms and pulled her to her feet.

She let out a cry of indignation and glared at him once she was standing. He shrugged. "You couldn't get up."

Every time he saw her, Celestine was doing something he didn't understand at all. Why had she been walking in the mountains early in the morning when she sprained her ankle? With a goddamned mountain cat, for crying out loud? What was she doing out at this time of night?

None of it made any sense. "I'll walk you back to your trailer," he said.

"That's okay. I'll be fine." She backed away from him on her crutches.

"It's my duty as a doctor to make sure my patient is okay," he added.

Her eyebrows came down. "What, right after you accuse them of sabotage?"

"I didn't say it was you. I just said it was suspicious."

"Which is an accusation."

Sam sighed. He didn't think she was suspicious or a threat to the Carnival. But what on Earth was she doing wandering around like this? "I'm sorry. I was concerned. Jack and Rilla have been filling me in on what has been happening around here. I guess I'm a little jumpy."

"We're all a little jumpy. No one likes it when the Carnival is attacked. But I wasn't doing anything suspicious. And I can walk myself back to my place."

Sam shrugged and continued to walk beside her as she awkwardly swung herself along on her crutches. "It's on my way."

"I thought doctors were supposed to be good listeners," she muttered.

"I've been out of the profession too long." Sam smiled. He liked it when she grumbled at him. Everyone else was on tenterhooks around him, worried about his fragile emotional state. Celestine didn't know or care about that. It made him feel a little bit normal again.

"If you're a fake fortune-teller, why did you join the Carnival?" he asked. He watched the emotions flit across her face before she controlled them. Irritation, frustration, fear.

"A girl's gotta make a living, right? I grew up on the circuit. I know the lifestyle, and I do a decent act."

"But why *this* Carnival?" Did she know and understand about the magic that swirled around them? Something in her story didn't quite add up.

She glanced at him, her eyes unreadable in the darkness. "I'd heard about Abba. People said he was a strong leader, who protected the people in his employ. And the Carnival itself is amazing."

"Did Abba live up to your expectations? Did he protect you from whatever you're running from?" Sam was taking a shot in the dark, but her quick glance told him he was right. She was hiding from someone or something. That was why she never spoke to anyone and covered herself up. She didn't want someone to recognize her.

"Abba was everything I needed and more. He was an amazing man... I miss him."

Sam caught the pain in her voice. It was the same with everyone here at the Jolly Knight Carnival. They'd loved their Ringmaster and the pain of his passing hung heavy around their necks. It made him wish he'd had a chance to meet him.

"I'm sorry I never got to know him."

Celestine nodded. "His death was a tragedy. For all of us."

They continued in silence for a few moments. It wasn't the kind he felt he had to fill; it seemed comfortable, despite everything that had just happened. Eventually they made it to her trailer, a small, old rickety number painted orange and white that needed to be attached to a car to go anywhere. There was a small lamp over her steps that offered a little light.

"Thanks for catching me," said Celestine, staring up at her door rather than at Sam.

"Look, Celestine—"

"It doesn't matter. Let's move on."

"No. I want to say this. I don't think you'd do anything to harm to Carnival. But nobody thought Christoph would do anything to harm it either. He's essentially a good man who was convinced to do something bad. I'm just trying to look out for my new family."

She glanced up at him, and he caught a flash of violet in her eyes. There seemed to be more of it than blue in that moment. He blinked. Must be the light.

"I'm part of that family too. I'm just looking out for them as well. And Christoph... He's a good man, but he's weak. He chose an outsider over the Carnival. I would never do that."

Sam paused. "Are you sure? You've got secrets that you're trying to keep, Celestine. It's as obvious as the nose on your face."

"They're not the kind of secrets that will hurt anyone but me," she whispered, her face suddenly stricken.

Instinctively, he put one hand out to touch her, but she flinched and pulled away. He hesitated then put his hand down.

"I can help you. Tell me what you're hiding from, and I'll help," he said softly. And he meant it. He wanted to save her from whatever was putting those shadows in her eyes.

"You can't help me. No one can." She turned and climbed the stairs. She didn't look back.

Sam stood looking at her closed door for a few moments, then turned back along the rows of campers to his clinic. They'd set him up with a bunk just off the main room, which was all he needed. He wasn't the kind of person to gather stuff or need more than a few changes of clothes.

In the distance, the low nighttime Carnival lights were on. The area was empty of people. There were no security guards patrolling or eyewitnesses to what Celestine had been doing. Unless... Abruptly, Sam changed direction.

He'd met Frankie a few times, and his impression of the younger man was that he probably didn't keep normal hours. Sam shrugged; he'd soon see. He knocked quietly on the door of the beat-up silver Airstream trailer, prepared for no answer. But within moments, it swung open to reveal Frankie, his hair mussed up, his eyes bloodshot, but holding a steaming mug of coffee in one hand. The younger man stared at him for a moment. "Come on in, then. If you must."

Sam hesitated, but he was here now. He would finish his mission. He entered the blue-screened haven of the agoraphobic Chancemaster.

"What do you want?" asked Frankie without preamble.

Sam appreciated that kind of straight up dealing. "I want to check the new security cameras around the animal enclosure from earlier this evening."

"What security cameras?" asked Frankie suspiciously.

"Jack told me about them. I know you had them put in," said Sam drily. "I need to see the feed around the animal pen from about a half hour ago."

"You think something happened?" Frankie's tone sharpened.

Sam shook his head. "Nothing serious. At least I don't think so."

"But you want to check anyway?"

It felt like he was betraying Celestine by not completely believing her story. But there was a mystery surrounding her that Sam felt compelled to solve, and getting more information was the best way to start. "Yes."

Frankie shrugged and turned to a large screen that held a series of black and white video images of areas around the Carnival. There were too many to keep track of for one person. "How do you even know what's going on in all of them?"

"It's essentially just a form of what they call big data. I've designed an algorithm to scrape information from all the cameras feeds as they come in. It'll alert me if anything happens that it thinks I need to see."

Sam nodded, although the technical jargon flew over his head. He'd stick to real people with real illnesses any day. "Sounds like you have it under control."

Frankie's face was blue in the darkened interior, and the eerie coloration hid whatever he thought about Sam's comment. He pressed a few keyboard buttons, and suddenly three different views of the animal enclosure popped up on the screen. Nothing was happening.

"Can you take it back about forty-five minutes?"

Frankie nodded and pressed another couple of keys.

Suddenly on the screen, Sam saw a figure trailing around the enclosure, touching everything softly with one ungloved hand. She appeared to be focusing hard, and her face was taut with concentration.

"What's she doing?" asked Frankie frowning.

"I don't know. That's what I was hoping we might figure out."

"My program should have picked her up. Movement and human forms at this time of night should have set off every alarm I have," he muttered as he typed on the keyboard. At the bottom of the screen computer code popped up in green, running in indecipherable lines across the bottom. At least to Sam. Frankie seemed to understand what it was saying. "She's been doing this for a while. Ever since we left the Compound in fact. The program decided she wasn't a threat."

"I thought you said—"

"I know what I said," snapped Frankie. "It's the damned Carnival interfering with my programming again. Damn thing won't let my machines do what they're supposed to without messing with them." Frankie pounded one fist onto the desk beside the computer, making the monitor and keyboard bounce.

Sam didn't quite understand what Frankie was talking about, but he hadn't taken his eyes off the screen, and he saw the moment Celestine touched George's kennel. He watched as she had another seizure, her body shaking uncontrollably. This one only lasted a couple of seconds, and she was able to remain standing.

She opened her eyes again and started searching for something at the back of the kennel.

What the hell was going on?

CHAPTER 9

*C*elestine looked up from shuffling her tarot cards to see who had entered her tent. She was in full Madame Fortune costume, her favorite red patterned scarf tight around her head, holding back her unruly hair and draped over her shoulder for best effect. She'd applied her usual smoky eye makeup, although the thick black kohl around her eyes was itching—she was concentrating hard on not scratching it away. It was always like this at the beginning of the season, when she wasn't as used to wearing the thick makeup.

She hesitated when she saw who had entered.

Alfie. Did he know what she'd done? She peered at him in the darkened confines of her tent, trying to see if his lined face indicated displeasure. She couldn't see anything in his expression, but the wiry Beastmaster had never sought her out before. Sam must have told him about the night before. "Hi, Alfie," she said cautiously.

"Hey, Celestine." He looked around at the draped walls of the tent, the excess of velvet and beads, and the low lamp. "This is some getup you've got here."

She smiled nervously. "Thanks."

Alfie hesitated.

Celestine tried to wait, to let Alfie say what he had to say, but she couldn't. "I don't know what Sam told you—"

Alfie frowned. "Sam? The new doctor fella?"

"You haven't talked to him this morning?"

"Nope."

"Oh." Celestine looked away, suddenly confused.

"Should I talk to him?" asked Alfie suspiciously.

"Uh. No. Definitely not. How can I help you today?" She smiled, trying to cover up her nervousness.

Alfie moved further into the tent, still taking in her elaborate mystic decorations. He looked about as uncomfortable as she felt. "I've never done this before, and I'm not sure I want to do it now. But the Carnival's been pushing me to come see you. To get a reading."

Celestine's heart dropped. This was the last thing she needed. Alfie was on the Nine, the ruling council. She couldn't let someone in charge find out about her.

Meow.

Artemis appeared in the doorway, and Alfie's face lit up. "It's been a while since I saw that cat of yours. She's a beautiful creature."

Artemis started purring, and strolled over to Alfie, putting one paw delicately in front of the other.

"Did you see that?" said Alfie. "That slight limp on her left front paw?"

Celestine looked down at Artemis in surprise. She shook her head and came forward, her fear of Alfie gone in the face of a possible problem with Artemis.

Alfie crouched down to pat Artemis, his gnarled hands running along her smooth fur. Artemis rubbed up against his side, but when Alfie tried to pick up her paw, and she hissed at him, backing off from his ministrations.

Alfie looked up. "Can you hold her while I check that paw?"

Sitting down on the floor next to Alfie, Celestine gathered Artemis into her lap. The cat was anxious, having now realized that its people intended something more than petting. She tried to escape, and only Celestine's strong grip kept the large cat in place. Celestine made a quick decision. The only thing that calmed Artemis down was skin contact. She was going to have to take off a glove. Holding Artemis close to her body with one hand, she managed to pull the other off quickly with her teeth. As soon as her bare skin touched Artemis, the cat stopped struggling.

Celestine glanced up to find Alfie watching her antics silently. She tried not to think about how much the perceptive animal trainer was finding out about her today.

Far too much.

But if he helped Artemis, she couldn't regret it.

Alfie reached out and smoothed one hand down Artemis's leg, the one that had been limping. He gently pulled it up and ran one hand over the soft pads underneath. "I can feel a thorn of some kind, stuck up next to one of the pads. I'm going to pull it out. The sooner that kind of thing comes out, the better."

Before she even realized what he was doing, Alfie had grabbed Artemis's leg in a firm grip, and used his other hand to pull at the thorn.

Artemis struggled, claws coming out. She scratched at Celestine's leg, although luckily she couldn't feel it through the thick-layered material of her skirt. Celestine automatically reached up to hold Artemis, to keep her from scratching Alfie, crooning to her cat the whole time. She was so focused on Artemis she didn't notice Alfie's hand still holding her cat. Her bare skin touched Alfie's hand, and Artemis immediately stopped struggling.

But it was because everything was frozen; time had paused for a moment to take stock of who she'd touched. She felt the familiar rainbow brightness surrounding her for a moment, and she let out a breath. As ever, she wished she could just stay in this calm, beautiful place a moment longer.

And then everything went wild.

The Blue Carousel, the beautiful antique carousel that was the centerpiece of the outdoors section of the Carnival, was spinning softly. Gentle music played in the background like a lullaby, and Celestine smiled. The carousel had always been her favorite place in the Jolly Knight Carnival.

Then someone screamed.

One of the barriers around the edge of the carousel broke as an enormous dolphin from the carousel leaped away from it, swimming through the air as if through water, still carrying the terrified punter who'd been on its back. One by one, the other creatures followed until the air around the carousel was filled with whales and dolphins, mermaids and giant sea horses, each with a person clinging to it. Shouts and laughter filled the air, both from those on the rides and others watching from the ground. At first it seemed wonderful, as if these people were being given an opportunity to experience their ride in free form without the structure of the carousel taking them around and around. The music played, and the creatures swam high in the air, graceful and poetic as they rode the air like it was sea currents. The air sparkled with magic, and the creatures danced through the moment as if they were made for it.

But something inside Celestine chilled. Her hands curled into tight fists, and her gaze was locked onto the scene. She felt like she was made of stone, she was so tense. Something bad was going to happen, and she could do nothing about it. It was always the same. She was just a witness, forced to watch.

On the backs of the sea creatures, the people were reacting in a variety of ways, many with excitement and delight but some with screaming terror. One woman was circling up high on her whale, throwing her hands high in the air, and laughing as the sea creature did dives and spins. In the background, the sweet haunting melody of the carousel continued to play.

Last to emerge from the carousel was an enormous swan, its feathers purest white with golden tips that shimmered in the sunlight. It was the only creature not from under the sea. It wasn't usually on the carousel, so Celestine knew it must be the Gift creature, created by their connection to the Mark and designed to draw one lucky punter into the Carnival so they could attempt to grant their deepest wish.

Sitting amidst the pure white feathers of this beautiful bird was the same young girl who'd been in her first vision of Sam's death. Tilly's little sister. Her face was calm, old beyond her years, but she clung tightly to the swan. She knew something bad was going to happen as well, Celestine could see it in her face.

Into the midst of all this chaos, Alfie ran, coming to a halt under the flying animals. He waved his arms in the air, crossing them over his head and then out wide again. "Bring your animals down to the ground!" he yelled. "Get them to the ground!"

But he was too late.

The gentle music came softly to an end, almost without anyone realizing it. The motion of the animals stopped in midair. They hung suspended for a moment, and Celestine held her breath, hoping.

But then gravity found them again. They plummeted to the earth, amid the broken screams of their riders. Most of the animals broke apart on impact, their bodies fracturing and spitting out from their center, breaking apart to varying degrees depending on how high they'd been when the music stopped. The people on their backs fared no better, their bodies smashed into their rides, the cries abruptly cut off. Pieces of the shattered wooden rides flew everywhere, hitting the people on the ground, while blood and flesh from the riders who'd fallen from the greatest heights splattered across the ground.

Silence fell. Then the low moaning of the survivors stirred the breeze.

Deep red blood, messy pieces of gore, and brightly painted sections of the broken animals were everywhere. Celestine wiped at her front, convinced she had someone's blood spattered on her. She searched desperately for Alfie, and finally found him crushed beneath the whale. His usually intelligent face was slack and his lifeless eyes stared up at her.

Celestine screamed.

"Hush, hush, child. It's okay. You're okay." The soothing voice calmed her, and brought her crashing back to reality.

Celestine opened her eyes to find herself being held in Alfie's arms, as he gently rubbed her back like he would with one of his animals.

She blinked repeatedly, trying to purge the image of Alfie crushed into the ground.

"They were flying, Alfie. Flying," she whispered, unable to hold it in.

"Who were flying?"

"The carousel animals."

"Don't worry about it, child. You're back now. Everything is okay." Alfie's soothing voice secured her back into the real world more quickly than usual, and Celestine pulled herself up into a sitting position.

"Thank you," she said. "I'm okay now."

"What was that?"

"I... uh..." She couldn't think of anything to say. The flying animals from the carousel still filled her vision.

"Some kind of fit?" offered Alfie.

Celestine nodded, seizing on his answer. "Yes. Yes. I get them sometimes."

"Nothing to do with seeing the future?" he asked softly.

Celestine hesitated. "No, of course not," she said, shaking her head vehemently.

"What did you see, child?" Alfie's eyes reflected the lights from above, and for a moment, he looked wise even beyond his years.

"Um." Celestine tried to think of something, anything that might put him off the scent. She remembered the previous night's adventure. "You have little tamarin monkeys?"

Alfie nodded, never taking his eyes from her.

"You're trying to get them to breed?"

Alfie shook his head. "Not really. They've only just recovered."

Celestine nodded. "Good. Because they won't be able to get pregnant. There's something wrong with the girl. You'll have to pull in a breeding female from somewhere else, if you ever want to do that. You should probably get her checked out." She hoped that would be enough to convince Alfie that she didn't know what she was talking about. He'd learn about the little female's pregnancy and think Celestine was nuts.

Alfie stared at her. "Is that what you saw just now? My tamarin monkeys? What about the flying animals?"

"That was just a crazy dream." Celestine crossed her fingers behind her back and tried to look innocent. She widened her eyes and thought of kittens and brown paper packages tied up with string.

Alfie nodded. He got to his feet, then held out his hand to help Celestine up. She quickly pulled on her glove and extended her hand, letting him drag her to her feet.

"You need to rest. You've been working too hard." He picked up her crutches from where they lay and gave them to her.

"Thanks, Alfie. I will."

With a nod, the animal trainer stalked out the door. He paused. "I'll send you some cream for Artemis. It'll help heal her paw."

CHAPTER 10

"*I*'m telling you, we need to keep a close eye on that girl. Something's up." Alfie was pacing up and down the small aisle in Jack's trailer. Jack and Sam were sitting cooped up in the booth. They'd been practicing Jack's absorbing when the Beastmaster had stormed in. Sam shifted uncomfortably in the dinette seat as he watched Alfie turn and stalk back to them. He'd decided not to tell Jack about the video footage of Celestine walking around the Carnival the previous night. He didn't want to get her into trouble until he was sure she was doing something wrong. Alfie's rant was making him wonder if he shouldn't have just said something.

"What are you talking about, Alfie?" asked Jack calmly.

"I mean, she was totally off base about the monkeys—little Suzi's pregnant, probably with twins," Alfie continued as if Jack hadn't spoken.

"Congratulations, that's fantastic news," said Jack. He hesitated, looking from Sam to Alfie. "Isn't it?"

"Yes, yes. It's fantastic," Alfie said, nodding impatiently. "But that's not the point. She told me they'd never get preg-

58

nant, and I'd have to get another female to breed. Completely off base, but it made me go and check Suzi pretty closely, so I've found out earlier than I might have."

"So we have yet more proof that Celestine's the world's worst fortune-teller?" said Jack drily.

Even though Jack was right, Sam had to force himself not to speak out in defence of Celestine. She *was* terrible at fortune-telling. Everyone said so.

Alfie took another couple of steps. "Yes. And no. She had some kind of fit while I was there and woke up raving about the animals on the carousel flying."

Sam clenched his fist. Another fit?

"That sounds a little farfetched, even for us," said Jack.

"I'd usually agree. But I was gettin' the heebie-jeebies while she was sayin' it. I can't explain it. Part of me was convinced she was tellin' the truth." Alfie hesitated then turned to glare at Jack. "And it was like the Carnival itself was pushing me to go see her. I've never felt anythin' like it."

"But she got the monkeys wrong?"

Alfie shook his head. "I know I sound crazy. But I'm telling you, I think we need to keep an eye on her."

Jack took a deep breath. Then he looked at Sam.

"What?" said Sam suspiciously.

"She had a fit when she was up the mountain with you, as well?"

Sam nodded. "She said she gets them sometimes."

"I need you to do a complete physical on her. We can't have someone who's ill working the circuit. It could be dangerous."

Sam froze. "You're not going to throw her out, are you?" He couldn't keep the accusation out of his voice.

Jack glared at him. "I'm not Veronica, Sam," he said quietly. "Indigo is heading home today. She can take Celestine with her back to the Compound if you tell me she's not fit enough to finish the season. We take care of our own."

Sam let out the breath he'd been holding and his shoulders slumped back down. "Of course. Sorry. I just…."

"No need to explain." Jack's expression was grim. "But I do need you to check on Celestine for me right away. If Alfie says there's a problem, there's a problem."

Alfie shook his head. "I'm not sayin' send her home. But there's somethin' going on that we don't understand."

Sam nodded, relieved he was going to be the one to assess her. "I'll go now, if that's okay? If Indigo needs to leave soon, it will help to find out as soon as we can." He moved out from the bench and stood up.

"I need you to be honest in your assessment, Sam. Don't feel sorry for her or let her stay out of pity," warned Jack. "We need everyone to be in top condition for the circuit, or we're not going to make it through the season."

Sam hesitated by the door. "I'll let you know what we should do," he said, then escaped through the silver entranceway.

His mind was whirling as he stalked along the row of trailers toward Celestine's place. Did they think she was a danger to the Carnival? He knew she wasn't; at least he hoped she wasn't. That was why he'd kept quiet about the late night visits.

But maybe his judgment of people wasn't the greatest. He'd been trapped next to Veronica's side for the last ten years. That had to mess with a person's perspective. And before that, he'd trusted her enough to join The Experiment. That was the worst decision in the world.

He knocked on the door of Celestine's small trailer. He heard Artemis's meow in the background, then a murmuring from Celestine. A moment later, she opened the door, her crutches tucked under her arms.

"Hi."

"Hello." The first thing Sam noticed was the dark smudges under her eyes.

"I'm here to check on you. Make sure your leg is okay."

She stepped backward. "I'm not used to house calls from a doctor. We've gone up in the world around here."

"All part of the new service," he said as he climbed the steps in to her small space.

He indicated that she should sit on the one chair not attached to the floor, a bright yellow wooden seat with a flower-patterned pillow.

He sat down across from her, on the bench seat, and indicated she should lift up her leg. She hesitated.

"I'm a professional. I'm not going to molest you or anything." As soon as the words were out of his mouth, Sam wished he could take them back. He looked at Celestine, and his eyes caught hers. The violet at the edges seemed to burn brighter for a moment, deepening until it seemed to cover her whole iris. He held his breath.

Perhaps she did have reason to fear him because all he wanted to do was take her lips against his, to crush her beneath his body and hold her tight.

He cleared his throat.

"You know I have a thing," she said. "I don't like to be touched. That's why I wear the gloves and the long clothes. I need you to respect that."

Sam nodded, his visions of touching her body all over turning to dust as he remembered her strange quirk. "I can look at your ankle without touching it if you help me."

It was awkward, but between them, they managed to get her bandage off. The swelling had gone down a little, courtesy of the fast healing that being part of the Carnival afforded them. "It looks good. We can rebandage it for now, but you'll be able to take it off pretty soon."

"Thanks, Sam. I appreciate it."

He waited until they had the bandage firmly back in place before bringing up the other reason for his visit. "Alfie came to visit Jack."

She hesitated a beat. "He told you I had another seizure?"

"Yes. We need to talk about it." Sam paused, wondering how to say it. "Jack said you can go back to the Compound if you're not well. They'll look after you there. You don't need to force yourself through the pressure of a season if you're not well enough for it." He leaned in, about to put his hand on her arm, before he remembered. He pulled back.

"I'm fine. I feel fine." Her jaw tightened.

"You've had three seizures in the last two days. Has that ever happened before?"

She shook her head. "Not for a long time. But I can be more careful. I was taking risks by being out there alone."

"Why *were* you up the mountain?"

"You'll think I'm stupid. You'll laugh."

Sam shook his head. "No I won't."

Celestine hesitated. "I was trying to give Artemis a sense of the mountains. It's where she came from. The Savannah breed is just one step away from being wild cats."

Sam glanced over to where Artemis sat on the windowsill, her half-closed eyes focused on Celestine. "She doesn't seem that wild."

"She's not. But I was trying to let her find her wild side."

Sam felt his lips twitching. "You're right. I *am* going to laugh at you," he said, before letting a bark of laughter come out. It sounded rusty, and he realized he hadn't laughed in a long time.

Celestine smiled, the warmth in her eyes letting him know she wasn't upset. "Okay, fine. It's wasn't my best plan. What were you doing up there?"

"Running."

"More of a mountain climb than a run."

"I like to push myself. To make it harder. The incline seemed like the perfect opportunity."

"Why do you push yourself like that? Is it because of Veronica?"

As quick as that, the good humour he'd been feeling died. "What do you know about Veronica?" he asked sharply.

"I know she's going to do everything she can to destroy you."

"I'll be ready for her when the time comes."

"You'll need more than being physically fit to beat her," she said softly.

"What makes you so sure?" said Sam harshly. "You've never even met her."

"You can't make your whole life about getting revenge. You have to move on." Her violet-blue eyes were huge on her face as she watched him.

Sam ran one hand through his hair. "I can't move on. Not until she's gone. As long as she's out there, the possibility of her return haunts me." The words flowed out of his mouth almost without his permission.

"She did a number on you, that's for sure." Celestine's voice held pity.

"She forced me to stay by her side for ten goddamned years as she tortured and killed people in order to make her way to the top. She has to pay for that." His voice shook, and Sam tried to understand why he kept answering her questions with the truth. Perhaps he should be the one heading back to the Compound for the summer.

"Jack and Rilla and the Nine have it under control. You don't need to be the one who takes her on."

"*I'm* the one working with Jack to make it happen. I'm doing it because I need to be part of her downfall. I did too much. I saw too much to leave it be, Celestine. Can you understand that?" He was pleading now, trying to get her to understand why he was compelled to follow this path. There was no other option for him and his sanity.

"As I understand it, she forced you to do the things you did. You were never a willing participant."

"But that's exactly why. She took away my control for *ten years*. I couldn't be myself or do the things I thought were right. I didn't know who I was anymore. It got to the point where I didn't know what was right or wrong."

"You seem to know now."

Sam sighed. "The only thing I know for sure is that I need to stop Veronica from hurting anyone ever again. And I will do everything in my power to make that happen, which includes dying." The words came unbidden from his mouth, and Sam realized they were true.

He was going to kill Veronica, or die trying.

CHAPTER 11

"That's what's going to happen, you know. You're going to die, and she's going to win." The words hung in the air between them for a moment. Celestine held her breath, hoping it might be enough to convince him.

"You don't know that for sure." His eyes were bleak.

Celestine hesitated, wanting to keep her secrets. The image of Sam's lifeless, blood-splattered body flashed into her head and she shuddered. "I do know it," she blurted. She put one hand over her mouth in a belated attempt to stay silent. What was she doing? The only reason she'd stayed safe for so long was because she'd kept her secrets to herself.

Sam shook his head. "No one knows what will happen."

Celestine let out a tiny breath of air and took her hand away from her mouth. He didn't believe her. She could stop now and it would be okay; she could stay hidden in the Carnival.

But could she ever forgive herself if something happened to Sam, and she knew she could have prevented it? "When I touched you up the mountain, I had a vision. I saw her kill you. Then I saw it again that night by the kennels." The words hung in the air, and Celestine had the sense of her own destiny changing.

Sam leaned forward, his movement tentative. "Everyone I speak to says you're a fake, Celestine." He hesitated. "They say you never get the future right."

The air was thick around them, like something important was happening, but she didn't know what. She only knew she had to convince Sam to change his path, or he was going to die. And she knew for certain she didn't want that. "I do it on *purpose.* I tell them the opposite of what I see. I don't want anyone here to know what I can do."

"Why would you do that?" Sam's voice made his disbelief clear.

Celestine almost growled in frustration. The trouble with carefully setting up a reputation for being a fake was that everyone believed you *were* a fake. She'd gotten so good at pretending, it was second nature to her. She'd almost convinced herself that she was normal.

But she wasn't. And the visions were stronger and coming more regularly ever since she had touched Sam. She didn't seem to be able to keep her gloves on properly these days.

She let out a sigh and tried to decide what to say. Perhaps she could convince him without telling him everything.

It wasn't that she thought he'd let her secret out, at least not on purpose. But the fewer people who knew the better. If her brothers even caught a hint of a rumor about her, they'd come check it out. And as soon as they were in the same vicinity as her, they'd be able to find her using their connection. She wouldn't stand a chance. She'd almost been caught in the weeks before she arrived on Abba's doorstep, and she never wanted to feel like that again.

"I'm hiding from..." She took a breath. "No one can know

I'm here. This is the only safe place for me, and I have to pretend to be something I'm not to stay safe."

"I don't want to hurt you, Celestine." Sam reached out one hand as if to touch her then pulled it back. "But I'm not going to pretend to believe you when I don't."

Celestine stared at Sam, taking in his serious brown eyes, and the lines on his face that had etched in the pain he'd already experienced in his life. He was a good man. A worthy man. He didn't deserve to die. She took a fortifying breath. "I'm hiding from my brothers. They want me to do the full show, to touch hundreds of people every night and tell them their futures. But... I can't." She gripped her hands together tightly in her lap.

"What happens when you touch that many people?"

"It... takes something from me if I use it too much. Like I have to start using pieces of my soul to make it work. My mother..." Celestine broke off. She couldn't say the words, but the image of her mother's wild, irrational eyes filled her head; they were burned into her memory. Her mother hadn't known who she was, let alone how to tell a fortune toward the end.

Sam hesitated. "I believe you're hiding from someone, so it makes sense that it's your family," he said softly, his eyes filled with pity. "But nothing you predict ever comes true, Celestine. I'm sorry. Everyone knows it."

It hurt. She admitted that to herself. Something about Sam had made her feel they were connected, right from the start. To hear him say he didn't believe her was painful. She took a deep breath. Then let it out. Behind her, Artemis meowed. "The reason I don't like people touching me is that I get my strongest visions when I touch people skin to skin." She felt soft fur against her side and looked down to see Artemis curling her body against hers. She put her arm around the cat and smoothed one hand down her furry body.

Sam frowned. "I think that bump to your head was harder than I realized. I'm going to take you for an MRI."

Celestine let out a frustrated huff of breath. "I'm fine, Sam. I'm not making this up. I know what I saw. Veronica knows you, she knows all about you. You were with her for ten years. Don't you think that's going to help her as much as it's helping Jack and Rilla to make plans? She's not going to be easily beaten."

Sam sat back in his chair, staring at Celestine, his expression pensive. "I don't believe that you can see my future. I'm sorry. I just don't."

"Then let me touch you again, see if I can catch a vision that will prove to you that I'm telling the truth." Again, the words were out before Celestine could think better of them. Why was she so determined to prove herself to Sam?

Sam stared at her for a moment, his dark brown eyes unreadable.

He was going to say no, she could see it in his face. Celestine's insides curled in on themselves as she tried to think of another way to prove what she was saying.

"Okay," he said.

"Pardon?"

"You can touch me. See if you can find out anything useful."

For a moment, time seemed to stand still. He was giving her a chance. Sam hadn't completely given up on her. A small part of him was willing to give her the benefit of the doubt, despite what he was being told by everyone else.

Her heart leaped as she realized what his agreement meant. She was going to touch him, skin to skin. Her heart started beating faster, and she surreptitiously wiped her suddenly sweaty hands on her skirt. "It works better if I can hold both your hands in mine," she whispered. There was so much riding on this. She had to get it right.

He silently held out both his hands, watching her intently. Celestine awkwardly pulled off her gloves. After so many years of wearing them constantly, taking them off felt like she was undressing for Sam. She hadn't touched another person's skin except by accident for a long time. Holding out her suddenly trembling hands, Celestine hesitated just before touching him. Sam held his own hands motionless, waiting patiently. She took a quick breath, then lurched forward, grasping both his hands in hers. Her blood pumped through her body like she was about to leap off the side of a ravine.

Perhaps she was.

His hands were gentle in hers, and her gaze caught and held Sam's eyes. She tightened her grip, wanting to let him know how important this felt to her.

Time stopped. It hung in the air around them, and Celestine used the time to get herself under control. Bright lights flashed and sparked around her, and rainbows of color filled the air. She felt the warmth of the sun on her face, and then she was standing in the field outside the Carnival. Sam and Veronica were standing opposite each other. Veronica held a small handgun pointed at Sam's chest.

"You'll never win," said Sam.

"I already have," replied Veronica. "Everyone you hold dear is dead, and while you were unconscious, I replaced the block on you with a stronger one. You're mine again now."

Sam took a step toward Veronica, his face a mask of rage, and then he stopped. Panic and a horrible kind of fear appeared on his face. He was straining to move another step in her direction. His face went red, and veins stood out on his neck.

"There's no point trying, Sam. It's done."

"No! I won't. You can't make me do it anymore."

"Oh, but I can, Sam. You know I can." Veronica turned

and started to walk away. She turned back. "Come, Sam. We're leaving."

The raw desperation on Sam's face was enough to make Celestine cry out. But no one could hear her in that place, a future that hadn't happened yet.

Sam started moving after Veronica, his feet moving in an awkward shuffle that suggested he was struggling against every step he took. He glanced back at the Carnival behind them, as if hoping someone might see.

No one came running.

The vision ended, but Celestine went back to the rainbow brightness. She needed more than that to convince Sam. She needed something concrete, something that would happen soon, that would convince him to listen to her. For the first time ever, she tried to focus her talent. She needed a vision of the next day.

She floated into another vision. This time it was the familiar surroundings of the Carnival's main strip, in the middle of an afternoon show. Crowds of people were wandering through the area, eating popcorn, hot dogs, and candied apples, laughing and chattering as they enjoyed the Carnival atmosphere. Sam was standing with Frankie, the Chancemaster, next to a food truck selling churros. Frankie was munching on one of the long donut snacks and had a dusting of sugar around his mouth.

"We need to keep watching her. She's up to something strange," Frankie was saying.

"Alfie's worried about her too," replied Sam. "He told Jack we need to keep a watch on her."

"I'll keep monitoring the video surveillance, see if she does any more nighttime walks. And I'll have one of the kids watch her during the day, see if we can discover anything useful."

Celestine's skin tingled. They were talking about her; she

knew it. Sam thought she was a danger to the Carnival. Not only was he suspicious of her talents, he was suspicious of her, full stop. She wanted to let go of his hands, to move away from him right then. But she couldn't move while she was inside the vision.

Sam nodded absently. "It can't hurt to keep an eye on her. Just to make sure."

Frankie finished the churro and wiped his face with one hand. He pulled out a deck of cards and started flicking them in his hands, the cards blurring, they were going so fast. "The chances are good that she's hiding something. And with the way our luck's been recently, it's likely she's stirring up trouble for us."

"She'll never know we've been watching her, will she?"

"No. Joey and the other runners are subtle. And she doesn't know about the cameras around the Carnival, does she? No one else does. Jack was pretty clear on that point."

"Then we watch and wait, see what she does." Sam glanced around as if looking for someone in the crowds. His eyes settled on Celestine, staring right back at her as if he could see her even in the vision; goosebumps rose along her arms.

Frankie was nodding at Sam as the vision faded out.

The rainbow lights appeared briefly again before she returned to her shaking body. She was on the ground, lying in Sam's lap, his arms holding her steady. She blinked.

"You were shaking so badly," said Sam, his voice uneven. "It lasted longer than last time."

She stared up at him, her hazy after-vision thoughts focused on the warmth of his bare skin against hers, and the delicious feeling of lying in a man's arms. Sam's touch against her body was gentle, like she was a fragile flower he didn't want to break. He gazed down at her; this close she could see flecks of gold inside the deep brown of his eyes. She wanted to reach up and caress her fingertips across his cheek, feel his lips against her skin. She never wanted it to end.

"Are you okay?" asked Sam. His arms tightened around her.

Celestine realized she'd been staring. She blinked again and the things she'd seen came flooding back. He'd been talking about her with Frankie. Agreeing to have her followed like she was a suspect in a criminal case. It was like having a bucket of cold water thrown over her. She tried to sit up, to move away from him and get her traitorous body back under control. As soon as she moved, a huge wave of dizziness overcame her and she fell back with a moan.

Covering her eyes with one arm, she told herself that it was nothing to do with him and the safety she felt in his arms. He was going to betray her. It might not have happened yet, but it would. She just needed a few moments to recover from what was essentially the first time she'd ever had a double vision. No wonder her body was taking a while to recover.

"You need to speak, Celestine. I need to know you're okay."

She nodded slowly. "I'm fine. That was just... It took it out of me." Her voice sounded weak, even to her own ears.

Sam moved restlessly. "I'll tell Jack you're going to cancel your show today."

"No. I'm fine. This is a normal reaction. I'll be fine in a few moments." Celestine tried to control the accelerated beating of her heart, to force her body to recover faster.

"This is the fourth seizure you've had in as many days, Celestine. That's not a normal reaction."

Celestine hesitated. He really didn't believe her. He'd arranged with Frankie to watch her using secret cameras hidden around the Carnival. That was more than just not believing in her ability to see the future. He thought she might be in league with their enemies.

"I saw you with Veronica again," she whispered. "She had you outside the Carnival. She'd put a block on you again."

Panic flared in his eyes before being doused again. "You can't see the future, Celestine. Your brain is sending you crazy messages while you're having seizures. That's all."

She gritted her teeth together. "I saw you talking with Frankie about me. He was eating a churro. You saw me on the secret cameras that Jack has had placed around the Carnival," she ground out. "You arranged with him to have me watched."

Sam stared at her wide-eyed for a second or two. But then he shook his head. "I don't know how you know that, but it's not because you can see the future. I'm sorry, Celestine. I don't believe you."

CHAPTER 12

S am couldn't get the idea that Celestine knew about the cameras out of his head. It meant she was working with someone who knew more than they should, or that she was way more observant than anyone else at the Carnival... or that she really was able to see the future.

Instead of heading back to his trailer like he'd planned, he headed toward Frankie's.

"What are you doing here?" were Frankie's only words before the younger man let him in. As always, it was dark inside, lit only by the blue light of the multiple screens.

"Do you ever turn a light on in here?"

Frankie glanced back at Sam as he sat down in front of his huge monitor. "You don't like my place, you can always leave."

Sam held up his hands. "It's not that. It's just... You could hurt your eyes, living constantly in this kind of environment."

"What are you, some kind of doctor?"

"Um, yes?"

Frankie let out a bark of laughter. "Oh yeah. I forgot."

Sam peered over Frankie's shoulder as he pulled up the multiple camera monitor showing the people around the Carnival. The crowds were starting to filter in for the thrill rides and the sideshow. The actual circus performance would be later that night.

"Have you seen anything interesting?"

"Aside from the Carnival protecting your fortune-teller?" Frankie shook his head. "No."

"Do you know Celestine?"

Frankie shook his head, turning in his chair to face Sam. "Not really. I'm here most of the time, except when Jack can get me out. I don't meet a lot of new people. Except on the screen." He gestured to the computer screen behind him.

"Do you think she can tell the future?"

Frankie shrugged. "People can do all sorts of things around here. Magic's all around us. Who knows what she can do."

Sam nodded. "What about Veronica? Have you found anything through your networks yet?" He needed to think about something other than Celestine and her predictions.

Frankie shook his head. "She's gone to ground. I've searched online for her family and have only come up with an uncle she hasn't seen since she was a kid. She has no friends, no other connections aside from her brother. The Experiment is closed up and is being offered as a foreclosure sale for the land."

"Her parents are dead?"

"Her parents died in suspicious circumstances not long after her brother had his accident. Knowing what we know about her now, I'd say she killed them."

"She never talked about them. She was focused on Marco and making him better," said Sam, thinking as he spoke. "What about some of the other people in The Experiment?

Have you managed to locate any of them? Could they be helping her?"

Frankie shook his head. "They've all dispersed. She no longer had power over them, and they disappeared. From what you've told me, it was a fragile ecosystem based on fear and intimidation, not loyalty."

"Have you checked on the uncle?" asked Sam, beginning to pace in the tiny space. Nothing seemed to be going their way.

"He's part of a circus that runs a circuit down near Florida. I've done the numbers, and I think it's unlikely she'd go down there. She hasn't seen him in a long time and had a grudge against her parents. Given the way she thinks, I'm pretty sure she'd consider her mother's brother culpable somehow."

"She might go to him if she's as desperate as we think she is. Someone needs to go and check it out."

"And you want to be that someone?" asked Frankie drily.

"Who else?"

"Maybe someone who isn't focused on getting revenge? You're not thinking clearly, and she's still powerful. We don't know if she could get another block on you, especially given the amount of time you were connected to her last time. It's too dangerous."

A chill curled down Sam's spine as he recalled what Celestine had said. According to her, Veronica *did* get him back under her power. He clenched his fists. He refused to be afraid of his former captor. "I can go down there and do some recon. I won't confront her without backup."

Frankie shrugged. "You need to convince Jack, not me. But I don't think the odds are on your side in this one. You need to be careful around her."

Sam nodded. "I will. And I'm going to talk to Jack right now about going to Florida."

Frankie lifted a hand in farewell.

Sam was already halfway out the door and didn't slow down. He needed to be doing something, to have some kind of forward action in the hunt for Veronica. If this uncle was all they had, so be it.

He walked with long strides to Jack's trailer, not paying attention to anything else around him. When he banged on the door, it was Rilla who opened the door.

Sam had opened his mouth to start convincing Jack, but he closed it with a snap. He didn't know Rilla as well as Jack, and he didn't know how to approach her. "Uh... I was hoping to talk to Jack?" he said.

"He's not here. But you can talk to me instead," said Rilla. Her voice was neutral, but her eyes held an edge; she clearly wasn't used to being passed over in favour of Jack.

"Uh. Okay, sure," said Sam. He didn't want to offend her this early in the season. He climbed the steps.

"So how can I help you?" asked Rilla. She waved him to the dinette but didn't join him. Instead she leaned against the counter, one hand curled around a cup of coffee, her brilliant blue eyes focused on Sam.

Sam didn't sit. He put his hands in the pockets of his jeans, wondering about the best place the start. "I was just checking in with Frankie on Veronica's whereabouts, and he has a lead."

Rilla nodded. "The uncle in Florida?"

"Yes. I want to go down and check up on him, see if he's seen her."

"By yourself?" Rilla's eyebrows raised. "You think that's wise?"

Her sharp eyes were focused on him. She clearly knew everything that was going on in the Carnival, possibly even more so than Jack. He steeled himself. He had to convince her that he was the best person to go. "You need everyone else here."

"We need you here too."

He let out a small laugh. "Not really. The Carnival protects everyone from the worst harm, and even if something happens, you all heal quickly. Celestine had a sprained ankle two days ago, and it's almost back to normal."

"Tell me about Celestine," said Rilla, abruptly changing the topic. She took a sip of her coffee.

Sam opened his mouth to tell her he didn't want to talk about Celestine, but Rilla's expression brooked no argument. In this moment, she was the Ringmaster and he was crew. "What do you want to know?"

"Is she a real fortune-teller?"

Sam's eyes widened in surprise. Hadn't Jack said Rilla knew Celestine was a fake? "I don't think so. Everyone says she's not very accurate."

"But what's *your* assessment?"

Sam hesitated, not wanting to give in to the little tendril of doubt in his mind. "I hope she's not a real fortune-teller," he blurted. "Because every time she tells my future, it's bad."

Rilla's eyes sharpened. "What's she said?"

"First that I was going to die. Then that Veronica was going to force a block on me again." Even just the idea of it made him start to breathe faster. He'd rather die than be under Veronica's power again.

"Why would she tell you these things if she didn't believe they were going to happen?"

Sam hadn't considered that angle. "You're right. She's not mean or vindictive. I think she truly does believe she can see the future. But I think it's more likely to be something to do with her seizures; her brain is taking the things she's thinking about and turning them into these vivid visions. Everyone says she's never accurate."

Rilla nodded. "I have to admit, I've heard the same thing. Still, it doesn't hurt to be prepared. I need you to watch her closely, make sure she doesn't do anything dangerous."

"What about my trip to Florida?"

Rilla frowned. "There is no trip to Florida, Sam. Frankie needs to gather more information before we can act on that. To be honest, if someone is going to act on it, it's not going to be you. You've already suffered too much at Veronica's hands. I can't risk sending you off after her just to be captured again."

"I wouldn't—"

"Sam, that's my decision. When Frankie finds out more, we'll revisit. For now, I need you to keep an eye on Celestine."

Sam snapped his jaws together. His hands clenched into fists, but he managed to nod and turn away from Rilla, leaving the trailer without spilling any of the anger and rage he was feeling.

There was no way they could keep him here if he didn't want to stay.

CHAPTER 13

*L*aughter bubbled in the alleyways between the sideshow acts. Punters were everywhere, going in and out of the stalls and sideshow tents. Celestine waited patiently in her darkened tent for her next visitor, the low light from the one lamp creating shadows in the corners and making the room glow red. The dangled beads glinted as they swayed in reaction to the movement of people outside.

She was in her full regalia. Scarf over her head, long flowing dress with another floaty shirt layered over it, and a shawl around her shoulders. Rings adorned her fingers, and bracelets jangled up her arms. A heavy layer of kohl surrounded her eyes, and smoky eye shadow made her seem otherworldly. At least that was the look she was going for when she put it on in the mirror.

In front of her on the table were her crystal ball and a deck of tarot cards. She didn't need either to see the future, but they were the expected tools of the trade. She picked up the cards and started shuffling them absently. In a business like this, it was about giving the punters what they wanted, rather than giving them the unvarnished truth.

While she waited, she thought about Sam. She admitted to herself that she was hurt he still thought she could be a part of a plot to harm the Carnival. It was upsetting to realize he thought so little of her.

Her hands gripped the tarot cards. She had to remember that he hadn't known her for very long, and he'd just been released from what was essentially indentured servitude to a woman who was unhinged. Of course he was suspicious of everyone.

He'd been through so much. She kept thinking of her vision and the terrified expression on his face when he'd realized Veronica had him under her power again. Her hand clenched. She was determined to save him from the future she'd seen. She would get him off the collision course he was on with Veronica—she just didn't know how yet.

She leaned down and grabbed her water bottle from under the table. Her hand trembled as she held the bottle to her lips. The two visions she'd had while touching Sam had taken it out of her; she still felt queasy and shaky.

But it didn't mean she wasn't going to do her part.

The tent flap was pulled aside, and Celestine looked up, keeping her face unsmiling. She always aimed for mysterious and all-knowing, and that didn't involve being too friendly.

The figure who appeared was familiar. "Sam," she said. "What are you doing here?"

For a moment he looked wild, his eyes reflecting the red glow from the lamp beside her. Emotions skittered across his face, and she thought she could see fear, anger, frustration, and uncertainty, before it was gone, and he was hidden behind his usual mask. "I just saw Rilla, and she wanted me to check on you. Make sure you're up for doing a show."

It looked like Rilla had talked to him about something else as well, given his reactions, but she just nodded and gestured for him to come further into the tent. "I feel fine."

"Then why is your hand shaking?"

"Just a little residual side effect. It'll be fine."

"You don't need to go through with the show today. Rilla is happy for you to sit it out."

Celestine shook her head. "You don't understand. I *need* the show as much as I want to do it." It was a delicate balance —too much and she'd end up crazy like her mother, overwhelmed by the multiple futures she was seeing all around her; too little and she'd feel like she was about to explode with the sheer pressure of the futures trapped inside her.

Sam frowned. "What are you talking about?"

"I get... I don't know, feedback, I suppose you'd call it, if I don't use my talent. If I go too long without using it, I get worse than this." She held up her hand; it was still shaking from her earlier reading.

"That's not normal, Celestine." Sam took several steps into the tent, his eyes on her hand. "I think I need to get a scan done on you. The next stop has a hospital. I'm going to call ahead and book an MRI." He lifted his gaze to her face.

Celestine put her water bottle down abruptly, frowning. "No, Sam. I'm not unwell." She stood, and walked around the table. "This is just part of my gift, I promise. I feel perfectly fine." Holding out her hands, she tried to give the impression of being in top health. It was difficult when she was tired and sore and shaky.

Sam narrowed his eyes at her. "You need to take care of yourself, Celestine. Seizures can be serious."

"Stay and watch to make sure if you want." She gestured behind her. "There's another room back there with a viewing hole through to this room."

He raised his eyebrows. "Who usually uses that?"

Celestine shrugged one shoulder. "It's an old tent. It used to be my mother's. Family members would watch and protect her while she worked." Images of her father and then her well-muscled brothers standing behind that viewing hole filled her with a familiar shaky panic. They'd watched her mother like a hawk, monitoring her every movement, pushing her even when she was too tired, forcing her to keep going. They'd bullied her every moment of her life, and she'd had no choice but to do what they said. It was no wonder her mother had been the way she was.

"To protect her?"

"So they said." Celestine shrugged, taking a breath to calm her jittery anxiety.

"And you don't need the same protection?"

"I never have, no. My mother didn't need it either." Celestine bit her lip, aware she was telling Sam far too much about herself.

"I'll hide behind here and monitor you. If I see you getting tired, I'm going to come out and cancel your show," he warned.

"I'll be fine."

Just as Sam closed the curtain, someone pulled aside the front opening of the tent. This time it was two pretty teenaged girls, both wearing brightly colored shorts and T-shirts, giggling and egging each other on.

Celestine sighed. It was a common sight. "Welcome to my sanctuary. Please, sit." Her voice low and commanding, she gestured to the chairs on the other side of her table.

The girls sat, nervously glancing at each other. "We want to know if Bernie is going to ask Julia on a date," said the girl with curly brown hair and cute freckles, giggling at her friend.

A wave of intense emotion rolled over Celestine, and at first she didn't know where it was coming from. She clenched her hands together in her lap. It was stronger than anything she'd ever felt when doing readings. She'd always experienced a kind of low-level hum of emotion emanating from customers that helped her to expand and create a reading. But this was strong and specific. The girl—Julia—didn't like Bernie, but she was pretending for the sake of her friend. The friend had a big crush on Bernie, but she wasn't as pretty as Julia, and she didn't think she stood a chance with the football captain.

This was way more than she usually had to work with. Something was happening to her powers. Was it because she'd fallen on her head up the mountain? She wasn't touching the girls, or even particularly close.

A shiver of fear ran along her spine—what if she could feel this level of emotion from people when she was just walking next to them from now on? Would she have this kind of emotional feedback coming at her all day long? She'd end up a worse recluse than her mother had ever been.

One of the girls cleared her throat. Celestine blinked and remembered what they were doing here.

"Bernie—" Celestine waved one hand over the crystal ball and, sensing movement, the internal light came on. "—I see a tall boy, strong and true." He was a football player, what else would he be?

"Yes, yes, that's him." The friend nodded enthusiastically.

Celestine waved her hands over the ball, widening her eyes as if she'd just seen something on her side. "I don't see him with Julia." The girl, Julia, glanced at Celestine in surprise. Her long, dark hair fell softly around her pretty face. Her wide, blue eyes were framed by long, black lashes.

Celestine glanced at the friend. "I see him with you," she said.

The friend gasped and glanced at Julia. "That's not true. I would never...."

"Julia does not want him," said Celestine. "She wants another boy."

Julia gaped at Celestine. "How...?"

"Always follow your heart," whispered Celestine. "Don't go where the crowds push you."

"Does he—" The girl swallowed. "—does Bernie feel the same for me?" she asked.

Celestine narrowed her eyes and looked down at the crystal ball. She had no idea. "Follow your instincts. They will not lead you astray," she said, vaguely waving her hand over the crystal ball. The glowing light from inside the ball intensified briefly, and Celestine held her face in the way that gave off the creepiest shadows over her face. Then the light disappeared.

"The spirits have gone. I can read your cards if you would like?"

Julia shook her head, her eyes wide as she dragged her friend out of the tent, only glancing back over her shoulder as they passed through the opening.

Her next visitor was an older woman on her own. "I left my son and my husband on the thrill rides. I can't bear them," she said in a confiding voice to Celestine.

"What would you like to know? What can the spirits advise you on?"

"My daughter. She... disappeared five months ago." The woman's face lost its joviality. "Is she still alive?"

Celestine took a breath and closed her eyes. She reached out across the table but stopped just before she touched the woman's arm with her gloved hand. That was all she needed to see anger and frustration, raised voices. "You fought with her?" she said. She pulled her hand away.

The woman nodded and a tear leaked out from her eye. "I was trying to make her see reason, and I just pushed her away."

"What was it that she wanted to do?"

"She wanted to go across country to college. I didn't want her to go." The woman wiped the tears off her cheeks with one hand. "I'd let her go anywhere she liked, if only I knew she was okay."

Celestine took a breath and placed her gloved hand on the woman's arm. She needed a little more contact for this one. She closed her eyes. Flashes of light and impressions of people talking came into her head. A young woman wearing a flowing dress and a sad smile. "She's alive. She's living where she always wanted to live. It's hard on her, she misses you, misses her family. But she's determined to succeed."

Pulling her hand away, Celestine took a deep breath. It took a little bit out of her. She tried to limit that kind of a reading—only when there was a genuine need.

"Where she always wanted to live?" The woman closed her eyes. "I know exactly where she is. Thank you, thank you."

"Don't thank me until you find her."

The woman stood and smiled shakily. "Thank you so much. You don't know how much this means to me."

Celestine just smiled her mysterious smile and let the woman walk out. She'd never see her again, but it would be okay, because the woman would find her daughter and they'd be fine.

A couple holding hands, maybe in their thirties, walked through the tent flaps next. The man seemed reluctant; he probably didn't believe in the "fortune-telling malarkey," but the woman came straight up to the table. "We want to know if we're ever going to have a baby," she said, looking down at Celestine. Her gray-green eyes reminded Celestine of the sea.

"Please, sit." She waved them to the chairs.

Again she felt much more than usual from the couple. There were conflicting emotions coming off both of them.

The woman was sad, and scared, but excited as well. The man was reserved. So reserved in fact that it seemed like he didn't actually want a baby.

"How long have you been together?" she asked.

"Why don't you tell us?" interrupted the man. "Isn't that what you're supposed to do?"

Celestine narrowed her eyes. "I don't think you've been together long. Maybe less than a year."

"What gave it away? Some kind of body language clue?" said the man.

Celestine shrugged. "You don't seem comfortable enough with each other to have been together much longer than that." She hesitated. "You're trying for a baby?"

The woman glanced at the man. "Yes. We both want children."

He smiled across at her, but on the inside, her boyfriend was radiating a very definite desire to *not* have children. His every cell radiated negative thoughts toward what was being discussed. For some reason he was pretending to his girlfriend. Celestine narrowed her eyes and looked at them both carefully.

The woman was wearing a rather lovely dress, with small flower patterns, a sweetheart neckline, and a belt at the waist. Her hair was pulled up and off her face into a French twist and her makeup was flawless, enhancing her natural beauty.

The man was classically handsome, but he was... *less flawless*. His edges were frayed. Except he was managing to hide it well. The unshaven cheeks said rugged rather than untidy, and the holes in his jeans could have been designer rather than just well used. He had less money to spend on his appearance, but he hid it well behind a mask of studied unconcern.

Celestine was almost certain he was a gold digger.

She debated silently with herself for a moment over how she was going to handle the situation. She never told couples outright that they weren't right for each other, although she'd certainly seen many in that situation in her tent. But the vibes that she was getting off this guy were so ruthlessly focused on getting what he wanted that she was afraid for the woman.

"I see *you* having children, yes, at some point in the future," she said, speaking directly to the woman, hoping she would catch the subtle hint that she shouldn't have kids with this current jerk. There was a definite vibe of younger children surrounding the woman.

"You will live a long and happy life surrounded by a loving family." Celestine tried to emphasise the fact that it would be a long life. Perhaps this man wasn't as deadly as she feared. But if he were, perhaps he would be put off by the idea that she'd outlive him. With many children.

"That shows how much you know," sneered the man. "Marie's been told she's infertile by a specialist."

Celestine glanced at the woman, who now radiated desperation. "I'm sorry. Marie, is it?"

"Yes."

"You will have children. They may be adopted or perhaps a blended family. But I definitely see children in your future."

Tears appeared in the woman's eyes, and she reached out and grasped Celestine's arm before she could stop her. "Thank you," she whispered.

Celestine simply nodded as a crashing wave of hope washed over her, clearly coming from the woman. It was more emotion than she could easily deal with, and she carefully pulled her arm back from under the woman's hand.

"Come, Marie. I've had enough of this nonsense." The man pulled Marie to her feet and put his arm around her shoulders. "Don't let some fraud at the local fair give you false hope."

Marie glanced back, just like the young girl Julia, as she was leaving the tent. There was a knowing in her eyes that Celestine hadn't seen there before.

She let out a breath.

CHAPTER 14

From where he stood in the anteroom, Sam watched the couple walk out again. He'd caught Celestine's hint to the woman that she ought to ditch this guy and wondered what she'd seen in the woman's face. He was uncomfortable with the idea that she was giving people relationship advice, telling them to leave their partners, but she'd done it in such a way that if it hadn't already been in the mind of the woman, she probably wouldn't see it. The man's face had darkened, so perhaps he would show his true colors soon. Sam frowned. He hoped the woman would be all right.

The next visitor was a tall gangling boy, holding a plate of food and a drink container. Joey, Frankie's runner.

"Here you go, Celestine. Your favorite." He held the plate and cup ceremoniously in front of her, and Celestine smiled warmly in response.

"Thank you, Joey. You're awesome." She took the food and drink and put them on the table.

Craning his neck, Sam saw a thick juicy hamburger on a whole wheat bun and bursting with lettuce and tomato, plus a bright pink slushy in a cup. He pushed the tent flap aside and came out. "Hey, Joey," he said.

Joey looked up and grinned. "Sam. If I'd known you were here, I'd've brought more food."

Sam shook his head. "I can leave at any time to grab something for myself. It's Celestine who needs the energy."

"Joey, what did you do to this slushy to make it taste so good?" asked Celestine around the straw that was in her mouth.

Joey shrugged. "Nothing to do with me. Tami saw a watermelon farm on our way here and stopped to get some. It's early in the season, but she still managed to buy a few."

Celestine closed her eyes and sucked on the straw. "It's delicious."

"I'll let Tami know you said that." Joey saluted casually at them. "I gotta run, have to do the food rounds for the rest of the sideshow. I'll see you later." He raced out of the tent without looking back.

"Do you get that kind of service every day?" asked Sam.

"Only when there's a show on. We can't take breaks, not really, so Tami makes sure that everyone has something in their belly to keep going into the night."

Sam glanced at his watch. It was dinnertime, exactly. "Everyone takes care of each other around here. It's nothing like The Experiment. It was sink or swim around there."

"And you managed to swim?"

Sam shook his head. "Not at first. It took a few years for me to learn how to survive."

"How did you do that?"

He paused, thinking back to his early years in The Experiment. "She didn't show what she was like at first. I didn't realize for a long time the kind of place she was creating. I guess I was naive. Idealistic. I believed Veronica's babble about creating a better world, a utopia for circus people."

"When did you find out?"

Sam paused. "The first time I watched her torture someone for disagreeing with her," he said quietly. He remembered every moment of it, the terrified screams of her victim, the smile on Veronica's face. And the words she'd said at the end. "You are forbidden to help her, Sam. If she survives, it will be on her own."

He'd tried to break the block that night, had fought with everything he had, and it hadn't been enough.

"She's a terrible person," whispered Celestine.

Sam nodded. "She is. That's why I have to destroy her. It haunts me, the idea of her doing what she did to me to someone else."

Celestine opened her mouth to say something else, but the tent opening rustled, and she shooed him back toward his hiding place. She put the empty plate of food down under the table alongside her half-finished slushy.

A woman came in followed closely by a young girl of maybe nine or ten. "Hi there. We're here to get our fortunes told," said the woman with forced cheer. The girl clung to her side.

Sam gazed at the pair through the special hole in the velvet tent, and wondered what Celestine saw. They were both well dressed; the young girl had long, blonde hair held back by a ribbon, and the woman had an attractive bob cut. There was tension etched on the woman's face, but the girl seemed a little blank.

"Please, take a seat," said Celestine. She was back in her Madame Fortune persona, her voice low and intense.

The woman sat down with the young girl on her knee.

"What would you like to know?" asked Celestine.

"Just a general reading. Maybe something about Bethany's future," said the woman, smiling nervously.

The girl looked up at her mother and shook her head

forcefully. She definitely didn't want to know what was in store for her.

Celestine waved her hands over the crystal ball, gazing down into it for a few moments. The silence hung heavy in the room before she spoke. "You've had a hard time recently," Celestine said softly. "It's been tough. But it's going to get better now. It's just the two of you, but you'll do much better without him."

The woman glanced owlishly at Celestine. "What?"

Celestine stared back. "You need to protect her above all else, do you understand me? No one else is more important than your daughter."

The woman nodded. "I know that now."

"If you follow that rule, you will both be fine. Bethany will grow up strong and bright. You will find a life you both love."

Tears appeared in the woman's eyes, and she stood. "Thank you," she whispered. Taking her daughter's hand, she walked out of the tent, her shoulders straight.

The next two hours were the same. A steady stream of people coming through the tent, Celestine telling them one or two insightful comments that made them walk away deep in thought.

It didn't make him believe in her ability to tell fortunes. It made him believe in her ability to read body language and people's expressions. She was very talented, but not with magic. He'd planned to leave after a little while, to sneak out the back without anyone being the wiser, but he became fascinated by the stream of humanity flowing through her tent.

She was masterful when it came to talking the right way to the right person. She would be gruff and difficult with one person and then soft and gentle with the next. It always ended with the customer walking away satisfied that they'd been given some vital piece of information. It was amazing to watch, and not because she was telling the future, because she did very little of that. She told the people what they needed to hear in that moment, gave them something to hold onto and allow them to hold their head up high as they walked out the door again.

No wonder she was so popular.

Something moved against his leg, and he jumped slightly. Looking down he recognized Artemis, rubbing him with her enormous cat body and trying to get Sam's attention. She meowed. Crouching down, Sam patted the enormous cat, earning himself a rumbling purr. "What's the matter, Artemis? You just want some attention? Or are you hungry?" He briefly considered picking the cat up but didn't think he'd actually be able to do it. So he settled into a cross-legged position and scratched behind her ears and stroked her fur.

"Having fun?" said a voice a while later, and Sam looked up, startled at Celestine. He had Artemis curled up in his lap, purring as he patted her.

"She just wanted to say hello," he said.

"Artemis doesn't usually like other people," said Celestine, her eyebrows raised as she looked down at her cat.

Sam smiled. "I have this effect on people. They can't resist me."

Celestine rolled her eyes and then came to sit down next to Sam. "The circus show has started, so the crowds have thinned to nothing. I thought I'd take a break." She reached out her hand and stroked Artemis's back. The cat butted her head against Celestine's arm. "Traitor," she said.

"Is it always like this? So many people?"

Celestine nodded. "This wasn't even a busy night. The longer we stay in a place, the more people find my tent."

"Word of mouth. They hear about you from other people." After what he'd seen tonight, he wasn't surprised.

She nodded.

"Isn't it tiring? Talking to all those people? Some of them were pretty emotional."

Celestine shook her head. "It's like a drive inside me. I like talking to them, trying to help them. If I haven't done it for a while, I feel like I'm blocked up. Over the winter it's actually quite difficult, because I walk around feeling clogged all the time, and my head hurts like I've got a cold."

Sam knew what she was telling him, that it was some kind of magical block. But he thought it was probably more of an emotional block, where she liked to feel like she was healing people. It meant she was a pretty special kind of person, one who cared about others more than she cared about herself.

He'd never met anyone like her before in his life. After years of standing next to a woman who did things for herself first, it was soothing to find there were people in the world like Celestine.

Celestine leaned forward again to scratch under Artemis's chin, bringing her delicate face near to his own. Her violet-blue eyes were bright with pleasure as she gazed down at her cat, and she had a soft smile on her lips. His whole body ached to be closer to her, and Sam let out the tiny breath of air he'd been holding.

He took a chance, giving in to his desire. He leaned forward as well, catching her eyes, putting one finger under her chin. Then he kissed her gently on the lips.

CHAPTER 15

right lights and terrible images flashed into Celestine's head. Blood, screaming, people running. The images were raw and fierce, the colors stronger, and angles sharper. It was like she was seeing it through some kind of extreme filter that made her vision even worse. She gasped and pulled back, away from Sam and his soft, gentle lips.

Artemis stood and hissed at Sam. The cat leaped off his lap and streaked out the tent and into the dark night.

She scrambled up, her heart pounding in her chest. She'd seen what he planned to do, and she hadn't stopped him; she should have known better. All she'd cared about was feeling his lips on hers.

"I'm sorry. I can't do that. I can't...," she said, shaking her head frantically, and took off after Artemis.

It was a dark night sky overhead, no stars visible, but the lights of the Carnival made everything around her bright. She felt freezing cold, despite the early summer warmth and the mild night. Tears spilled down her cheeks, and she wiped them roughly away. She didn't have space in her heart to feel sad, to cry over not being able to touch a man she was attracted to, to kiss him or be intimate with him.

"Wait! Celestine, wait up!" Sam called out to her.

She glanced back and then ducked behind a tent, using her superior knowledge of the layout to avoid him. She couldn't talk to him right now, couldn't explain what had just happened. She'd tried telling him the truth, and he didn't believe her. What did that mean for them? They couldn't be together, not if he thought she was a loony tune.

And if she couldn't touch him... Well, that was just stupid, thinking that a man would want to be with a woman who couldn't touch him.

She didn't know when she'd started thinking about Sam like that, but she knew she wished they could have kept kissing. She wanted to bury her hands in his hair, to touch his face softly, to run the tips of her fingers over his stubble. She wanted to kiss him so deeply that part of herself was left behind when they separated.

But that would never happen, because she couldn't touch anyone. A sob broke free from her chest, and she rounded another corner and bumped into a solid surface.

She looked up, tears streaking down her cheeks, into a weathered face. Viktor.

"Ah, just the person I wanted to see," said Viktor, firmly ignoring her tears.

"Pardon me?" she said, confused. Perhaps he couldn't see them in the dark?

"I want your opinion on something. I have this idea you're the right person to ask for advice."

Celestine hesitated.

"It won't take long." Viktor put one arm around her shoulders and guided her along the alleyway toward the thrill rides where he was usually found at this time of night.

"Where were you going?" asked Celestine. She sniffed and tried to surreptitiously wipe at her tears.

"To find you, of course. I have a gut feeling about this."

Viktor firmly led her toward a ride she'd never seen before. It stood to one side, huddled beyond the haunted hotel at the end of the thrills section. "This is your new ride?" she said incredulously.

"Well, it needs a little bit of work to be sure. It's one of Abba's old ideas. I thought I'd give it a go."

In front of her was the open mouth of a cat, sitting in a sphinxlike position, yawning wide, with its teeth on show. The little carriages were moving through the mouth of the cat and into its darkened interior.

"A giant cat?"

Viktor looked chagrined. "It's not quite right, is it?" he said.

Celestine moved forward, intrigued despite herself. She touched one hand to the side of the cat's face and felt a rumbling of emotion. She couldn't sense enough, so she surreptitiously pulled off her glove and touched her bare hand to the new ride.

Optimism and a renewed sense of purpose popped into her head. There was excitement mixed in, and a sense of pride in what they'd managed to put together. Trepidation about whether the punters would like the new ride.

She caught a glimpse of the future and saw the same ride, but as a huge lion, its jaws open wide to welcome people in as they rode on small carriages. They were laughing and pretending to be scared as they entered the lion's mouth.

"He's a beautiful cat," she said.

"But...?"

"He's not the right kind of cat. You need something fierce, something that will give people that little thrill of fear they come to the Carnival for."

"A big cat? Like a tiger? Or a lion?"

Celestine nodded. "Yes. A lion would be perfect. The King of the pridelands. What's the rest of the ride?"

"It's a mini roller-coaster for the younger kids. We haven't finished the theme on the inside yet. So we could change it to the savannah, and have lions and giraffes and zebras inside." Viktor was nodding his head. "Yes, we're onto something here. Lots of noise from the animals, grasses popping up everywhere, that kind of thing. I knew you were the right person to ask." Viktor grinned and thumped one hand on her back. Celestine stumbled forward slightly, but she was smiling. It felt good to help.

"Can we go through its mouth? I'd like to see the inside of the ride." She was suddenly lighthearted and just wanted a bit of fun. She wanted to prolong this feeling for a little longer.

"Sure, go on in."

Before she could stop him, Viktor grabbed her bare hand, and started to pull her toward the closest ride car.

Immediately time slowed, then stood still. Viktor's concerned face hung in front of Celestine for a moment and then was gone, replaced by the bright lights and the rainbow colors that came before one of her full visions. Celestine scrambled for a second, trying to get her bearings before the images of the future appeared to her. After a long afternoon and night of fortune-telling, a full-on vision like this was going to hit her hard.

And then nothing else mattered; she was in the future. The Blue Carousel was spinning softly, while laughter and sounds of enjoyment floated in the air around her. She shivered. She still hadn't recovered from what she'd seen of the carousel in her vision with Alfie.

Viktor stood next to the slowly turning ride, working on a metal box that was attached to one side. He was frowning, his face concentrating as he used a small screwdriver to unscrew something inside the box.

"Come on, Mommy, I wanna to go on the carousel," yelled a little boy, his face filled with excitement. "I want to ride the dolphins!"

His mother laughed at the expression on his face and gathered him up into her arms. "Of course you can go on the carousel. We'll just wait here until it stops and lets these people off. Then you can ride your dolphin."

Celestine shifted away from the mother and son, moving closer to Viktor. He was mumbling under his breath, and she couldn't quite hear the words. "Thinks she can... Won't work... Wait until she sees...."

"Ah, Viktor, there you are," said a soft cultured voice. Celestine recognized it by now, she'd heard it so many times in her visions. Veronica. "Not trying to escape me are you?"

Viktor turned his head and a look of panic crossed his features.

"I did give you some very specific instructions as to what I wanted you to do, didn't I?"

Viktor nodded.

"And you understand what will happen if you disobey me, don't you? That block you have inside you will cause you so much pain, you won't know what hit you."

Viktor opened his mouth to speak, but nothing came out.

"And did you forget something else? I have your precious granddaughter. If you do anything other than what I tell you, that sweet little baby will suffer before she dies."

Viktor's face went white, and he stumbled. He put his hand out to hold himself steady against the metal box. "I'll do what you want, Veronica," he rasped out. "Just don't hurt the baby."

"Then set up that spell inside the carousel and come back to your trailer. That's an order."

Celestine felt herself moving backwards, being pulled back to the rainbow-colored dimension, where she hung motionless before returning to the real world. She opened her eyes and saw a metal roof. It took her a moment to realize she was sitting in the carriage of the ride with Viktor sitting next to her, fanning her face.

"Oh, thank the Gods. You're back. You were shaking so bad, I thought you were having some kind of lethal fit."

Celestine put one hand to her head and tried to keep everything straight in her head. "I saw you."

"Just stay calm, child. It's going to be fine." Then Viktor put his hand against her bare one again.

Celestine dipped back into the vision world, the rainbow colors dimmed and fractured. She saw Viktor again, but this time he was in a small, darkened van workshop, making something. He held it up, and the metal surface shone in the light from the single overhead lamp. "It's done," said Viktor. "It's finally done."

The door opened behind Viktor, and his son Henry came in, followed by a woman with bright green eyes and curly blonde hair. "Dad, come on, everyone's waiting on you."

"I just wanted to finish this. It's important."

"So's your birthday. Come on."

"Just one more minute...," Viktor said.

"Dad. You're going to miss the big announcement. It's all planned."

Viktor frowned. "What big announcement?"

Henry grinned at the woman and squeezed the hand he was holding. "You won't know if you don't come to the party."

Viktor glanced from one happy face to the other. "You're pregnant!" he said and then gave a whoop and a holler, throwing his cap into the air. He surged forward and hugged his son and daughter-in-law. "I'm so proud of you!"

CHAPTER 16

"I tell you, son, she needs to head back to the Compound. That girl's got some serious problems going on inside her head. That fit was scary. She was shaking and moaning." Viktor was holding his cup of coffee with both hands, and leaning across the breakfast table toward Sam. They were both up early, so they were mostly alone in the food tent.

"How did she seem after the seizure?" asked Sam.

"She was shaken up, if you can excuse the pun. Told me that my Henry wouldn't have a baby for years to come."

"And?" Sam leaned closer to Viktor.

"I went straight to Henry and Fee, and asked them if they was tryin'. They admitted they'd been going to tell me on my birthday in a couple of weeks. Fee just found out she's pregnant. It's still early days, so keep it under your hat." Viktor beamed with pride, his ruddy cheeks glowing.

A strange feeling curled around in Sam's stomach. Why would Celestine give what she would have thought was bad news to Viktor like that? Given the way she'd responded to the people the night before, he was sure she wouldn't have just blurted out that someone was going to remain childless for years. It seemed tactless.

She'd been so good at handling all those people and their reactions.

He was missing something.

Except, perhaps she'd been upset? She'd run away from his kiss and then, by all accounts, had run into Viktor and had gone with him, then had another vision. She'd probably been just too exhausted to do more than blurt out what she thought she'd seen.

"I'll talk to her again. Jack will probably agree with your assessment of the situation."

Viktor nodded. "She's a good girl. I wouldn't want her to get hurt. Gave me some excellent ideas for the new ride, to make it more accessible to the kids."

Sam nodded absently. "She understands people really well. I watched her yesterday in the fortune-telling tent."

"One of the most popular sideshows, that's for sure." Viktor nodded.

"Do you think she might be right sometimes? I mean...."

Viktor shook his head. "She's a lovely girl, has a real good grasp of people and the way their heads work, but she ain't no fortune-teller. These fits she's having, they're messing with her head. Her brain is telling her things she thinks is real. She's one of us now. We've got to protect her from herself."

Sam nodded. "You're right. I'll talk to her." A small part of him wanted Celestine to be right about her abilities. He wanted her to be able to tell the future, because then she would be okay. The seizures would have an explanation, and it wouldn't be that she potentially had a serious physical disorder inside her brain.

But he needed to get over that. He needed to acknowledge that he was attracted to her, and that it was messing with his ability to see things clearly. He shouldn't have tried to kiss her yesterday. He'd forgotten all about her touching phobia in his desire to be closer to her. He was her damned doctor, for crying out loud.

She wasn't someone he should be trying to get closer to.

But something inside him kept going back to her. "I'll go talk to her now, Viktor. See what she says."

Viktor nodded and waved him off, a funny expression on his face as he watched Sam go.

Sam shook his head. Viktor was a smart old bugger. If he said that Celestine was a fake, then she was a fake. He strode quickly through the Carnival into the camper and trailer area at the back. They were due to move on tomorrow, so people were starting to emerge from their homes, packing up what they could in advance. He nodded at a few of them but didn't stop until he got to Celestine's little trailer.

He knocked on her door and waited impatiently. There was movement inside but it was slow. He knocked again.

"I'm coming, I'm coming," Celestine grumbled from inside. Her voice was low and croaky.

When the door eventually pulled open, Celestine looked down at him, her face showing her dismay.

"I'm here to apologize," said Sam. "I shouldn't have tried to kiss you. It was unprofessional, and I promise it won't happen again."

Celestine's eyes widened slightly.

"Can I come in? I need to do an assessment. Viktor told me you had another seizure last night?" He kept his voice even and efficient.

Celestine made to shut the door, but Sam shoved a foot in the way. "You need to let me in. Jack will do whatever I say when it comes to sending you back to the Compound. If you want to stay here, I'm your best chance."

"That's blackmail!"

Sam shook his head. "No, that's me trying to convince a hardheaded woman that I'm a doctor and I have her best interests at heart."

"But you don't know what's best for me," said Celestine. "You don't even believe what I tell you."

"Let me in, and I'll do a quick check up. Otherwise you're going straight home."

There was a charged silence, and then Celestine opened the door wider, a sulky expression on her face. "It's still blackmail."

Sam shrugged. "Whatever works to keep everyone healthy." Climbing the steps, he glanced around and saw Artemis sleeping on Celestine's rumpled bed in the far end of the trailer. A few dishes were on the countertop, and yesterday's clothes were draped over a chair. It was the messiest he'd ever seen her small home.

"Come, sit over here, and I'll take a look at your ankle first."

Celestine sat in front of him but didn't say another word. She was clearly annoyed with him.

"Hold up your ankle, and I'll try not to touch you," said Sam.

She did as he asked. The ankle was showing colorful bruises, but the swelling had gone down and it was healing fast.

"I need to check your eyes. If you could sit under the light over here and open them wide for me."

Her eyes were fine as well. She seemed in tip-top condition this morning—aside from her annoyance at him. "You hit your head when you fell in the mountains, correct?" he asked.

Celestine nodded. "But you said it wasn't a big deal."

"I thought that at the time. But now that you've been having these visions, I think we should get a second opinion."

"What are you talking about?"

"Our next stop has slightly better medical facilities. I'm going to book you in for an MRI. " He tried to indicate just by his tone of voice that he would accept no arguments from her.

"I can't possibly afford anything like that," said Celestine, her eyes wide.

"It's all covered under the insurance Jack got at the beginning of the season. I'll talk to him about it."

"I won't do it." Celestine crossed her arms. "You can't make me."

Sam glared down at her. "I can, and I will. If you don't go with me to get an MRI, I will tell Jack that he and Rilla need to send you back to the Compound. You shouldn't be performing when you've got a potentially serious issue like this. You could get hurt."

"I keep telling you, I'm perfectly fine. This is normal behaviour for someone who can see the future."

"It's an MRI or the Compound, Celestine. Your choice."

"What happens if the MRI comes back with something bad?"

"Then we'll get you the best medical treatment our insurance can buy."

"You'll send me back to the Compound anyway."

"It's not a death sentence. If that happened, it would be because we wanted you to get better again. You'd heal, and then you could come back on the circuit."

Celestine heaved a big sigh, clearly torn. "Fine. I'll go with you. But it's because you're forcing me."

CHAPTER 17

"What I don't understand is how you managed to get us an appointment for an MRI so quickly," said Celestine. She was walking slowly across the hospital parking lot in Nampa, Idaho, trying to delay the inevitable.

"It was actually Rilla and Viktor working together to pull a few strings," said Sam. "They come through this place every year, so they know a few of the locals. Just happened to know a few of the right ones." He shrugged.

They'd left the rest of the Carnival folk setting up on the outskirts of the city, and Sam had borrowed a pickup truck to bring Celestine in to the hospital. She'd tried every argument she could think of to get out of the MRI, but Sam was adamant. There was no stopping him now that he was on a mission.

The hospital loomed over them, at least ten stories high with glass reflecting the morning sun. They pushed open the doors, and she could immediately feel the emotions of everyone around her, lots of fear and anxiety mixed with sadness. She bit her lip, trying to control the urge to turn and run. Her abilities were getting stronger, and she didn't know why.

Celestine was shaking by the time they made it to the radiology department.

"Now, dear, it's not going to hurt a bit," said the nurse kindly as she handed Celestine a baggy hospital gown. "Put this on, and we can get started."

As she changed behind the screen, Celestine tried to get her desperation to leave under control. As soon as she'd left the main corridors, the waves of other people's emotions had calmed down. Thankfully the nurse was happy and uncomplicated, so she wasn't leaking emotion like so many other people in the hospital.

She'd never reacted like this before. She'd always been able to control how much of other people's emotions she absorbed in public.

She took a deep breath. All she had to do was lie down on the patient table; it wasn't so difficult, right? She looked down at her gloved hands. The gloves were staying on. The last thing she needed was to accidentally touch the nurse and have a vision while she was in the MRI.

When Celestine emerged, the nurse and the doctor looked at her gloves, but Sam cleared his throat. "Celestine has a phobia about people touching her bare skin. It's important to her that you keep that in mind."

"Of course, darling," said the nurse to Celestine. "We see all sorts in here." The nurse moved forward and placed a sheet over Celestine's body. "To keep you warm and cozy," she said.

"You'll need to keep as still as possible so we can take some clear pictures of your brain," said the radiologist. "This will allow us to take better images, and also hold your head still while we do the scans," she added as she clipped a round piece of equipment over Celestine's head. It made it difficult to see around her, and Celestine could no longer move her head from side to side.

The radiologist nodded to Sam and gestured that he should precede her out.

Celestine glanced wildly at him, suddenly realizing she was going to be alone in the room. Her heart pounded in her chest as she reached out her arm to him. "Don't go," she whispered, her voice coming out strange and husky.

Sam grasped her gloved hand and leaned over so he could see her through the gaps in the head shield. "It's going to be fine. I'll just be in the next room. You can do this." His eyes seemed to bore right into her skull and somehow managed to steady her a little. She swallowed hard and nodded slightly inside the equipment holding her head still.

He squeezed her hand and then left the room, the door banging heavily on the frame.

When the platform started moving backwards into the large cylinder, she twitched but managed to remain where she was. She shut her eyes, trying to block out her emotions, and stay calm.

The table stopped and she shuddered. She was encased in the metal tube down to her knees. Close all around her was the white circle of the MRI, pushing in at her. The cold metal soaked into her back, making her shiver.

"Can you hear me, Celestine?" said a tinny voice next to her head. It was the radiologist talking to her through a speaker.

She blinked open her eyes. "Yes." Waves of emotion washed over her. Celestine swallowed, trying to push it all away.

"Just keep still, and we'll have you out of there in no time.

You're not alone in being nervous. Most people who do this procedure feel the same way you do."

Like a light coming on, Celestine realized what was happening. It wasn't her own emotion—at least not totally—that was making her react this way. She was soaking up the emotional residue of people who'd had MRI procedures before her. They experienced such strong feelings while they were inside the MRI, it was like being dunked in a pile of ghostly emotional remains.

A red light went on to one side, and she was hit with a fear so terrible it made her gasp out loud and clench her hands.

"Celestine, I need you to hold still, please. The images we're getting still aren't clear enough yet." The radiologist's stern voice came through the speaker.

Celestine squeezed her eyes shut and tried to control her shaking. The emotions inside her were building up; layer upon layer of people had been lying here in precisely the same position, wondering what was wrong with them, wondering if they were going to die, wondering why it was them here and not someone else. Their emotions were wrapping themselves around her like a heavy cloak, suffocating her until she started gasping for breath. She could hear their voices, soft murmurs and cries as they suffered through the torture of an MRI.

Celestine couldn't hold it in any longer. She was trapped inside this circular tube, soaking up the fear and anger of a million people before her. Her eyes were scrunched tight, and her nails dug into the palms of her hands.

If she could have moved, could have gotten out of that chamber, she would have. Almost on its own, her back lifted itself slightly off the table and then slammed back down. An angry crackling sound came from the speaker. Celestine heard a loud crash, and a sound like a small explosion. A bright light flashed outside of the tunnel and the smell of smoke filled the air.

Then the lights went off inside the MRI tunnel and Celestine screamed.

CHAPTER 18

*S*am watched in horror as the MRI machine on the other side of the one-sided glass window came to a shuddering halt. It seemed to shake internally, and then everything went dark. He heard Celestine's scream, and everything inside him clenched.

"What the hell just happened?" asked one of the technicians.

Not waiting to find out, Sam raced into the room, closely followed by the radiologist. "How do we get her out of there?" he asked urgently. Celestine was writhing on the platform, her legs kicking under the sheet. His stomach curled in on itself. It was his fault that she was here, in this machine.

"There's a manual override button on the panel," said the woman as she opened the side of the machine and pressed a button.

"It's okay, Celestine, we'll get you out of there. We're coming." Sam touched her leg over the sheet, and immediately her legs calmed. He could hear her small sobs from inside the machine.

He'd done that to her.

A screeching of metal sounded as the patient table moved back out. Celestine was pulling at the equipment still around her head, and Sam tried unsuccessfully to unlock it. The radiologist came to the other side and unclicked it, setting Celestine free.

Celestine almost leaped up off the bench and crushed herself into Sam's arms. She was trembling uncontrollably and her face was pushed hard against his shoulder. Her arms were locked around his neck like she was never going to let go. He felt her skin against his but didn't say anything, figuring she needed the comfort of his arms.

"I'm terribly sorry about that," the radiologist was saying. "It's never happened before. I've never seen anything like it."

"Did you get any useful scans before it went up in smoke?" asked Sam.

"I think the machine was acting up before it exploded," said the radiologist, shaking her head. "The results made no sense. All we got were rainbow colored lights all over the brain scan."

Sam glanced down at Celestine. If he believed her about being able to see the future, then perhaps that would explain the scans. He shook his head. But he didn't believe her. The MRI had broken. It was a complete coincidence. Still... "Can you send me the scans?"

"We'll have to fix the MRI and get you back in for another set. The ones we took aren't worth diddly-squat."

"I'd like to have a copy of them for my records. It could be an interesting comparison."

The radiologist shrugged. "Sure. I'll send them to you. But they won't make any sense."

Sam nodded. "That's fine."

"We'll need to book you back in for another scan." She frowned at the big machine in front of them. "But we'll have to get someone in to look at it first and tell us how long it's going to take to get it fixed."

He nodded absently. They would probably be long gone before they could get back in again. "Let us know how it goes. You've got my mobile number?"

The radiologist nodded. "I'm so sorry about this." She waved her hand at the MRI.

"I think we'll get her dressed and go now." He picked up Celestine and carried her now limp body behind the screen. "Come on, Celestine, you're going to have to help me here," he said softly. Celestine murmured something and pulled back. She was dazed, like she was on drugs. He was going to have to get her dressed. He was a doctor; it wasn't like she had anything he hadn't seen before. But she did have an intense dislike of being touched and had run from him only two nights before after he'd kissed her. He had a feeling he was going to hear about it when she woke up properly.

But for now, he had no choice.

Luckily she'd left her bra and panties on under the gown, so he just had to get her into her top and skirt. He undid the hospital gown, and she managed to hold out her arms while he pulled her top on over her head. He drew the long floating skirt up her legs and managed to get it over her hips while she sat on the chair. He'd had to touch her bare skin a few times, and he waited for her to have some kind of reaction to it, but she stayed in the same limp position on the chair the whole time.

When she was dressed, he crouched in front of her, and put his fingertips under her chin, where it was drooped onto her chest. He pulled her head up until she was facing him again. Her eyes focused slowly on his face. "Celestine? I need you to wake up now. Come on. Snap out of it. It's over. You're out of the machine."

Celestine blinked. "I can still feel it. I need to get out of here," she whispered.

Sam nodded, leaning down to pick her up again. "Put your arms around my neck," he said. At this moment, he would do whatever she asked; the memory of her terrified face was still etched into his mind.

She leaned in, like a trusting kitten, and curled up against his chest.

When he emerged from behind the screen, the room was empty. He managed to get the heavy door open and then strode off down the hallway, swearing to himself that he would never bring Celestine back to this place again.

He emerged into the early summer sunlight outside the hospital, and Celestine raised her head, holding her face to the warm light. She seemed to be gaining strength with every yard they moved away from the hospital and the MRI machine.

"I'm okay again now, Sam," she said. "I can walk."

"I'll carry you to the car, just to be sure."

"It's fine. I'd rather you put me down." Her voice was already sounding stronger, and more annoyed.

Sam started breathing easier. "I'd prefer to carry you," he said.

Celestine shook her head. "I need to walk," she said firmly, her voice clear for the first time since she'd emerged from the MRI.

Sam stopped and gently put her legs first to the ground. She held him a moment, steadying herself, then nodded and stepped away. "Where are we parked again?" she said.

"That way," he said pointing to the far corner. He lingered patiently beside her, waiting for her to move off in her own time.

She took a few small steps and then started walking a little faster, her skirt swishing against her legs. She was just getting her stride back, when she stopped, her gaze caught on a massive light pole with a brightly colored poster attached to it.

Celestine went pale and put one hand to her mouth for a moment and then crumpled toward the ground.

Sam leaped to her side, only just managing to grab her before her head hit the hard concrete.

CHAPTER 19

*C*elestine opened her eyes. The world was spinning. She closed them again and groaned. The seat was moving beneath her. She vaguely remembered Sam bundling her into the beat-up blue truck they'd borrowed for their trip to the hospital.

"Are you okay?" Sam asked from beside her.

She opened her eyes again, this time battling the nausea to stare at Sam. He was in the driver's seat, both hands on the wheel. He flicked a quick glance in her direction. She was buckled into the passenger's seat, and they were driving along the road that led to the Carnival's new camp.

Nodding slowly, she put one hand to her head, trying to remember what had happened. She'd escaped from the MRI, Sam had been carrying her. She made him let her down. She'd been walking across the parking lot—

The poster.

She'd sensed it before she'd seen it. It had traces of her younger brother's emotions all over it. He'd put it up, and he'd been resentful and angry as usual. He was part of the advance team for the Marber and Mayhew Circus. It was his job to go around putting up posters and signs letting everyone know about the circus that was coming to town. It had been so familiar and so fresh; he'd only been there a few days before. She'd seen the dates on the poster—they'd already started their shows—and her old fear and desperation had risen to the surface. He was here, in the same town as her. They probably both were. On top of everything else, it had been too much.

She'd fainted.

"I didn't go back into the hospital," Sam said apologetically. "I figured I could treat you back at the Carnival just as easily."

"Thank you," she said weakly.

He turned into the back entrance of the Carnival camp and parked the truck back in its place. He turned in his seat. "Now tell me what it was that made you faint like that."

Celestine blinked, trying to think. "Nothing. I... It was just another reaction to the MRI."

Sam shook his head. "No. You were recovering from that just fine. You were looking at that poster. Is that your old circus?"

Celestine held her breath. Sam was so quick, she sometimes couldn't keep up with him. "What makes you think that?" she asked.

"You told me about your brothers. I assume they're still out there, working the circuit."

She nodded slowly. "Yes, they're out there. Which is why it's such a gamble for me to be out here too." She took a breath. "Do you know, in all the time I've been with the Carnival, I've never so much as caught a whiff of my brothers? And now, when things are going all haywire and my power is doing weird things, I suddenly find them."

"You don't think that it's a coincidence?"

"There's no such thing as coincidence."

"What about the MRI?"

"I knew I didn't want to go in there from the moment you mentioned it. I'm not afraid of small spaces. I don't have claustrophobia. Some part of me just knew what was going to happen in there."

"What happened?"

"I was hit with all the negative emotions of every single person who'd ever gone into that damn machine. It hit me all at once. I think I made it explode somehow."

Sam opened his mouth to say something, but Celestine held up her hand. "Don't you dare tell me it's all in my head, and that it was my own fear and terror. It wasn't. Somehow my abilities are getting stronger, and I'm reading the emotions not just off the people around me—I don't even have to touch them anymore—but also from the places they've been." Her voice wobbled. She didn't want her abilities to get stronger. It was bad enough that she could see the future and read people's emotions.

She didn't want more.

A figure sprinted toward them, waving his arms. "Sam! Sam! Come quick. There's been an accident in the big top. Jack says to come quick!" Celestine recognised Joey as he arrived at the door of the truck, his breath coming in gasps.

"Who's been hurt?" said Sam, opening the door and slamming it shut. "Come on, Celestine, I might need your help."

Celestine sat for a second, trying to figure out what kind of help she could possibly be to Sam when she couldn't touch anyone. But she had to do whatever she could. She jumped out of the old truck, slammed the door, and raced after Joey and Sam.

It was late morning, and the show proper wouldn't be starting until early evening. The three-ringed big top had been set up, but many of the thrill rides were still in the process of being put together. Celestine caught a glimpse of

Sam and Joey racing into the big top and followed through moments later.

Inside, it was chaos. The rigging above the high wire was still being set up, and in the air high above, one of the building crew was hanging upside down, his leg caught in a dangling rope. Celestine saw the problem immediately. The safety net wasn't in place; if he fell, he would die.

"Who is it?" asked Celestine.

"It's Davos," said Joey.

Celestine gasped, putting one hand over her mouth. Davos was one of the Nine, the leader of the build crew, and one of the most experienced men in the Carnival. How had he gotten himself into this mess?

Before she could say another word, Sam had disappeared in the direction of the rigging ladder. He was halfway up before Celestine thought to object to him climbing. She glanced around. Viktor was preparing a safety net, to be held by the remaining members of the build crew, and Jack was issuing orders to members of the crew who were spread out high up in the structure above.

She ran forward, trying to get a better look at what had happened. The crew members still in the rigging seemed to be trying to get close to Davos, but the structure was rickety, whole sections not quite in place yet. Wood and rope groaned against each other every time one of them tried to move closer to their leader.

"Don't move," yelled Jack, gesturing with his arms to the men. "It's going to come down on everyone."

Celestine crept closer, pulling off her gloves and putting one hand on the base of the ladder that lead up into the rigging. Emotions flashed through her head. Mainly determination to get the job done. But there was also an underlying sense of eagerness, of excitement. Of revenge.

It had been set on purpose.

A shout high overhead made Celestine glance up. She gasped along with everyone else in the room, as Sam swung across the top of the tent on a rope, his foot wound through a loop at the bottom. The rope was tied to the far section of the rigging that seemed more stable, and Sam had swung out into open air, rather than relying on the unstable rigging.

He grabbed hold of Davos, who reached out with his arms. The ropes swayed and jerked as they connected, but the two men managed to stay together, held in place by the two ropes. Sam helped Davos pull himself upward, so he was at least upright, despite his leg being snarled up in the rope. Sam leaned down and started cutting at the rope around Davos's foot with a small Swiss Army knife.

It felt like everyone down below was holding their collective breath, all eyes on Davos and Sam. The rigging creaked and grated above them, swinging a little as the other men in the rigging now worked to steady the rest of the structure.

Sam was hacking at the rope, but he was having trouble cutting through the thick material around Davos's feet with his small knife. Davos reached down and grabbed the knife from him and took a turn attempting to pull the blade up through the rope. The older man's huge muscled arms bunched as he worked. Taking turns, they managed to weaken the rope, and eventually began pulling at it, trying to fray the edges. Their efforts slowed, and Celestine could tell, even from a distance, that both men were weakening.

Sam was leaning out, his rope on a long angle, only attached to Davos and his rope because they were holding themselves together. Sam held the knife and yanked it across the rope; it came apart in his hands.

The movement jerked Sam backwards, and his foot slipped out of the loop in the rope. Above him, Davos, who had both hands firmly wrapped around Sam's rope, swung back towards the stable rigging, his heavy weight dragging the rope out of Sam's hands.

For a moment, it was as if Sam hung in the air, stunned. Then he plunged toward the hard-packed earth, a yell forced out of his throat.

Celestine screamed and ran forward.

CHAPTER 20

*A*s Sam fell through the air, Celestine felt like the air had been punched out of her lungs. She locked her eyes onto his falling body as she ran, as if she could stop his wild descent through sheer force of will.

But nothing could stop Sam from falling.

He came crashing down to earth… and landed in the middle of a jury-rigged safety net that sprang up from the ground just as he was falling. It was held in place by more than twenty muscled Carnival crew, including Jack and Viktor; their faces were tensed, the straining muscles in their necks and arms showing how much effort it cost them to hold the net in place as Sam bounced back up into the air and came down again.

While she'd had her eyes locked on Davos and Sam in the air above, Viktor had been working tirelessly with the remaining crew to pull out the safety net, preparing for the worst.

There was silence for a moment and then a whoop of relief from members of the building crew. They lowered the net to the ground, and two men raced forward to check on

Sam, while others ran over to where Davos was climbing down the rigging. His strong arms and legs were making short work of it, and it wasn't long before he landed on the ground, and Celestine could see his face close up.

She shivered. His jaw was clenched, his eyebrows were lowered into a deep scowl, and his face was flushed. He looked livid. His long strides ate up the ground as he strode over to where Sam was lying on the ground. Celestine took a step forward, meaning to protect Sam from Davos's obvious anger.

But as soon as he arrived, the big man helped Sam to his feet, and enveloped him in an enormous hug.

"You damn well saved my life," Davos said. He slapped Sam on the back.

Sam grinned sheepishly. "I almost got us both killed."

"Not on your life. I was a goner. That was a deliberate trap." Davos shook his hand, then hugged Sam again. "Thank you, son."

At Davos's words, Jack's expression darkened. "I think we need to talk," he said grimly to Davos. The Buildmaster nodded and gestured to a couple of his crew to start the clean up without him. He followed Jack and Viktor out of the tent.

Celestine watched with trepidation. Did Davos think someone else was trying to sabotage the Carnival? She glanced at Sam. Would he think she had something to do with it? He'd seemed worried that she was up to something in the vision with Frankie.

There was nothing she could do about it, if he did. They wouldn't find any proof; the worst that could happen would be that they might throw her out of the Carnival. The thought chilled her and sent goosebumps up her arms. She was happy here; she didn't want to leave.

She waited in the shadows, trying to avoid the worst of

the crowd. Now that they were back at the Carnival, she didn't seem to be taking on the emotions of everyone around her in the same way. Perhaps the Carnival itself was protecting her from it? The thought was tantalizing. It meant she was connected to it just like everyone else. That it considered her one of its own. Her skin tingled as she considered what that might mean for her.

She studied Sam as he stood talking to some of the other build crew. After the initial thank you from Davos, he didn't look as elated as he should. He seemed grim and received the thanks with a measured expression. She caught his eye after a while, and he gestured with his head toward one of the exits. She nodded.

Celestine cautiously moved around the edges of the tent, trying to avoid contact with the crowds. She made it to the exit first because Sam was stopped several times to be congratulated for what he'd done. Anger started to boil inside her as she watched him make his way to her. He'd done it without thinking and with people far better suited around him, who knew how to safely climb the rigging and who worked with ropes every day. Jack had called him to come quickly, but not for his skill on the high ropes. It was because the Ringmaster had feared a serious accident was about to happen and he wanted Sam's medical expertise.

Sam had recklessly risked his own life by climbing up there, and she knew why.

Because he didn't care about dying.

Veronica had done such a number on him that she'd convinced him that he was worthless. He thought he deserved everything that was coming his way. It made her insides churn with anger.

When he finally arrived next to her, he didn't say a word, just held the canvas aside for her to go through. She ducked under his arm and strode off, leading him along the alleyway back to the trailers. She didn't say anything, but her anger was simmering just below the surface. She didn't know who she was more angry at—Sam or Veronica.

When they arrived back at her place, Celestine paused outside her door. "Do you want something to drink?" she asked.

Sam shook his head. "I would come inside and do a check up on you, but I don't think I'm thinking clearly myself. I might have to come back later." He gave an exhausted half smile.

Without thinking about it, Celestine reached out and put her bare hand on Sam's arm. She had to see if his future had changed after what he'd done today.

Time froze, the rainbow colors were so bright they hurt her head, and then she saw Veronica again. She was standing over the bodies of Sam and Rilla, a smoking gun still in her hand. They were outside the main tent, and people were running all around them.

"I wanted you for my own," murmured Veronica, gazing down at Sam. "But if I can't have you, no one can." She looked up and smiled at someone, and Celestine saw herself. She had ripped clothing and blood dripping from a wound on her arm.

Veronica raised her gun directly at Celestine and fired.

Celestine jerked awake in Sam's arms, on the grass in front of her trailer.

CHAPTER 21

*A*s the last tremors stilled from her seizure, Sam lifted Celestine into his arms and carried her into the trailer. His adrenaline high from saving Davos was long gone, and he was left with just a throbbing headache and a feeling of nausea deep in his stomach. But he managed to get her onto her bed.

"What did you do that for?" he asked softly, brushing a strand of her curly golden hair from her face.

Celestine didn't ask him what he was talking about. She looked up at him, her violet-blue eyes swirling with mystery. "I needed to see if your future had changed."

Anger rushed to the surface. Her belief in her abilities felt like an insurmountable barrier between them. "Don't tell me. I don't want to know," he growled.

He stomped to the kitchen area and grabbed a cup from the shelf, pouring water from the fridge into it. He was sick of the pretence, of the way she believed in something so clearly false. He'd hoped the MRI would show something conclusive that would prove to Celestine that she couldn't see the future; that it was just her brain deceiving her.

"Thank you," she said softly as he handed her the cup. Her eyes looked bruised and her skin had a transparent look to it. His anger collapsed between one breath and the next. She'd been through so much, he couldn't hold it against her. He longed to run his fingers down her arm, to soothe away the aches and pains, and make her forget all about the future.

"I'm going to my place to sleep now," he said abruptly, unable to stop himself from wondering what it would be like to kiss her soft lips again. He turned and stalked away from her. He was almost out the door when Celestine spoke again.

"Sam."

"Yes?" He stopped but didn't turn around. His carefully erected control was close to the breaking point. If he looked at her right now, he might just break all her rules about no touching.

"Take care of yourself," she whispered.

He nodded. "You too." And then he almost ran out the door.

He didn't know where he was going, and he expected to end up at the door to his clinic, so he could sleep off his raging headache. But moments later he found himself knocking on Frankie's door.

Frankie answered with an annoyed frown on his face. "What is it now?" he asked. "You're practically moving in."

"I just wanted to check how it was going."

"And crow about your performance in the big top?" said Frankie, holding the door wider.

"How did you—"

Frankie waved one arm vaguely toward the computer screen behind him. "The cameras. They're everywhere."

"Even so, you'd have to be watching them all the time to pick up everything."

"The algorithm, remember? It finds the unusual occurrences and movements on the camera feeds for me."

"Did you figure out why it didn't pick up Celestine?"

Frankie narrowed its eyes and held up two fingers. "Two possibilities. One is that the Carnival is messing with me, which is a likely option. The other is that the program considered Celestine's night time activities a normal occurrence based on previous surveillance." Frankie moved over to his computer and brought up a series of videos on the screen in a montage. Each one showed Celestine walking around in the middle of the night. "She's been doing her midnight walks regularly since we left the Compound."

Sam looked down at the screens, trying to figure out what she was doing. It seemed to involve a lot of touching. She had her gloves off and stroked her fingers over all the equipment. It was blurry and black and white, but Sam was mesmerised by watching her move around the silent Carnival.

A knock on the door interrupted their contemplation.

"It's like Grand Central Station in here today," grumbled Frankie as he went to open the door.

Jack stood on the grass below. "I came to see if you wanted to get out for a while," he said. "I need your take on something."

Frankie didn't even hesitate. He grabbed a pair of dark glasses from the counter beside the door. "Come on, Doc, we're outta here."

"I didn't realize you could leave your trailer," said Sam. "I thought you were agoraphobic?"

Frankie shook his head. "Only when the magic is working. It's something the damned Carnival cooked up to keep me here. But Jack can absorb the magic around me, and get me out of here." He clapped Jack on the back. "My savior."

"My pleasure, Frankie." Jack gave a mocking bow. "At least my absorbing works for someone."

"You'll figure it out, Jack. It's just a matter of time," said Frankie, his expression serious for the first time.

Sam nodded. "We're already making progress. Did you talk to Rilla about the 'hour of power' idea in the mornings?"

"Yes, and she's happy for us to try it out. We can have a quick gathering post-show tonight to get everyone on board. Then I'll try it in the morning."

"What're you going to do?" asked Frankie, eyeing the food stalls they were passing. Delicious-smelling snacks were being prepared for the Carnival's imminent opening.

Jack gestured for Sam to explain.

"Jack needs to find time every day when he can just let his absorbing powers loose, to gather the magic to him, then set it free again. It would be good practice for when he actually needs it."

Jack smacked Sam on the arm with the back of his hand. "I'm willing to give it a go, if everyone else agrees." His face held a mix of trepidation and intrigue.

Frankie nodded and sniffed the air. "I smell churros. The good kind, the ones that Tami makes." He broke off to wander over to the van that was advertising authentic churros in big red letters. Instead of going to the front window, he went around the side. He could soon be seen inside the van talking and smiling at Tami, the red-haired leader of the food crews.

"He's so happy to be out of that trailer. How does he cope stuck in there all the time?" said Sam.

Jack hesitated. "Sometimes he doesn't. Rilla says it's better now I'm here and can take him outside. We all try to support him, to make him feel part of the community."

"I'm guessing having the cameras has helped him," said Sam drily.

Jack let out a snort of unexpected laughter. "Well, it hasn't hurt." He glanced up to where they both knew a camera was hiding. "I wish it wasn't necessary. But we need to keep an eye on the Carnival, try to avoid the kind of sabotage we had before you came. We can't let another person like Hugo take advantage of us."

"Veronica was always in the background of Hugo's attempts. Did you know that?"

Jack nodded. "We've since realized they were connected. Veronica is a very smart woman. Hence the cameras." He paused. "I don't want anyone else to know about them, okay? Frankie knows to keep quiet, and I'm sure you do too," he said in his Ringmaster voice.

Sam nodded. "Of course." He thought about Celestine. Technically he hadn't told her, she'd just known about them.

Frankie walked back to them. Whatever he'd said had charmed the older woman—he had two large churros, one in each hand. "The best ever," he said, closing his eyes for emphasis. Sugar dusted the side of his mouth.

Jack looked at his watch. "I have to meet Viktor quickly about a new ride. You'll be fine here for a few minutes?"

Frankie nodded. "As long as you don't go too far away, I'll be fine."

"It'll be a good test of my ability to pin point my absorbing. I'll be back in a few minutes."

Frankie waved him away, and Jack strode off toward the thrill rides.

"Did you tell him about Celestine?" asked Sam.

Frankie shook his head. "For some reason, I'm reluctant to do it. That's usually my intuition at work, and I like to trust that." He shrugged. "I'm the Chancemaster after all."

"Do you think she's involved in something bad?"

Frankie shook his head. "But we need to keep watching her. She's up to something strange."

"Alfie is worried about her too," replied Sam. "He told Jack we need to keep watch on her."

"I'll keep watching the video surveillance, see if she does any more midnight walks. And I'll ask one of the kids to watch her during the day, see if we can discover anything useful."

Sam nodded absently. "It can't hurt to keep an eye on her. Just to make sure." Why did he feel like this was familiar? He looked at Frankie's sugar-coated mouth. Hadn't Celestine said something...?

Frankie finished the churro and wiped his face with one hand. He pulled out a deck of cards and started flicking them in his hands, the cards blurring they were going so fast. "The chances are good that she's hiding something. We can't take any risks, not right now."

"She'll never know we've been watching her, will she?"

"No. Joey and the other boys are good at what they do. And how is she going to know about the cameras around the Carnival? No one else does. Jack was pretty clear on that point."

"But she does know," blurted Sam. "She told me about them after she had a seizure." Sam felt a strange tingling along his skin. Celestine had described this scene to him. Frankie eating a churro with sugar on his face. Watching her with cameras.

His skin felt clammy, like he was sweating all over, but he was cold to the bone. "She knew. She saw this in her vision," he whispered. "She really can see the future."

CHAPTER 22

*C*elestine felt like she was trapped inside the small tent. The velvet walls seemed to press in on her, and she wiped the small round table for the third time. Her hands were shaking as she worked.

What was she going to do about Sam? How was she going to keep him safe from Veronica? Not to mention herself. She'd seen her own death wrapped up in his future now. She still remembered the look in Veronica's eyes as she fired the gun. There had been glee as well as an unholy sense of satisfaction.

The woman had enjoyed every second.

Artemis curled around her legs, and she dropped into the chair with a sigh. The massive cat immediately jumped onto her lap and bumped her head into Celestine's chin. She smoothed her hand along the cat's back. A rumbling purr erupted from Artemis's throat, and Celestine laughed. "You always make me feel better, don't you Artemis?"

She rubbed herself along the side of Celestine's hand and curled into a lying position on her knees.

"You're too big, Artemis. You're almost falling off." Celestine held Artemis around her sides, keeping her in place.

"Hello?" The voice was hesitant. "Anyone here?" A slight figure pushed her way through the tent flap and into the small space.

"Uh... Hi, Missy." Celestine only knew the star trapeze performer fractionally; their paths didn't cross much.

Missy rubbed her palms on the sides of her jeans and gazed around, wide-eyed. "I've never been inside a fortune-teller's tent before. You'd think I'd know more about it, given I've lived here my whole life."

Celestine smiled, liking Missy's candid style. "It's just the same as the other sideshow tents, except for the mood lighting." She gestured to the small lamp to one side.

Missy laughed. "I guess it is."

"Come, sit down." Celestine gestured to the chair. "Tell me what brings you to this part of the show."

Missy hesitantly moved forward and perched on the edge of the wooden chair on the other side of Celestine's table. She noticed Artemis for the first time. "I wondered what that noise was. Sounds like a small motor."

"He's a big softie."

"I can see." Missy paused. "I should be checking on everyone in the sideshows more regularly, I guess. I *am* the Showmaster."

Celestine nodded. "Christoph used to come by and say hi every few days."

Missy blinked at the reference to her father. "I guess I don't know as much as I think I do about what he did."

"He's a good man. He just made some bad decisions," said Celestine softly.

"Yeah, maybe." Missy shifted awkwardly in her chair. "Jack told me you've been having seizures."

Celestine's heart stopped in her chest. Sam had promised

her he'd talk to her first before he said anything more to Jack. "It's okay. I'm fine."

"I need to make sure you're up to your job. What would happen if you had a seizure while you were with a punter?"

Celestine shook her head. "That would never happen. It only happens when I've touched someone on their bare skin."

Missy stared at Celestine, her hazel eyes shadowed. "Look, I know you're not a real fortune-teller. That's okay, you draw in the crowds, and you're good at what you do. But it means your seizures are a problem. You can't control them, and I doubt they'll stick to being only when someone activates your bare skin phobia."

The words made Celestine breathe out slowly, as if through thickened air. She'd created this reputation. This was what she'd wanted, how she'd decided to survive in hiding. She'd needed everyone to believe she was a fraud, a fake.

Her brothers could find her at any minute, and she didn't need the growing reputation of a real fortune-teller drawing them in.

But now it was coming back to bite her on the butt. Missy was going to tell her she had to go home. If she really was having random seizures, perhaps she'd agree and go quietly.

But she wasn't.

A strange feeling of calm came over Celestine. This was it. "I'll prove it to you." She slowly removed her gloves, finger by finger, as Missy watched, a bland expression on her face. "Put your hands out on the table."

Missy did as she was told, and Celestine grasped Missy's hands in hers.

Time froze, Missy's expression held still, and then the bright rainbow lights appeared around her. She'd left the real world behind.

Celestine was in the big top, and Missy was practicing

high above with the new trapeze artist, Alphonso. They wore matching black and silver outfits, and there were black silks dangling from the rigging high above. They slowly moved through a matching routine, showing off their skills and their strength. Celestine had watched these kinds of acts her whole life, but had never seen anyone as graceful and talented as Missy. Alphonso seemed just as good.

The ribbon practice was beautiful and mesmerizing, but nothing happened, and eventually Celestine felt herself falling away from the vision. When she opened her eyes again, she was still holding tight to Missy's hands across the table and could feel the remnants of her shaking.

"Are you okay?" Missy leaned forward. "I didn't know what to do. I didn't want to let go, in case you tumbled off your chair."

"I'm fine. I..." Celestine fumbled for something to say. Nothing in the vision would convince Missy of her talents. She'd failed. "I didn't see anything useful. Just you and Alphonso practicing for a new act."

Missy looked at Celestine with genuine pity in her eyes. "I'm sorry, Celestine. I know you want to stay. But these seizures are getting serious now."

"Just let me stay a bit longer. I need to be here." If she left, Sam was going to continue on his collision course with Veronica. He was going to wind up dead, and he was going to take other people with him. She had to stop it.

Missy was shaking her head.

"What about if I don't do my show, but help out in other ways? Maybe with Sam in the clinic?"

Missy hesitated. "You can stay till the end of the week. But you're taking up space and food here. We need you back at the Compound, getting proper medical treatment."

"Sam's not proper?"

She sighed. "Sam's great, but he's one man. And he doesn't seem to see things clearly when it comes to you."

Celestine frowned at Missy. "What does that mean?"

"He said to Jack that you should stay. But clearly,"—she gestured to Celestine—"it's not okay. You're still having seizures, and it's not fortune-telling. I'm sorry." Missy stood up decisively. "You can come back later in the season maybe, if you manage to stop the seizures."

Celestine stood. "Missy—"

"I'm sorry, Celestine. My mind is made up."

CHAPTER 23

*T*he two men were as different from Celestine as it was possible to be. Tall and broad, with long noses and dark eyes, they stood out because they were head and shoulders over most of the other punters.

But something about the way the shorter one stood—or perhaps it was the expression on his face—made Sam hesitate on his way to talk to Jack.

The Carnival had just opened, the first flow of people were streaming into the area. Lighthearted music danced through the air, and the sweet smell of candied apples and churros assaulted his nostrils. The thrill rides would be starting up soon, and the sideshows were filling with hopeful punters. Most people were chatting excitedly or laughing as they headed toward their favorite section of the show.

But these two guys weren't looking around, at least not in excitement. It looked more like they were casing the joint.

He followed them down the alleyway toward the contortionists and the tattooed lady. They barely looked at the tents and their splashy advertising. They looked like they had a specific destination in mind. Celestine's tent was toward the back, out of the way of the main stream of people. He'd always thought it was a good idea, but now that he was following the two large men, he had changed his mind.

Should he stop and get reinforcements? Everyone was busy, and he wasn't entirely certain he was right. Maybe they weren't Celestine's brothers. He looked around and didn't see anyone he could recruit. His eye caught a flash of sunlight on something metallic. One of the cameras. He waved at the camera and pointed to Celestine's tent. He mouthed the word *help* as obviously as he could, waved and jumped a little more, then kept going. Hopefully that was enough to alert Frankie, who could then send in the cavalry.

If not, he'd have to figure something out.

The bigger of the two men saw the fortune-teller's tent and stopped suddenly. He nudged the other man's side, and pointed. They both nodded and slipped back behind another tent in a manner that could only be described as lurking.

That was it. They were definitely after Celestine, whether they were her brothers or not. Sam ran down the alleyway, past the two men and Celestine's tent, trying to pretend that he was on some kind of urgent mission that had nothing to do with whatever they were doing. Then he turned down the narrow strip between tents and came back around behind Celestine's tent.

He pulled aside the tent flaps. Celestine was standing by the front entrance, talking to Missy. It didn't look like it was a happy conversation. "Celestine. You need to get out of here," he whispered urgently, striding into the tent. "I think your brothers are outside."

Celestine turned at the sound of his voice. She stared uncomprehendingly at him for a moment, and then her face paled, and she took a step back from the entrance. "It's not possible." She shook her head.

Sam's heart lurched; she looked terrified. What exactly

had her brothers done to her? "I don't know for sure, but there are two men, and they're definitely interested in you." He moved to stand closer to her, wanting to protect her.

Celestine stared wide-eyed up at him. "I would feel them if they were close…" Her voice stumbled to a halt. She paused, her expression going vacant for a moment. "Oh God, it's them. I can sense them now." She put one hand to her flushed cheek. "How did I not notice?" She glared over at Missy. "I was too busy trying to prove myself to you. I should have known better than to try."

Missy frowned. "What's going on?"

Ignoring Missy, Celestine looked frantically around. "I have to get out of here. They can't find me. I can't get close to them."

Missy glanced at Sam, then gently placed her hand on Celestine's arm. "You need to tell me what's happening," she said, standing so that Celestine had to look her in the eyes.

"My brothers will force me to go back with them. I can't do it. I *can't*." Tears sparkled in Celestine's eyes, and her movements were jerky and agitated.

Sam stepped around Missy and put his arms around her shoulders. "It's going to be fine. We'll protect you from them."

"They can't make you go anywhere with them; we won't let them," said Missy, nodding in agreement. "You're part of *our* family now."

"You don't understand…," Celestine's voice trailed off, glancing between Sam and Missy.

"We need a distraction," said Sam, moving back slightly. He untied Celestine's scarf from her head. "Here Missy, put this on. If they come in, you can pretend to be Madame Fortune." He hesitated, glanced at Missy's clothes, then removed the shawl Celestine had wrapped around her shoulders. "Just keep them here until I can get Celestine away."

Missy glanced down at her T-shirt and jeans. "I'm not sure I'll be that convincing."

Celestine dragged down her long floaty skirt, revealing tight leggings underneath. "Here put this on as well." She handed Missy the skirt, but kept her gloves and long sleeved shirt firmly in place.

Sighing, Missy pulled up the skirt and walked over to the table. "When this is done, you're going to tell me exactly what is going on," she said in as stern a voice as Sam had ever heard her use.

Sam nodded his head firmly. "Absolutely," he said, although he wasn't entirely certain he knew the full story either. He grabbed Celestine's hand and pulled her behind him, out the back of the tent.

"Why do they have such a hold over you?" he whispered as they crept along the back of her tent.

Celestine shook her head and refused to speak until they were a few tents away. She crouched down low and dragged Sam down beside her. Her breath was coming in gasps, and she was trembling all over. "I have a foreseeing talent." Her violet-blue eyes met his. "Whatever you may think about that, it's true. My brothers have one very specific ability; a persuasion talent they can use on me. I have no choice but to do what they say."

Sam glanced back at the tent. "Is Missy going to be okay?"

"It doesn't work on anyone else. Just me."

"So they can force you to go back, just by insisting that you come with them?"

Celestine nodded. She was huddled next to Sam, and he felt rather than saw the tremors shuddering through her body.

"That's terrifying." He'd thought having Veronica's block was bad enough, but at least Indigo had been able to remove it. This was permanent.

She nodded again, wrapping her arms around her body. "I can't tell you how terrifying. My father had the same power over my mother. He forced her to keep doing the shows, even when she was exhausted and it was hurting her, making her sick. He worked her into the ground until she was nothing more than a shell of a person. And then he made her do some more. She went crazy because she had too many futures flying around inside her head. He *killed* her." Celestine's words were coming low and fast, as if she'd released a dam and was unable to stop them coming out.

"And you think your brothers would do the same?" Sam leaned in closer, lending her his warmth and trying to let her know he wouldn't let anything happen to her.

"I *know* they would. They already did, before I ran away. They see me as their meal ticket; that's how our father taught them to think. Without me, they're just the guys who put up the posters."

"How did you get away from them?"

"Their persuasion talent only works when I'm nearby. I realized I had to put some distance between us and then just stay in hiding. So I was perfectly behaved, and they relaxed around me. One day in a town on the circuit, I managed to buy some sleeping tablets and crushed them up into their evening meal. When they fell asleep, I took everything I could and ran. I stole their truck and packed up all my mother's things—I couldn't bear to leave them with my brothers." The violet in her eyes darkened with the memories.

A gust of wind swept up between them, blowing Celestine's hair across her face. Sam leaned over and used a finger to brush it back. "I can help you, Celestine. I won't let them get you," he said softly.

"You won't be able to stop it. If they see me, they'll take me with them." She turned her head, as if to hide her face. "I'll tell you I want to go with them. I'll resist anything you say. Because once they have me, they'll be able to persuade me to do whatever they want."

"I won't let that happen. I know what you want." He grabbed her into a tight hug and after a moment's hesitation, Celestine hugged him back. She was careful to keep her skin away from his, but it was a start.

He leaned back and looked down into her eyes. "I think you should take a look, make sure it's them," he said softly.

Celestine shook her head vehemently, her curly hair spilling wildly over her face. "I can't. I won't."

"We'll stay well back out of sight. I'll go first, make sure they can't see you."

"I can feel them. I know it's them," she whispered.

"What if I've made some kind of mistake? Maybe I've spotted the wrong guys. They could be some of Veronica's goons, or a couple of completely innocent customers." Sam peered around the corner of the tent, trying to see if the two men were visible. There were too many people walking up and down the alleyway; he couldn't see them.

"Do you really believe that?"

He glanced back at her. "That I'm wrong? No. But we need to make sure. From a distance, I promise."

Sam put her gloved hand in his, and they crept around the back of the tent where they'd been hiding. "We need to get closer."

Celestine reluctantly allowed Sam to lead her back toward her tent. They were behind the adjacent tent when Sam heard raised voices from inside Celestine's red velvet tent. He tensed.

"It's them," whispered Celestine. "I recognise their voices." She crouched down beside the canvas of the next-door tent.

Sam hesitated, but he couldn't leave Missy on her own with two over-muscled bullies if they were going to get aggressive with her. "Wait here," he said. "I have to check on Missy."

Celestine clutched at his hand. "Don't leave me."

Sam crouched down next to her and pulled both her hands in his. "It's going to be fine. We're part of the Carnival now. These people take care of their own. And *I'm* not going to let your brothers take you," he vowed.

She shook her head sadly. "You won't have any say in it. That's not how the magic works."

"We'll find you somewhere to hide while I make sure she's okay. They won't find you. Then when they've gone, we'll figure out how we're going to make this work." Sam crept back to the contortionist's tent, two down from hers. He found an open flap at the back and urged her inside. "Stay here and don't move. I'll come back for you as soon as I make sure Missy is okay." He touched her arm gently. "It'll be fine. They won't find you here."

Celestine regarded him with her violet eyes, doubt swirling in their depths. Sam hesitated, wondering if he really should be leaving her—but he had no choice. He couldn't just leave Missy on her own with those thugs.

He ran back out onto the main alleyway, and sprinted towards Madame Fortune's tent. Pulling the flap aside, he peered into the dark interior, just in time to hear Missy speak.

"You can both get out of here right now. I've had enough of your stupid questions," she said sternly.

The two men were looming over Missy, their eyes narrowed to mean slits.

"What's going on in here, Missy?" said Sam.

The two men turned at the same time, identical expressions of contempt on their faces. "Nothing's going on. We're just asking this pretty fortune-teller some questions."

"That she doesn't appreciate from the sounds of it. You

can leave now, or I can have security throw you out." He hoped he sounded more certain than he felt.

"No one's going anywhere," snarled the bigger of the two. "Who do you think's gonna win in a fight? Me and m'brother here, or a pip-squeak fella like you and a *woman*?"

Sam made a mental note to start taking Garth's capoeira classes in the mornings, so that if someone ever spoke to him like that again, he could give them the shock of their lives. But for now, it was probably true. "I wouldn't underestimate carny folk. We can be pretty slippery."

The bigger man sneered. "You think you're any different to us? We're carnies as well, mate, and that's nothing that's gonna protect you."

Sam took a step forward, wondering how many bones these two were going to break on his body. He could see Missy gesturing behind them, but he had no idea what she was planning.

Seconds later, when she leaped on the back of the smaller man, he assumed she'd been telling him to take the larger brother. He managed to duck under a punch from the big man, who was slow with his fists, but the second punch got him in the stomach. Sam stumbled back, winded. He put his hands over his belly, struggling to breathe.

The next punch got him on the side of his head, and Sam slammed onto the hard earth, trying desperately to get his bearings. His attacker loomed over him, his leg pulled back for a kick, when a flurry of action at the entrance made him turn.

Several figures rushed into the tent. A couple of them converged on the larger brother, dragging him away from Sam. Others helped Missy to bring down the smaller brother.

Through his blurry vision and the ringing in his head, Sam vaguely recognized Davos, a couple of Viktor's sons, and Jack. They had the two men well in hand, pulling their hands up behind their backs.

"You okay?" asked Jack, still panting from the exertion.

Sam nodded weakly from his position on the ground. Everything was still a little bit woozy inside his head, but at least he wasn't about to be kicked.

"We'll take care of these two. You both stay here. Recover for a minute."

Jack led them out the door before Sam could even pull himself up.

"You alright?" said Missy, putting her hand out to grasp Sam's.

"I've been better," he said, groaning as he came to his feet.

"Where's Celestine?"

"I left her hiding just down from here. I need to go get her." He managed to get to his feet, and move toward the door. He was unsteady, and when he got to the tent pole at the entrance, he hung on tight for a moment. The world was spinning, and the suddenness of the attack and then withdrawal had given him a strange adrenaline rush that was affecting his thinking.

He peered out the tent and in one direction saw the group of men, centered on the two brothers who were being pulled toward the main exit.

In the other direction, he saw Celestine peering around the edge of the tent where he'd left her.

When she saw Sam, she ran out onto the main alleyway and into his arms. "I saw them. It was my brothers. They were really here."

CHAPTER 24

"*I* have to leave. That was too close." Celestine paced up and down Sam's clinic, twisting her fingers together restlessly. "They might come back."

"They're just thugs who like to make trouble," said Sam from where he was sitting, drinking a cup of green tea. "They didn't see you, and Missy says they had no idea she wasn't the real fortune-teller."

"Then why did they make the effort to go into the tent? Why did they try to get more information from Missy?" All she could think of was escape, of getting as far away from her brothers as possible. "They probably recognised my mother's tent."

Sam shook his head. "I'm sure there are hundreds of other tents just like it. And maybe Missy said something they didn't like." He leaned back and put one hand to his stomach. "They didn't strike me as the kind of guys who think before they hit." He rubbed the spot where her brother, Alden, had punched him. It made her flush with shame to think that she had gotten him hurt.

"They must have been pretty sure it was supposed to be me."

"Or they could just try the fortune-teller at every new circus they come across. We can't know for sure."

Celestine took a deep breath. And another. Being this close to her brothers again made all the old fears and panic resurface. She thought she'd left all that behind.

But she could never leave it behind.

The thought brought another wave of panic crashing over her body, and she had to sit quickly on the clinic bed before she collapsed. She closed her eyes and lay back on the thin mattress. "What's the point in having a fortune-telling talent, if you can't even foresee this kind of thing?" she said softly.

"Celestine...," said Sam gently.

"Don't you dare tell me I don't see the future," she said fiercely, glaring over at Sam. "Not now. Just pretend for the moment that I do have it, and everything is possible, would you? Just for the next five minutes?" She closed her eyes again and tried to relax into the clinic's narrow bed.

She heard Sam's footsteps as he came closer to her bed. She opened one eye and regarded his solemn face.

"I believe you," he said.

She blinked open her other eye and stared up at him. "Pardon?" Had she heard him properly? She pulled herself up so she was sitting with her legs dangling off the edge of the bed.

"I know you can see the future. I believe you."

It felt like the air had been sucked out of her lungs. He'd been so adamant that she was injured. She frowned. "I don't understand... What changed your mind?"

He paused. "I experienced one of the visions you told me about in real life. Frankie eating churros and the two of us discussing...." He hesitated.

"How you were going to have me followed? That you didn't trust me?" said Celestine, lifting her eyebrows.

Sam shook his head. "I never believed you meant the Carnival harm. I just don't trust my instincts anymore. That was what got me into trouble with Veronica."

Celestine nodded again, something easing inside her as she saw that Sam finally believed what she had been telling him. He moved to sit next to her, his shoulder touching hers.

"I'm sorry I didn't believe you earlier," he said softly, bumping his shoulder against hers.

"I worked long and hard to build up the reputation for being a fake. I'd have been a little disappointed if you'd believed me straight away," she said with a half smile. It felt good, knowing he believed her, and that her secret was out. She'd had to work so hard to walk the fine line between bringing in the punters for the fortunes and convincing everyone else at the Carnival she was a fake. She'd had enough.

No more hiding.

But then she remembered her brothers and the reason she'd been hiding in the first place. Her momentary euphoria evaporated. She would always be hiding from them. Her hands tightened onto the edge of the bed. There was no way to escape.

"I could have been more open to it," insisted Sam. "I knew you were a good person from the beginning. There was no reason for you to lie to me."

Celestine looked at him and wished things could be different. His dark brown eyes drew her in; all she wanted to do was lean forward and touch him. To place her lips on his, to taste him, to feel his body against hers.

She hadn't been attracted to someone like this since she was a teenager and had had a crush on a gorgeous young contortionist. Only difference was that he'd never given her the time of day. Sam, however, was looking at her with his intense eyes, something dark and mysterious dancing in their depths. She was on the verge of doing something dangerous when a knock on the door made her jump.

Sam sighed before standing and heading over to open the door. For a moment he hesitated on the doorstep, then he waved someone inside. Looking up, she saw Garth towering over her. It figured.

"Did you have an uncontrollable urge to visit me, too?" she asked.

He was silent for a moment. "The Carnival says you're not the fake fortune-teller you've been pretending to be. Apparently it's been protecting you since it became strong enough to understand what you were doing."

His eyes were the expressionless all black they became when he was in the middle of the Gift. It made his face seem dark and unforgiving. Celestine just stared at him, not sure how to answer.

"Take off your gloves," ordered Garth. He sat down on a wooden stool next to the bed.

"Please," said Celestine.

Garth frowned. "Please what?"

"If you say please, I might be more inclined to help you," she said in a patient voice, determined not to be intimidated by him.

Garth bowed his head slightly. "My apologies. Please, Celestine, if you would take off your gloves and let me test your abilities."

Sam came over to stand beside the bed. Celestine sat on the edge, her feet dangling off the side. She removed her soft leather gloves, finger by finger. She seemed to be spending an awful lot of time recently with her gloves off, telling fortunes. She glanced up at Garth. "You say the Carnival knows I can tell the future? So it *was* the Carnival that sent you to me?"

"It sent Alfie, Viktor, and Missy too, if that's what you're asking." He stopped and seemed to consider his next words. "None of them thought you could tell the future after their visits."

Celestine nodded jerkily.

Garth cleared his throat. "I've just come from talking to Frankie. He thinks there's a good chance you can actually tell the future."

Celestine didn't know Frankie well, but people seemed to respect his opinions. She knew he was good with gambling and understanding the odds. It occurred to her that his ability was similar to hers, except he used a knowledge of the situation and a kind of fact-based intuition to figure out what might happen in the future. Less precise, but it could be used more widely than her own very specific talents.

"He talked to Alfie and Viktor after they saw you. They explained how your fortunes were completely off base, thereby proving you couldn't tell the future. But something they said convinced him you were for real." Garth's eerie eyes never left Celestine's face. "You were telling them the exact opposite of what was true. The *exact* opposite."

Celestine didn't know what to say. She glanced at Sam, who was grinning back at her.

"It's highly improbable that you'd get it so precisely wrong each time," said Garth.

"As much as I appreciate the fact that the Carnival believes in you, we've been through enough recently without being conned by a very clever fake." Garth bowed his head toward Celestine. "If you'll excuse the blunt talking."

"I didn't know," blurted Celestine abruptly.

"Didn't know what?" said Garth, frowning down at her.

"That Abba was going to die."

Garth had known and worked closely with their former Ringmaster. She didn't want him thinking she'd just stood by and let it happen.

Garth took a deep breath. "You can't prevent everything in this world, Celestine. Life still happens around us, even with our gifts to lead the way." His words took on a deeper tone, and Celestine felt a ripple of power.

"You're joined to the Carnival right now? Because of the Gift?" asked Celestine. Her heart beat faster. She had felt the rich beating heart of the Carnival when she'd first arrived. It had soothed her, enabled her to rest and recover. But its real power had been lying dormant. Now their enemies were defeated—or at least more visible—the power of the Carnival was resurfacing. She wasn't sure she wanted to touch Garth and be connected to that overwhelming magic.

"Yes." His lips tightened, but he didn't elaborate.

Celestine watched Garth carefully, trying to decide what to say to him. "I don't know what will happen when I touch you. It might be your future, or it might be the Carnival's." Celestine hesitated. "I haven't been seeing very good futures for the Carnival and its people recently," she said.

Garth nodded again, his face even more grim, if that was possible. "We must do it. If you can truly see our future, and it is not as we'd like it to be... We need to know."

Celestine let out a breath, relieved to be doing something. She had only ever wanted to help the Carnival, ever since Abba had taken a chance on her. She'd let him down by not being vigilant enough, and he'd died without ever being warned about it, but she could help Garth. "Hold out your hands."

He held them out, palms up in front of her. Celestine held her hands over his, hesitating for a moment. Before she could change her mind, she grasped his hands in hers.

Everything froze around her. Sam's warmth next to her, Garth's hands in hers.

Celestine looked up. The one thing that hadn't stopped was the swirling mists that churned inside Garth's black eyes. The power inside him stared out at her, and she held still.

The sparkling rainbow lights appeared, blocking out her surroundings. She didn't know if it would be for Garth or the Carnival itself, but she had an idea the Carnival was in control and very present in her vision space.

Images appeared, but they were different from usual, too many to see clearly, all laid over each other, until it was just a mass of noise and color. She couldn't make out individual people, or hear what was being said. Nothing made any sense, and she put her hands over her ears to block out the increasing level of noise bombarding her. But it didn't make any difference inside a vision; when she closed her eyes, she still saw the images flashing and her hearing was still perfect despite her blocked ears.

Celestine's heart thumped hard in her chest and knew that her real body would be shaking, in the grip of a seizure. This overload of sensation was too much for her to take in, and she could feel her body starting to shut down.

And then it stopped.

Only one image was left. The Blue Carousel, rotating slowly with the setting sun behind it, the internal hinges squeaking. The music was gone, and so were all the rides that usually lit up the interior. Cracked pieces of glass and plaster lay around the edges. There were stains on the ground that Celestine knew were blood. The scene of the carnage had been cleaned up, but some of the evidence remained.

A lone, silhouetted figure walked toward the carousel, limping slightly, a sad slump to his shoulders.

It wasn't until he was right next to the carousel that Celestine could make out who he was.

Garth.

But not the Garth that she knew, the strong man who had stood before her in the clinic.

This Garth had a long, fresh scar across his cheek, his clothes were ripped and dirty, and his expression held a vein of sadness so deep that Celestine couldn't breathe as she looked at him.

CHAPTER 25

*S*am held Celestine's shaking body in his arms. Despite knowing this was what happened whenever she looked into the future, his primal instinct was to protect her from it. If he had his way, she'd never do another reading.

"Is it always like this?" asked Garth, his black eyes shifting and spinning.

Sam nodded grimly. "She's never seen it, so she doesn't realize how bad it is."

Celestine slowly stopped shaking. Her body went limp, as it had the other times she'd seen the future in his presence. Sam held her tight against his chest, leaning back against the wall behind them on the clinic's bed. She opened her eyes slowly. He wondered how often she'd been surprised by a vision and had ended up on the floor with bruises and cuts to show for it.

Garth closed his eyes and then opened them. Instead of the all black they'd been only moments before, they now glowed bright with the colors of the rainbow, spinning and swirling across the surface of his eyes. Power emanated from those eyes, so bright that Sam had to look away.

"You truly do have the power of foresight, Celestine Rose Mayweather," he intoned in a strange voice. "The Carnival has seen what you saw, and it is a frightening future. We thank you for letting us follow you into your realm."

Sam felt a whisper of air against his skin and shivered. For the first time, he realized the Carnival was more than just a group of people. There was a presence with them in the room, using Garth as its conduit. It felt beautiful and magical all at once, a glorious outpouring of delight and happiness. The soul of the Carnival, the sum of all its people was here with them.

And then it was gone. Garth blinked again and his eyes returned to their inky blackness.

"We have to go talk to Rilla and Jack. All of us. This is more serious than we'd realized," he said.

Celestine nodded. "I just need a few moments to get my bearings." She tried to sit up, out of Sam's arms, but he held tight. After a moment, she relaxed back against his shoulder.

Sam shook his head. "She needs more than a few moments. That was a really big seizure."

"They're not—" Celestine began to protest.

"I know you're seeing something, and I understand that it's really the future," said Sam. "But to your body, here in the real world, it's still a seizure, and it's affecting you. It's not something to take lightly."

"I don't take it lightly," she snapped. "I just know what I'm capable of. You don't need to baby me."

"You've been taking risks all these years," continued Sam. He hated to think of all the times something could have happened to her. He thought of her brothers. They had probably made her do reading after reading, looking for the money, unconcerned with her health. His arms tightened around her body.

Garth bowed slightly and stepped back. "I'll leave you to your arguments. I must talk to Rilla and let them know what is happening."

"You saw it too?" asked Celestine.

"Yes. Through the Carnival's power, I saw my future. It's not going to happen if I can help it." Garth's expression was grim.

"I've never had that happen before."

"We're both connected to the Carnival." He shrugged. "It's more powerful than all of us combined." He nodded and left through the narrow door.

Celestine pushed herself back up into a sitting position, and Sam let her go. He moved so that he was leaning on the edge of the bed, right next to her.

"I'm not a child you know," she said.

"I never said you were."

"Don't boss me around."

"Did your brothers make you do it very often?"

Celestine hesitated and then nodded. "It brings in the most money, doing a skin-to-skin reading." Her eyes were shadowed with remembered pain.

Sam wanted to gather her up in his arms again, to sooth away that hurt. He knew what it was like to have someone else directing his every move. It was something he vowed he would never go back to, and he would never let the same happen to her. "I won't let your brothers find you again," he said.

"You can't control that." Celestine shook her head. "I still have to leave. They were suspicious of Missy." She stood up from the bed and started pacing again.

"You don't know that."

She turned and faced him. "The fact they stayed and tried

to argue with her tells me they suspect something. Even the way they decided to fight you so easily. They were angry because they thought you were hiding me." She hesitated. "They could probably feel my presence, the same way I felt them." She resumed her pacing.

Sam stood, stepping into the middle of the aisle and into her path. She stopped abruptly in front of him, and he placed his hands on her shoulders. "You don't have to go anywhere, Celestine. Stay here at the Jolly Knight Carnival. We'll all protect you from your brothers."

She shook her head. "But that's just it. I keep seeing futures where the Carnival has been destroyed. You can't save me if you're dead." Her words reverberated around the otherwise silent trailer.

Sam shook her gently. "Your visions of the future... Are they set in stone?" he asked.

Celestine blinked and looked up at him, her violet eyes staring right into his soul. "I... I don't think so. Your future has changed every time I've read you." She blinked again. "I don't usually see into people's futures more than once."

"Then you have to stay and tell us what you see. You can help change the futures you've been witnessing."

"Is that the only reason you want me to stay? To tell you what I've seen?"

Sam hesitated. He shook his head. "No. I want you to stay for me."

Celestine's eyes darkened, and she leaned forward, falling into his arms, her head against his chest. He held her tight, a warm bundle that he never wanted to let go. He kissed her on the top of her head, and Celestine leaned back, gazing up at him. He leaned in and softly kissed her, pulling her to him, and trying to let her know by touch how he felt about her. For a moment, there was nothing but sensation, the feeling of her against him, the rightness of her lips against his.

And then he felt her body shaking against his.

He pulled back; her eyes were closed and she was in the grip of another seizure.

His heart stuttered in his chest as he realized what he'd done. Through his own selfishness, he'd sent her off into another vision, exactly what he'd vowed he'd protect her from.

CHAPTER 26

Sam grasped Celestine under the shoulders and knees, lifting her back onto the clinic bed. He stood over her, watching her beautiful face, his heart wrenching in two. He couldn't ever kiss her again.

It wasn't long before she opened her eyes again.

"Are you okay? Are you hurt?" he asked.

"I'm fine," she said with a frown. "I keep telling you, it's completely normal."

"What did you see?" he asked.

She shook her head and looked away. "Nothing has changed."

"I'm so sorry, Celestine. I didn't mean to send you into a vision. I won't do it again."

She quickly turned her gaze back to him. "What do you mean?"

"We can't kiss again. I can't keep sending you off into visions every time I touch you."

"It *is* inconvenient," she said with a small half smile.

"It's not safe," Sam said, wishing she would accept how dangerous her seizures were.

"My mother and grandmother had exactly the same talent I do. They were both fine."

"I thought your mother died because your father forced her to continue reading fortunes for too long?"

"He forced her to keep going even when she was so exhausted. She could barely keep her eyes open. As long as I'm in control of them, I'm fine."

It was when others took control that there were issues, Sam thought sourly. Her brothers were a big problem. He'd have to talk to Jack about what they could do to help Celestine.

Celestine pushed herself into a sitting position using her elbows. "I need to talk to Rilla and Jack. You're right. I do owe it to the Carnival to tell them everything I've seen."

"Do you want a drink or something to eat first? Does it tire you out, having a vision?"

Celestine shook her head. "I'm fine. Let's go."

They were quiet on the way to the Ringmaster's Airstream, each of them lost in thought. It was still midafternoon, although it felt much later to Sam. So much had happened, he wondered how it had all been crammed into one day.

The door to the trailer opened as they approached, and Rilla poked her head out. Even outside of the ring, she was stunning; her straight, dark hair was arranged with not even a strand out of place, and her bright blue eyes were sharp as she gazed at Celestine and Sam. "You coming to see us?" she said.

"Yes," said Sam. "Is Garth with you?"

Rilla nodded. "He's been telling us an interesting story." She smiled at Celestine. "We need you to fill us in on everything. Come inside."

Sam stood back and let Rilla lead Celestine to the table. Jack and Garth were already there, cups of coffee in front of them, serious expressions on their faces as they considered whatever dark future Garth had seen. He knew Celestine had seen his death more than once. Perhaps Garth had seen a similar future. His brain refused to think too far on that topic—they just had to prevent whatever dark future Celestine had seen for the Carnival.

"Coffee, Celestine, Sam?" asked Jack.

They both shook their heads.

Rilla pulled a chair over from beside her bed, and offered Sam the other stool from the kitchen. Even in a trailer this size—one of the larger silver Airstream models—it felt cramped with this many people. He was still getting used to the idea of living in such small spaces and being so intimate with other people—he could actually see into the bedroom from his perch in the kitchen. At The Experiment, he'd had an entire house to himself behind the medical center. Veronica had given him every possible mod con and the best of everything.

He would rather be here with these people than back at The Experiment with her. A million times over.

Rilla cleared her throat and exchanged at glance with Jack. "Celestine, did my father, Abba, know that you were for real?"

Celestine shook her head, nervously twisting her fingers together on the table at the booth. "He knew I was desperate, and that I was hiding from someone. He never knew more than that."

"Those two men we threw out today," said Jack, "were they the people you've been hiding from?"

She nodded jerkily. "They're my brothers."

"We would have protected you from them," said Rilla softly. "You could have told us."

"You don't understand...." Celestine looked desperately over at Sam. "That woman Veronica, the one who held

Missy, she put a block on Sam, right? So he had to do everything she said?"

Rilla and Jack nodded.

"My brothers, they can tell me to do whatever they want, and I have to do it. One part of my brain knows that I don't want to do it, but it's hidden away, subverted by whatever part of me is linked to them. Once they have me under their control again, I'll happily tell you all to go to hell, to stop trying to protect me, and I'll leave with them." Celestine let out a hiccuping sob and covered her mouth with both hands.

Sam pulled his chair over and sat next to her, putting one hand on her back. He made sure he wasn't touching her anywhere near to her bare skin.

As he watched her pull herself together and face the others again, he realized something important. He'd been under Veronica's control for approximately ten years. He'd been in his midtwenties, a freshly minted doctor looking for adventure and exciting experiences when he'd crossed her path. He'd chafed and howled against the world when he realized he was stuck there with her, forced to do her bidding or receive bolts of unimaginable pain.

But Celestine had experienced the control of her family her entire life. She had always been under their power, and somehow she'd found the strength to fight her way out of that trap. She'd made it here and survived for three years on her own, living life her own way and with her own agendas. She was amazing.

"Did your brothers always have control over you, even when you were younger?" asked Rilla.

"No, it was my father up until he died a few years ago, just after my mother. The ability to control my actions passed from my father to my brothers."

"They both have it?" Rilla asked.

Celestine nodded again. "I think it's shared somehow. They can't do it without both of them present."

"You said your grandmother had it as well as your mother? So it's genetic?"

"Yes."

Cogs began to turn inside Sam's head as he listened to Rilla's questions. "So it's a talent that's been passed down. What about your mother? What happened to her?"

"She was powerful, more powerful than my grandmother. She was also pretty headstrong. She ran away a few times when she was a kid, because she hated my grandfather telling her what to do."

"Did he have the same power over her?"

Celestine paused, a tiny line appearing between her eyebrows. "I've never thought about it before. She never said so explicitly." She hesitated. "But he must have, and she hated it."

"How did she get away from him?"

"She ran away from home when she was sixteen and married my father."

"When did your father discover he could force your mother to do whatever he wanted?" said Sam softly.

Celestine put her head to one side. "Long before I was born," she whispered. "It was passed on from my grandfather to my father and then to my brothers."

Rilla leaned forward. "So if you marry, the persuasion magic passes from your brothers to your new husband?"

CHAPTER 27

*C*elestine swayed in her seat. The only thing holding her in place was the warmth of Sam's hand at her back. There was a way out of this? She could get her brothers to leave her alone? It was too good to be true.

But then reality hit, and she realized the other side of this new coin. "There must be a way to do it without having to give someone else control over me," she said. There was no way she was willing to do that.

Rilla nodded. "I understand, Celestine. We'll ask Indigo to research it for us in the archives. She might come up with a better solution."

"In the meantime, we need you to tell us everything you remember about your visions," said Garth, cutting into the discussion for the first time.

Jack nodded in agreement. "Garth's right. Tell us everything."

"I saw two different futures for Sam. And..." She glanced around the room nervously.

"What else did you see?" asked Rilla suspiciously.

"I saw you both die," she said in a rush, looking at Rilla and Jack.

Jack abruptly sat back against the padded booth seat.

"How? What happens?" said Rilla.

"Veronica. She's been in most of the visions. Definitely in all of Sam's futures. She gets him under another block. And Viktor as well. He... he sabotages the carousel because of her."

"What! Viktor would never...." Rilla hesitated, and Celestine didn't need to see into her head to know she was remembering Christoph's betrayal.

"She takes his granddaughter," said Celestine softly.

"Ruby?" blurted Jack, surprise in his voice. "She's only a couple months old. Surely even Veronica wouldn't stoop so low?"

Sam cleared his throat. "Yes, she would. She's done that kind of thing before."

Rilla and Jack gaped at Sam. "But a *baby*?" said Rilla.

"She doesn't have a sense of right or wrong. She only knows what she wants and then does everything she can to get it," said Sam quietly.

Celestine shivered. The thought that Sam had been in the power of someone like that for ten years made tears choke up her throat.

"What else, Celestine? Tell us everything."

And so, for the first time in years, Celestine told them precisely what she'd seen. When she'd finished, they looked shell-shocked.

"You're sure about all this...?" said Rilla hesitantly.

"As sure as I can be." Celestine paused. "Sam made a really good point. His futures have changed in the four times I've touched him. Nothing is set in stone." She glanced at Sam. "Although the last two times were the same."

"But if we make changes to the way we were going to do

things, we can change the way it happens, right?" asked Rilla, leaning forward.

"What if the changes we make are the changes we were going to make all along, and it leads us along the same path again?" Garth's voice was as sharp as a knife.

"I'm not an expert at this," said Celestine, just as sharply. "I've never tried to change someone's future before."

"What gets me is why Veronica is so determined to get Sam back," murmured Rilla thoughtfully. "Why isn't she just trying to kill him like the rest of us?"

Jack's gaze sharpened on Rilla. "You think he's special in some way?"

"I don't know." She turned to Sam. "Is it likely she'd go to all these lengths just to get even with you?"

Sam went still, his warm hand resting on Celestine's back. She turned so she could see his reaction.

His mouth was open as if he had something to say, but then he closed it again. He tried again. "All I can say is that in the past she's been content to kill people."

"Did she ever say you had a talent? Why did she keep you at her side all those years? Why you specifically?"

Sam looked from Rilla to Jack. "It's never occurred to me. I don't know. She could have had me killed any number of times, and sometimes I saw in her eyes that she wanted to. But she never did."

Celestine felt a ripple of power go around the room. "It's important. What you just said. I felt it," she said. She hesitated, thinking hard. "I think Veronica mentioned your powers in one of my visions. She said you were more powerful than you realized."

Rilla nodded. "I think Sam has some kind of latent talent that she was secretly using. Something that helped her. Otherwise, why would she be so determined to get you back?"

Sam nodded slowly. "That actually makes sense. Doctors like me are a dime a dozen. She could have replaced me at any time in the last few years. But she didn't."

"You don't have any idea what it might be?" asked Jack.

Sam shook his head. "No clue." He hesitated. "What if I have a power I could have used against her all this time?" Celestine could see the thought upset him.

"We need to figure it out," said Garth. His skin was ashen and his lips a hard slash across his face. Their possible future had unnerved him more than any of the others.

Rilla nodded. "What kind of talent would be invisible to Sam but valuable to Veronica? Something that gives her an edge."

"Wouldn't we have noticed his talent? Or the Carnival itself?" asked Jack.

"He has to become connected to the Carnival first. He's only been here a short time." Rilla glanced at Celestine. "We've had Celestine here for three years, and this is the first time we've realized she was hiding her talent."

"But that's because the Carnival is only just getting its full power back," said Jack. "Maybe in a few weeks—"

"We don't have a few weeks," interrupted Garth, his voice filled with raw emotion. "Veronica is an immediate threat to the Carnival and everyone in it. We need to know *now*."

Jack put one hand on Garth's arm. "We're going to be fine, Garth," he said calmly. "We won't let it happen."

Garth nodded, his movements jerky, but didn't say anything.

"Perhaps the Carnival could tell us what Sam's talent is," suggested Rilla. "What if we attempt to force Sam's connection?" She looked expectantly at Garth.

Behind Celestine, Sam's hand tensed on her back.

"You checked on me when I first arrived, Garth," said Jack. "Can't you do the same?"

Garth's black eyes swirled as they all turned to him. "I checked with the Carnival to see if Jack had good intentions toward us. It didn't tell me what his talent was. Forcing the Carnival connection to learn where Sam's hypothetical power lies could be dangerous. Mostly for Sam."

Celestine held her breath. Their current path meant Sam would die, but if he died while being bound to the Carnival, wasn't that the same thing? "How dangerous?" she asked.

"I don't know what his talent is. I can't predict how it might affect him." Garth pushed one hand through his hair in agitation.

Rilla looked at Sam. "Do you want to be part of the Jolly Knight Carnival, Sam? We'd be happy to have you, but I understand if you're reluctant after what happened with Veronica. It's up to you."

Sam paused. "I want to bring Veronica to justice. If that means bonding to the Carnival, so be it. Hopefully my ability involves being able to destroy her where she stands."

Celestine turned to look at Sam. "That's not the right reason to be part of the Carnival. You should want it in your bones." She put her hand on his arm. "To be part of something greater than yourself."

"Is that really how you felt when you arrived? Or were you just so scared to death that you would have agreed to anything?" said Sam, his expression grim. "There are many reasons to join, and this is one of them. Let's do it, Garth."

Celestine sat back, stunned by his harsh words. For the first time, she realized just how deep his hatred of Veronica went.

"Fine," Garth said. "No time like the present."

"What? Right now?" said Celestine, her voice almost squeaking. It was all so rushed. "Shouldn't we discuss this a bit more?"

"My decision is made," said Sam, nodding to Garth.

"And so is mine," said Garth. He closed his eyes and leaned back in his seat.

Celestine held her breath as she watched. Nothing happened at first, and she wondered if the Carnival had rejected Sam. Then the trailer started filling with power like a bathtub fills with water. It was as if they were floating in it, buoyed up by the sheer energy that emanated from Garth.

Celestine had never felt anything like it. It was luminous and thrilling; they were soon completely immersed in the magic of the Carnival. It sparkled and shone around them, filling the small space with a dream-like essence.

Her own process of being connected had been gradual, with never one moment where she could pinpoint being unjoined and then joined. She had a feeling Sam was going to have a very different experience.

Between one moment and the next, she found herself in another place. It was made up of light and air and power. She could see four bright lights standing next to her. She recognised them as Rilla and Jack, who were the colors of a rainbow, Garth, who was the brightest, and Sam, who was an unusual purple color and was standing off to one side. She looked down at herself and saw bluey-green swirls where her body should have been.

Garth moved toward Sam, his glow pulsating with power. Sam's light dimmed momentarily and then glowed a little brighter. Rilla and Jack moved around to the other side of Sam, so the three were surrounding him. Celestine knew, without knowing how, that Garth wanted her to join them.

She glided across to stand next to Garth and Rilla, with Sam in their center.

Garth moved forward, closer to Sam. Celestine and the others followed, until they were standing so close to Sam, their light was almost touching.

Then Garth took the final step, merging his light with Sam's, and again they all followed.

Suddenly it became a screaming furious mix of color and images; Celestine wanted to step back, away from the overwhelming mass of visions that were infiltrating her mind, but she couldn't move. She berated herself for not realizing this might happen. She was experiencing a vision here, in this place. But it was the kind of unreadable vision that was useless to them all, because she saw everything and nothing, every possibility that might happen, and other possibilities that would never happen. There was death and destruction, happiness and joy, babies and marriage, loneliness and old age.

She was seeing the Carnival's future, but it was multiple futures, in different worlds on different levels. It meant everything and nothing. The images took over her mind, and she couldn't see what was happening to the others, until suddenly they were back in the trailer, everyone looking like they'd just been hit by a train. Her head was swimming, and the room was swaying around her like she was drunk. Her breath rasped as she tried to get enough air into her lungs, and dots appeared in her vision. She felt like she'd just run a marathon—backward through thorn bushes.

Celestine lay her head in her arms on the table in front of her and tried to breathe calmly through her nose, so she wouldn't throw up on them all, then and there.

It was a few moments before she realized that she had something heavy leaning against her.

Sam.

She tried to turn around, but he was slumped against her, his body limp.

CHAPTER 28

*S*am came slowly awake, blinking his eyes open. He was lying down, his head on a pillow. He felt someone's hand holding his; his vision was blurry, and he couldn't see who it was. But he knew. Celestine.

"He's coming to." Celestine's voice was soft and musical. It sounded perfect to his ears.

He tried to squeeze her hand, but his body was filled with lead and he couldn't move. His head ached like he'd taken a knock from a championship fighter.

"Wh—" he cleared his raw throat. "Where am I?"

"You're still in Rilla's trailer. We put you on the bed. You passed out."

"How long?" Had it been days? A panicky part of his brain immediately went into overdrive.

"About ten minutes. We were starting to get worried."

Sam nodded, then wished he hadn't when a shaft of agonizing pain sliced through his head. He groaned.

"Garth says it was successful. You're part of the Carnival now."

Sam's heart rate sped up. He searched inside himself for

some kind of physical thing, some feeling like when he'd had Veronica's block inside him. But there was nothing. He didn't feel any different.

"He says it might feel terrible because you've essentially sped up a process that normally takes weeks, sometimes months."

He blinked again and turned his head slowly to look at Celestine. She looked tired too. Something had happened to her as well, but he couldn't remember anything after he agreed to do it and Garth closed his eyes.

"What did the Carnival say?" he croaked out.

"About your talent?" Celestine glanced back toward the other end of the trailer. He followed her gaze and saw Rilla and Jack talking quietly in a huddle with Garth.

"Yes," he said, feeling impatient.

"Garth didn't actually tell me."

"Get him over here. I need to know." He knew he was being rude, but he couldn't help himself. Blinding uncertainty had taken over his thoughts. He needed to know what it was that Veronica wanted from him. Then maybe he could figure out a way to bring her down.

Celestine nodded and went over to Garth and the others. Sam watched her out of hooded eyes. She'd had just as much of a revelation today as he had. She'd been told that she could get out from under her brothers' domination, but only by submitting to another person. The thought of the amount of trust it would require to let another person have that kind of control made him shudder.

He hoped Indigo could help her instead.

Garth and Celestine came back to stand beside his bed, leaving Rilla and Jack talking in low voices on the other side of the trailer. Sam didn't say a word, just looked up at Garth.

"The Carnival knows why Veronica wants you so badly," said Garth. He hesitated.

"Just out with it. It can't be that bad."

Garth shook his head. "It's not bad at all. You have the ability to amplify the power of those around you."

At first, the words didn't make sense. It wasn't what he'd been expecting to hear. "I make other people's talents stronger?"

Garth nodded. "While we were in the Carnival dimension, I learned that part of the reason the Carnival has been getting more powerful so quickly is because you were already starting to make the connection. Now you're fully joined to the Carnival, its magic has increased exponentially."

Sam thought through what Garth was saying. "I don't actually have a talent of my own?" he asked. Part of him felt cheated. He'd risked everything because he'd been sure it would help him end Veronica, and now he found that it didn't make a damn bit of difference.

Garth was shaking his head. "Your ability is very rare. By being connected to the Carnival, you make us stronger in the fight against Veronica."

Sam clenched his hand into a fist; it wasn't enough. They didn't understand the burning desire that churned in his gut. Veronica had kept him like a caged animal for *ten years*, forcing him against his will to harm others, leaving him broken and guilt ridden.

He didn't want to help others finish her off. He wanted— needed—to be the one to personally destroy her.

His face must have shown his inner thoughts because Celestine put one gloved hand on his arm. "You couldn't do it on your own, Sam. She beat you every time. I saw it. This way, we all work together to bring her down."

Ghosts formed at the edge of Sam's vision; all the people he'd seen her kill or who'd been harmed by Veronica. His stomach churned, and for a moment, he thought he might throw up. He blinked a few times, trying to make the faces disappear, but they weren't real, and his mind wasn't ready to let go of them.

He clenched his fists. The only way he could make up for what he'd done while he was chained to Veronica's side was to bring her down personally. This ability wasn't going to help him do that.

He nodded shortly. There was nothing he could do about it right now. Except he couldn't lie still any longer. Pushing himself up onto his elbows he attempted to sit up. The room swayed, then righted itself. Celestine leaped forward to help him, her gloved hands soft on his skin.

"You need to lie down again, Sam. You're not ready to be up so soon." Celestine looked like a broody mother hen as she told him off, and Sam smiled. She probably wouldn't appreciate the comparison.

Ignoring her words, he kept moving to sit up, but was breathing heavily and sweating by the time he was fully upright.

Just as he was seriously considering taking Celestine's advice and lying back down, there was a knock at the door. He straightened his spine and looked toward the door.

Missy and Viktor entered the small trailer, their faces grim. They nodded briefly to Garth, Sam, and Celestine before going into a huddle with Rilla and Jack. They talked with the Ringmasters—presumably about the latest developments—in hushed voices.

Sam leaned over his knees, putting his forearms on his legs to hold himself in place. He glanced up and saw Celestine looking at him with a frown. "I'll be fine. Just give me a minute."

Footsteps announced Jack's arrival at the bedside. "I'm going to start doing double sessions of my absorbing practice beginning tomorrow morning. Five o'clock to seven. I need to get it under control in case Veronica makes a play for us.

Any early risers need to be aware that their magic will be unavailable until then. I need all the members of the Nine to go out and spread the word." Jack looked at Garth who nodded.

"I'll start now." Garth looked down at Sam. "Don't move too far or too fast, Sam. You'll be weak for a while yet, I think."

Sam grunted, unable to think of anything smart to say to Garth, who nodded and headed out the door.

"How are you feeling?" asked Jack.

"Like crap," said Sam.

Jack nodded. "It's not unexpected."

Missy came to stand at the end of the bed as well, her long dark hair floating down around her face. "I hear you're one of the crew now," she said.

Sam nodded.

"You'll have to learn to fight better," she said with a grin.

Sam gave a tired half smile in return. "Feel free to teach me."

Beside him on the chair next to the bed, Celestine gave a small cry and started shuddering violently. She fell forward onto the bed, in the middle of a full seizure.

"What the hell's happening?" said Sam, trying to keep Celestine from tumbling off the bed. "She's not touching anyone!"

Adrenaline surged through his body, and he managed to pull her onto the bed beside him. She trembled against him, her body shaking uncontrollably.

"What's going on?" asked Jack.

"This is what happens when she's seeing the future," said Sam.

"Is it safe?"

Sam shook his head. "It's what I keep trying to tell her. As far as her body is concerned, she's having a seizure. Neurologically, it can't be good for her. She tells me I'm worrying over nothing."

They all waited in silence, watching as Celestine shuddered beside him. Sam wanted to tell them all to leave, to let this happen in private, but he understood their desire to know what she was seeing. It could be something important.

Eventually it stopped. Sam smoothed one hand down her hair, waiting for her to come around.

Celestine opened her eyes; a deep violet color spread over her whole iris. It made her look eerie, otherworldly.

Time hung still for a moment. The room was silent.

Celestine blinked. "I saw Missy fall and die," she whispered. "Sometime really soon."

CHAPTER 29

*C*elestine shook out her hands, trying to convince herself everything was fine.

But it wasn't.

The vision she'd had earlier had been jumbled with images overlapping each other until she couldn't tell what was happening or when. It felt like she was seeing every possible future, thereby negating every single one of them. But one thing had stood out to her. Missy falling from the trapeze at tonight's show into a broken safety net.

The only problem was that she'd also seen it not happening. She just didn't know which one was the real vision.

A shoulder bumped into hers and she glanced at Sam, standing next to her. They were near the backstage entrance in the top corner of the big top. As they watched, the audience was streaming in through the two official entrances, and the noise level was going up as more and more people filled the seats. Music from the orchestra flowed around in the background, and the striped tent loomed overhead, fairy lights twinkling down on them from the rigging around the high wire.

Her palms started to sweat.

"How often do you get to watch the show?" asked Sam.

Celestine shook her head. "I don't, not usually. I went to the Winter Spectacular last year. And I've seen Missy practicing a few times." She tried not to seem panicky, but it didn't work.

"You're always working?"

She nodded. "Even while the show's on, a few people wander the sideshows." Her vision this afternoon had been based on Missy, who'd been standing a few feet away. The implications of this weren't lost on her—it meant her power had strengthened, probably due to Sam's connection to the Carnival.

There was no longer a way to control when and how she dove into her visions just by keeping herself from touching other people. The thought made her cringe and her heart race.

She wished she hadn't agreed to come to the circus show. Her whole body was tensed in case she had another vision. To make it worse, the visions she was seeing were completely useless, just multiple images piled on top of each other.

Sam's ability was supposed to amplify her talent, but it was more like it had been taken away from her, leaving her with nothing but the seizures and the fear.

"Why are we doing this again?" she asked, her voice raw.

"We're searching for Veronica."

Celestine shook her head. "I think I'm going to faint. I need to get out of here." She turned, fleeing through the tent flap and out into the fresh evening air. Sam followed immediately behind her.

They were at the back of the massive tent, near where the circus performers dressed and waited for their turn. Circus folk milled around this area, but the huge swathes of punters were on the other side of the tent.

"You okay?" asked Sam, his expression concerned.

Celestine nodded. "I don't think I can do it. I'm...." She broke off. She couldn't admit she was afraid.

"I'm sorry."

She looked up at him sharply. "What are you sorry for?"

"It's my fault this is happening to you. My amplification abilities are messing with your talent."

"You're not doing anything to me on purpose. I don't blame you for any of it."

"It's still my fault, whether I'm doing it on purpose or not."

Celestine shrugged. "It doesn't matter." She hesitated. "But I can't go back in there. I think I need to go back to my trailer."

"I'll come with you," said Sam immediately.

"No, they need you. You know what Veronica looks like. We need someone to sound the alert if she tries to show her face at the performance."

Sam shook his head. "There are others who know what she looks like."

"I'll be fine. This is about protecting the Carnival. Go." She pushed at his shoulder, and Sam allowed her to guide him back toward the tent.

He glanced back over his shoulder. "I'll come check on you as soon as the show is finished," he said.

Celestine nodded. "I'll see you soon." She lifted one hand in a small wave and then turned, eager to get away from all the people. She felt twitchy, like her body was about to go into a seizure. It could happen anywhere, at any time. She glanced back toward the big top. What if she had a vision on her way home? She could knock her head or break something if she fell the wrong way. Maybe she should have let Sam come with her? She frowned. When had she become so pathetic? She could damn well get herself home.

Celestine walked quickly down the main strip. She just had to get through this section of the Carnival, and then she would be in the trailer compound.

As she passed the hot dog stand, a whisper of a vision slithered into her head, and she shivered. It was dark and smoky, not yet formed properly. She started to shake, but tried to fight it. She managed to stumble into the space between the hot dog stand and another stall before her knees buckled and she tumbled to the ground, holding out her hands to break her fall. As she collapsed, she grazed one leg against the rough wooden edge of a sideshow stall, and her head hit the metal pole keeping the stall in place. She landed with a thump on the ground, the breath knocked out of her, and spots appearing in front of her eyes. Nearby, the brightly colored Carnival signs offering massive stuffed toys in return for hitting the skittles wavered in and out of focus.

Then it all disappeared and she was in the misty rainbow world that preceded her visions. As ever, she paused to take a deep breath and prepare herself for whatever was to come. Her whole body trembled as Veronica's face appeared, contorted in rage. Red veins stood out on her neck and her mouth was snarled up like a rabid dog's. She looked like a wild animal running on violent instinct, no longer able to reason.

Celestine's heart was pounding like it was trying to escape from her chest, and she felt like she'd been running for miles. Veronica's fury was a palpable entity, like a vaporous mist that would poison all who strayed too close. Celestine instinctively held her breath, not wanting to breathe it in.

And then it was gone.

Celestine braced herself against the hard wooden side of the stall, trying to ease her trembling. Hard earth jabbed into the grazed and bleeding skin on her leg, and the sideshow wall was cold against her cheek.

What had she seen? Had it been Veronica's future?

She didn't know. It had happened so quickly, the vision had stopped almost before it started. She managed to pull herself up, rubbing her face.

She'd always thought of her ability to see the future as a curse. Growing up never able to say no to her father and then under the control of her greedy brothers had never seemed much of a life. When she'd been forced to run and hide, it had just seemed like an extension of the same curse. It had never occurred to her that she might one day miss it and wish for it back.

But that's exactly what was happening. Ever since she'd gone into the Carnival dreamscape, her powers had changed, evolved, but not in a good way. Seeing all possible futures at the same time was as useless as witnessing a close-up of Veronica in a rage.

In fact, she was no longer much help to anyone.

A sob broke out of her mouth, escaping into the air without warning. Another one followed, and after that, nothing Celestine could do would halt the flow of gut-wrenching sobs that emerged from deep inside her. She'd never cried about her life before, not when her mother died, not when her brothers forced her into working day and night for them, not when she was running from her brothers, desperate and alone. But it all seemed to gush out of her now. Who was she if she couldn't tell the future?

After a while the wracking sobs eased and she managed to start breathing normally again. She felt better for getting the pent up emotions out of her system, but it wasn't doing her any good lying here on the ground. She wiped her nose on her sleeve, wishing she were the kind of person who carried a handkerchief.

Celestine pulled herself to her feet. The evening lights twinkled across the sideshows and thrill rides, the warm black night providing a perfect backdrop for the fun of the Carnival. People walked past, everyone involved in their own private lives, none of them paying any attention to her problems.

She sighed and continued on to her trailer.

She heard boisterous applause from the big top, and checked her watch. The circus show was about halfway through. She was sure she'd have felt it if Veronica had turned up for the show. The more she thought about it, the more she became convinced that the image of Veronica had been her finding out that she wasn't going to be able to go ahead with her planned attack on Missy. Did that mean she was seeing things happening in the present as well? Her powers had never been so confusing.

Her home was dark and quiet when she let herself in. She went straight to the bed, unable to even think about getting changed. Her head hit the pillow, and she closed her eyes, smiling when a warm lump moved over to lie against her.

Artemis started purring, her large furry form rumbling against her side.

"You're always here for me, aren't you Artemis?" said Celestine.

Artemis rubbed her head against her arm, then lay down.

His purring soothed her senses and she was able to think clearly again. Now they knew the threat from Veronica was real and imminent, the Carnival would be on high alert. They'd be watching for the woman, and would probably be able to stem whatever mischief Sam's former boss and—what did you call someone who'd controlled you by force? His controller? It sounded too tame. Like a train conductor.

His owner. His master.

The woman who forced him to do things against his will.

She understood that. Her brothers had forced her to keep working when she was too tired to keep going.

But they'd never forced her to hurt or maim another person. And if she understood Sam's tortured words, that's precisely what Veronica had made him do.

She was evil. They needed every weapon they could use in the battle against this woman.

And her own ability, the one thing they had over her, was now useless.

Celestine punched the pillow and turned on her side. Artemis meowed grumpily as she repositioned herself.

How was she going to tell which of the many possible futures she was seeing was most likely to happen? She needed to find some trick that would help her discern which one was their most likely future.

Her mind was so busy she didn't notice the passage of time until her alarm clocked pinged. Glancing over, she saw that it was one in the morning. It was the time she'd often gone out to try to find problems to fix around the Carnival.

She was still wide-awake, her mind a jumble of thoughts and options.

Celestine shrugged to herself. She was still dressed; perhaps she could try some of the options she'd been considering on the Carnival, to see if she could make her talent useful again.

Walking out into the cool early summer air, Celestine took a deep breath. It could be worse. She was alive, and she had friends who would help her hide from her brothers.

CHAPTER 30

*I*t had been a long night. Sam walked slowly along the trailer alleyway, his hands in his pockets and the world on his shoulders. For some reason, Celestine had been convinced that Veronica would attend the show tonight and when they hadn't spotted her, it had been a huge anticlimax. At least it was for Sam. He felt like his skin was crawling with insects, making him edgy and uncertain.

He wanted to go for a run.

He'd meant to go check on Celestine after the show, but he'd been waylaid by Jack. The Ringmaster had taken one look at Sam's face and told him to follow him back to the trailer he shared with Rilla. They'd spent the last couple of hours drinking whiskey and practicing Jack's absorbing skills. It wasn't necessarily a good mix, but now that Sam was joined to the Carnival, Jack's absorbing ability was even stronger, and the Ringmaster was grimly determined to get it under control.

Another problem he was responsible for. He swayed a little as he stumbled along.

Around him, the main lights were out, leaving only the security ones glowing in the dark. The Carnival itself was quiet. Or at least as quiet as it ever was. The occasional soft voice carried across the still night air, and the whirr of generators was a faint comforting hum in the background. He knew Frankie's cameras were watching, but it still felt like he was alone out here. There was something soothing about being the only person walking around after the extreme crowds that had been there earlier. He took a deep breath and his lungs filled with clean fresh air mixed with cotton candy and French fries. He smiled.

Metal grated on metal somewhere behind him. Sam halted. Sound carried on a clear night like this, and the sound hadn't been from the trailer compound.

Someone was roaming the main Carnival.

Sam took another breath. It was probably nothing. A stray cat checking out the strange tents in its territory.

Or maybe it was Celestine's brothers. Or Veronica. He swayed and righted himself against the nearest trailer.

They had too many enemies for him to take something like this lightly.

He ran as quietly as he could back toward the main strip, where the noise had come from. His heart pounded in his chest. What if it was Veronica? What would he do with her? The thought was tantalising.

Then his heart stuttered and he slowed to a fast walk. He still had nothing to use against her, no useful magic that could knock her out. What if she put another block on him?

The thought was almost enough to make him turn around. But he clenched his hands into fists and kept going. He wasn't going to give in to the fear. Veronica no longer owned him, and he could make his own choices.

A small voice was telling him that this was the wrong choice, but he made it anyway.

The strip was empty. He stayed to the shadows and

peered up and down the alleyways, trying to find the source of the noise.

He heard it again. Metal clanged somewhere, and he crept closer to where the sound came from. His throat was suddenly dry and he swallowed. This was it. He was going to see Veronica again after all these months.

How would he react? He didn't know; his brain was too full of the terrifying ghostly images that thinking about Veronica always gave him. People hurt and dying. Calling out, asking, begging for his help.

His attempts to help them.

Pain. Terror. Death.

Everything around him started spinning, and he grabbed the side of the nearest stall to steady himself. His breathing was coming in ragged gasps, and his heart was pounding. He felt like he'd just done a hard-core run up the side of a mountain. If he confronted Veronica right now, she'd win. It was a fact. He knew it.

But he also knew that he couldn't leave her to rummage around in the Carnival by herself, doing who-knew-what to their equipment.

He stood up properly again and took the last few steps to the corner of the stall. He looked around the edge, where the noise had been coming from.

There was a slight figure down the end of the small alleyway.

He rubbed his sweaty hands against his trousers. "Hey! Leave that alone," he called out.

The figure jerked back as if they'd been stung. It was a woman, he could tell that much. She turned, and he let out his breath.

Not Veronica.

Celestine.

"What on earth are you doing here?" he asked, more harshly than he meant to.

Celestine came forward, and the tears rolling down her cheeks became more obvious. Sam moved forward, pulling her into his arms without thinking about it.

She hesitated and then laid her head on his shoulder with a sigh. But he knew she'd made sure there was no skin-to-skin contact before she did it.

"What's the matter?" he asked, softly this time.

"It's not working anymore," she said. "At least it is, but it's not working the way it should. I'm seeing every possibility, instead of the most likely right now. "

"Is that why you had to leave the show?"

She nodded against his shoulder. "It's just a jumble of confusing images."

"We'll talk to the others. There must be something we can do."

Celestine shook her head miserably. "What if there's not? What if this is how it is for me from now on? I can barely concentrate. I have multiple images of you being captured and killed by Veronica in various places around the Carnival going through my head right now, and I don't know how to deal with it."

"I thought you had to be touching the person?"

"Not anymore. Just being close to them is enough."

"Is that what happened with Missy? I thought she must have touched you somehow."

Celestine shook her head. "I really thought Veronica would be here tonight. That particular image was more powerful than the others." She wiped one hand over her face. "I even thought I felt Veronica earlier. Like I'd walked past her or something. But I don't know if it was real or imaginary."

"Come on, let's go back to your trailer. It's late at night. Too late to be wandering around like this."

"I used to be able to help the Carnival. Protect it. But now I'm useless."

"You're not useless. We'll figure out how to make this better. I promise."

"Don't make promises you can't keep," said Celestine softly.

They walked back slowly to Celestine's place, Sam holding Celestine around the shoulders. She must have been distracted, because she let him do it. He figured it wouldn't matter if he was just walking beside her or holding her—she was going to get visions either way. At least it didn't seem to be giving her seizures for the moment.

He managed to get her up the stairs and into her tiny home without hassle and helped her crawl back into her bed. She closed her eyes and curled up, facing Sam.

"I'll leave you now," he said. Unable to help himself, he reached out, holding his palm against her cheek. "Get some sleep."

"Stay," whispered Celestine. "Stay with me. I don't want to be alone." She moved over and patted the bed beside her.

Sam hesitated. But Celestine, who was already half asleep, didn't mean anything more than just lying next to her. He kicked off his shoes and crawled into the small bed, fully clothed.

She snuggled in next to him like a cat, and he put his arms around her, holding her against him. He let out a breath. "Are you still getting visions about me?" he whispered.

"No. They've settled down," said Celestine softly, slurring and half asleep.

Sam tucked her head under his chin and closed his eyes. "Good night, Celestine."

"G'night Sam," she murmured.

~

SAM OPENED HIS EYES, and the unfamiliar surroundings caused a wave of panic along his body. For a moment he was convinced that Veronica had managed to capture him while he slept.

But then something warm and soft moved next to him, and he remembered. Celestine's body was curled up against his, and his arms held her close. He wanted nothing more than to lean in and press his lips against her neck. Only the memory of what had happened last time kept him still.

Outside it was still dark, but early morning birds were singing, and he knew it would be time to get up soon. He lay watching the flowery curtain flutter in a faint breeze from the window. Celestine murmured and moved against him. Was she having visions in her dreams? He wondered if he should move away, but he couldn't bring himself to leave the warm comfort of her arms.

He didn't notice at first when she started moving next to him. But as she turned in his arms, snaking her hands around his waist, he smiled down at her. When she placed her lips against his neck, he pulled back.

"What are you doing?" he asked.

"I'm not getting visions," she said with a small half smile. "I think Jack's absorbing our talents. I thought I'd test it out." She moved her hand up to touch his cheek, pulling his face back down to hers. She was warm and soft, still half asleep.

Their lips touched and Sam's whole body felt like it was going up in flames. She was beautiful, her lips soft and malleable over his. He touched the side of her face, his hand running reverently over her velvety skin. He deepened the kiss, trying to let her know through touch how he felt about her.

It was like they were in a bubble, a slip of time where

nothing and no one else mattered. Sam kissed her cheeks, her eyes, her neck, running his lips over her skin, losing himself in the sensation. When he felt her hands on his shirt, pulling it off, he looked down into her eyes.

"Are you sure?" he asked.

She nodded. "Never been more sure," she whispered, slipping her hands inside his shirt and running her fingers over his body.

Sam groaned, closing his eyes and giving in to the sensation. All he knew was that he wanted to get closer to Celestine.

He wanted more.

CHAPTER 31

*P*ulling her shawl closer around her shoulders Celestine walked a little faster. Images were pulsing through her head now, and she didn't know how to stop them. She didn't even know who they related to. The early crowds for the sideshows and thrill rides were starting to fill the Carnival grounds, and with the new amplified version of her powers, she felt like she was seeing all possible futures for all of them.

Her head was full, and her stomach was rolling about like she was on a small boat in a big sea. It was too much.

While Jack was practicing his absorbing, it had been so peacefully quiet this morning that she'd almost forgotten she even had a problem. She had just been able to enjoy being with Sam. It had been sweet silence for a short period, but it made the return of all the noise and imagery even worse.

There was no way she could live like this. She didn't know what she should do, but she had a horrible feeling it involved leaving the Carnival and finding a new home away from Sam.

Her steps faltered for a second and she only just managed

to avoid tripping over her own feet. Instead of slowing down, her steps became faster as she blindly walked, trying to outpace her thoughts. She had no idea where she was going, but at the moment, all she needed to be was *away*. Jack had agreed that she couldn't do her show like this, and she'd been given the day off. But now, all she had were the fearful thoughts of living the rest of her life like this. It would have been better to work through the confusion.

She left the bounds of the Carnival, trying to put some distance between herself and the crowds. Perhaps that would ease the pulsing images in her head. She longed for the quiet of the morning, for Sam's arms around her, and his lips on hers. It had been beautiful and had held the promise of better things to come.

Then Sam had left to meet with Jack, and those promises had seemed false, and the possibilities had become limited. She couldn't live with these images in her head. Which meant she couldn't live with Sam.

She sucked in a sobbing breath.

Why had she let herself get so close to him? She'd always had a rule about keeping distance between herself and everyone else. It was how she'd survived so long. When had she started to let go of that idea? When exactly had Sam become so important to her? She shook her head. She couldn't think of an exact day or moment, but he'd managed to worm his way into her life. And now the idea of leaving him behind was breaking her in two.

She wiped roughly at the tears streaming down her face. They didn't solve anything. She was long past crying about this kind of thing. Her mother had cried, and where had that gotten her?

Celestine kept putting one foot in front of the other, stomping out her fears and her heartbreak. She knew what she had to do. But she didn't want to do it.

She got to the edge of the field where the Carnival was set up and looked around. She could either go along the edge of the road or head for a forested patch in the distance. She chose the forest. She quickened her pace until she was almost running. It felt good to use her lungs, to stretch her body out of its usual routine. Perhaps she should take up running with Sam?

Except that she wasn't going to be around long enough to do that. She broke into a sprint, her long skirts swishing about her legs. Sweat was running down her neck and her body didn't have the spare breath to cry any more.

A streak of yellow and black swished past her, and Celestine smiled. Artemis.

She raced ahead, then stopped and turned around. She stood in front of Celestine, and meowed, rubbing against her legs when she came close enough. Celestine crouched down in front of Artemis and smoothed one hand from the top of Artemis's head along her back and up her tail. The cat leaned into the pat and started purring. She head-butted Celestine's knee and demanded attention.

The wooded area was only a few yards away, and it suddenly seemed dark and unforgiving. Celestine didn't want to go in there. She sat down on the ground and crossed her legs. Artemis responded by jumping lightly to land on her legs and settled herself on Celestine's lap.

Behind her the sounds of the Carnival drifted on the breeze. Laughter, shouts and the sound of the thrill rides wove through the air. Everyone was happy.

Except her.

In front of her, the wooded area waited. But she had lost the desire to lose herself among the trees. They seemed too dark, too creepy now. She didn't understand what had happened between one breath and the next, but she was

194

staying where she was for now. The images had left her head, and that was what mattered.

Movement to one side of the trees caught her eye. Two figures. One a lot taller than the other. At first she didn't recognize them. But then Artemis growled.

Celestine felt her heart leap up into her throat as she recognized her brothers running toward her. She tried to stand but it was already too late. They had her in their control.

She couldn't move, so she remained on the ground, stroking Artemis, who'd stood up and was arching her back and hissing. "It's okay, Artemis. My brothers just want me to go with them. It's okay." She knew something was wrong, from the way Artemis was reacting. But she couldn't for the life of her figure out what it was.

Smiling up at her brothers as they arrived, Celestine looked closely at them. They looked more worn and world weary than they had when she'd left them. Clearly it had been tough.

"You ready to come with us, Celestine?" asked her older brother, Alden.

"Of course," she replied.

Artemis hissed again when Alden tried to lean down and pull her to her feet. She struck out with her paw and drew blood from Alden's hand.

"Get rid of that ball of fur or you'll regret it," he growled.

Celestine pushed Artemis off her lap and stood up. "Go back to the Carnival, Artemis," she said. "Go home." She pushed the cat in the direction of the brightly colored tents behind them. Artemis stood her ground, hissing at her brothers.

"I'm going to kick her into the next life," muttered Leptune, taking a step forward. Celestine cowered back, putting herself in front of Artemis. She didn't want her brothers to harm Artemis. But she would hurt the cat herself if her brothers told her to.

"Go," she said harshly to Artemis, pushing the cat away.

Before she could do anything to stop him, Alden aimed a kick at Artemis. The cat managed to leap out of the way, and instead of catching the full boot across her head, Alden's foot grazed her side. Artemis meowed in pain, falling to the ground and then getting up. She backed away, watching all of them.

"Go," said Celestine again.

This time Artemis turned and ran back to the Carnival, her yellow and black body streaking across the grass.

"Come on, Celestine. It's time to go," said Leptune.

Celestine nodded. "Sure," she agreed. Her brothers knew best. They always had.

CHAPTER 32

"So, all in all, it was a successful experiment?" said Indigo from the computer screen. They were crammed into Frankie's trailer for a video call with Indigo. She had the most knowledge about the way the Carnival worked, even more than Garth.

Jack nodded. "I was absorbing the whole Carnival. And I managed to control it, rather than letting it control me." He was happier than Sam had ever seen him. This morning's experiment had been a total success—in more ways than one. Sam thought of Celestine lying naked beside him. It had been glorious—no, *she* was glorious. He still couldn't believe it had happened.

He wished he was still there with her, instead of here in this darkened room with Jack and Frankie. He wasn't really sure why they needed him in on this, other than some vague idea that there should be a doctor present. The others all knew much more about the magic of the Carnival than he did, even Jack.

A knock at the door made them all turn. When Frankie

opened it, Joey stood at the base of the steps, his face creased with worry. "Celestine isn't in her trailer," he said.

Sam rubbed at the goose pimples that appeared on his arm.

"And?" said Frankie.

"She said she'd eat some lunch if I brought it to her. She promised."

"She's probably just went for a walk and forgot. Her new powers are messing with her head a little," said Jack, glancing at Sam for confirmation.

Sam tried to be calm about it, but something had felt off as soon as he'd seen Joey. A little ball of panic had burst into life in his chest. "We need to find her," he said, already heading for the door. "Something's wrong."

Jack hesitated, then nodded. "All right. Let's break off this meeting here. We were almost done anyway." He turned to Indigo's face on the computer screen. "We'll talk later," he said. "Joey, start searching the Carnival for Celestine. Use your other runners. Tell everyone we're looking for her."

Joey ran off.

"We'll find her somewhere silly, hiding out," said Jack to Sam. "I'm sure she's fine."

Sam was already out the door and striding back to Celestine's trailer when Jack caught up with him.

"We'll find her. The Carnival is connected to her. We just have to get Garth to do a search for her."

"Really? He can find her?"

"He can give us some more information, certainly."

They changed their direction and headed for the big top where Garth usually practiced in the afternoons. He often led a crowd of Carnival folk through the complicated self-defence moves that his father had taught him. They'd been passed down the Giftmaster line for at least a century and were designed to help with the practical craft of being a clown in the ring. But they actually served the dual purpose of helping people protect themselves when they needed it.

They strode into the big top, and Sam skidded to a halt. Instead of just two or three people, the class had expanded to about thirty. They were all doing the slow moves that incorporated Capoeira moves with Tai Chi and ballet.

Sam edged around to the front of the class. "Garth," he whispered.

Garth looked over, his eyes the full black of a Gift in progress.

Sam barely noticed. "You need to do a search for Celestine right now. We think something has happened to her."

"It can't wait until we're finished?" he said.

"No. She's missing. Something's wrong."

Garth sighed and stood up. He gestured to one of the others to take over the class and walked to the side of the big top with Jack and Sam. "You think Veronica has her?" asked Garth.

Sam's heart stumbled. "I was thinking her brothers had her." It had never occurred to him that Veronica might have been behind it.

"We don't know where she is. She could have wandered off and gotten lost, for all we know. But we need to find her, just in case. She's not in her right mind at the moment."

"Since the forced joining?"

"Yes," said Sam shortly.

Garth winced. "I didn't know she'd be affected like that, or I'd never have let her be a part of the ceremony."

"None of us did. But we need to protect her." Sam ran his fingers through his hair agitatedly.

Garth sat down on the bottom tier of the audience bleachers and closed his eyes. Sam felt a low-level hum, a prickling of his skin, and then Garth opened his eyes again.

"She's not inside the Carnival grounds. I can tell that much."

"Anything else?" Sam's stomach felt like it was climbing out via his throat. What was she doing outside the Carnival?

"She's fuzzy. Like she's unconscious. I can't get a good read on her." Garth looked at Sam's face. "I don't think she's hurt," he said quickly.

"Then where is she?"

"I don't know." Garth shook his head. "I'm sorry, she's just too indistinct to find."

Sam started pacing. "What good is it to be part of this place, if we can't protect her?" He glared at Jack and Garth. "I thought the Carnival was stronger than this. If we can't even keep Celestine safe, how are we going to catch Veronica?"

Jack let out a frustrated breath. "That's why we're doing everything we can to research Veronica. We're not going into an altercation with her blind."

Sam felt like punching someone. "I'm going to search her trailer," he said abruptly. "Something might be in there that will help us."

"I'm coming with you," said Jack. "With the kind of enemies we've got around us at the moment, I don't want anyone rushing off on their own, especially not you."

"Me too," said Garth.

Sam almost growled at his honor guard, but he led the way to her trailer without saying anything. He opened the door to the small space, and her scent hit him in the face. He took a deep breath in. He would find her. There was no way he would let Veronica or Celestine's brothers—or whoever the hell had her—hurt her.

"I'm going to look through the drawers in here," he said pointing to her bedroom. "You two check in the front."

At that moment, a streak of yellow and black raced in through the open door. Artemis leaped straight toward Sam, scrambling for purchase when she landed half on Sam's shoulder, scratching his skin with her long claws. She was meowing and growling at Sam as he tried to pull the enormous animal off him.

"What the hell's the matter with that cat?" said Jack. "I've never seen her like that."

"Something's wrong," managed Sam, as he held the wriggling cat. The feeling was like a snake slithering over his skin now.

Artemis stopped struggling and leaped down. She ran down the stairs and stopped outside, meowing and looking back at them.

"If I didn't know better, I'd say that cat is trying to lead you somewhere," said Jack.

"I was just thinking the same thing," said Sam.

"She knows she's not Lassie, right?"

"I'll call her by any damn name she likes if she leads me to Celestine," said Sam, already halfway out the door.

Sam raced off after Artemis, who was travelling fast through the Carnival. She looked back occasionally to check that Sam was still following but just kept running in an almost straight line through the crowds. They reached the edge of the Carnival and went out into the massive field that was behind the set up. It was empty.

Halting for a moment, Sam watched as Artemis raced across the long grassy field. "Is this what we should be doing? Chasing a cat?" he asked Jack and Garth as they ran up behind him. The three men stood at the edge of the grass.

"I've done stranger things since I've been with the Jolly Knight Carnival," said Jack.

Sam nodded and started running again. They were across the other side of the field, and almost at the wooded copse when they finally caught up with Artemis. She sat very precisely in the middle of a flattened area of grass. Sam looked around, trying to find some kind of clue, something that would tell them if this was really where Celestine had been.

"This isn't helping us find her," said Garth.

Sam turned in a circle where he stood. "There must be something. Some clue." He was beginning to feel desperate. A patch of yellow in the woods caught his eye, and he ran over to the edge of the tree line.

It was a piece of material. A yellow shirt.

Very like the one Celestine had in her wardrobe. He hadn't seen her dressed today, but he'd bet money that it was from her shirt. "Here," he said, lifting it up for the others to see.

"So we have evidence that someone was sitting here, and a scrap of yellow material. It could mean anything," said Jack.

"Or it could mean that she was out here by herself and her brothers, who had been waiting for an opportunity, came out of the woods and grabbed her."

"Why wouldn't she fight them or run from them? She wasn't sitting that close to the trees. Shouldn't there be evidence of a struggle?"

"She can't fight them, remember?"

They stood silent for a moment. "We have to go check their circus."

"I saw the poster. They're in the old Hanson field on the road to Boise," said Sam.

"We'll take my car," said Jack. He pulled the keys out of his pocket and sprinted off toward the Carnival parking lot.

The shadows were lengthening around them, and Jack had to put on the headlights to see where he was going in the dim dusk light. It wasn't long before they were travelling at speed toward the rival circus.

"What do you know about the brothers? Other than that

the big one has a bruising left hook?" asked Jack. He didn't take his eyes off the road.

"Their only ability is to make Celestine do anything they want." Sam rubbed his hands down his legs, trying to ease the dread he was feeling.

Jack glanced in the rearview mirror at Sam in the back seat. "She's likely to fight us? If we try to get her out of there?"

"Yes." Sam's stomach lurched. "We'll have to bring her against her will."

"Then we have to do it as fast and as quietly as we can. Preferably without alerting the brothers."

Sam looked grimly out the window at the dying light. "I don't think there's much likelihood of that happening," he said.

Jack shrugged. "Then we make it happen any way we can. I promised to protect her. I refuse to let her brothers take her like this."

CHAPTER 33

"Wake her up. She's been asleep for too long anyway." Alden's voice hadn't changed in the last three years. Her younger brother was still rough and whiney. "She can help us with the last of the packing." Someone punched her in the shoulder, and she moved back, yelping in pain. They were in the trailer she'd grown up in; everything was familiar and comforting.

"Wake up, Tiny," said her older brother, Leptune, using her childhood nickname. "We gotta get going. Show waits for no man." He paused. "Or woman."

She rolled away from him but got up as he'd asked.

They were almost done, which was surprising, because in the old days they would have waited until she'd done most of it and then rolled in to help with the final bits and pieces. Clearly their time without her had done them good. The thought came in and flittered away again, like a butterfly that had lost its way.

She stood up. "What do you want me to help with?"

"We need to get you ready to set up the fortune-telling

tent straight away when we stop at the next town," said Alden. "Put your stuff all together."

Celestine shook her head. "I can't do it anymore. It's broken," she said. The pain she'd felt before was gone; now she was simply numb and accepting.

"What?" Alden stopped and stared at her, a large sheet of canvas folded neatly in his arms.

"It's broken. I helped with a Carnival ritual, and it's done something to my ability to see the future. Now I see all of the possible futures, not just the most likely one."

"What does that even mean?" asked Leptune.

Celestine shrugged. "I can't tell the real futures from the possible ones anymore."

Alden dropped the canvas he'd been holding. He took a threatening step toward Celestine. "Don't think you can con us with your stories, sister. You think because you've hidden from us for so long, you can trick us? Think again."

Celestine blinked. The warm feeling that had been covering her split open for a moment, and she knew that she didn't want to be here with her brothers. They were forcing her to do something she didn't want to do.

But then it was gone. "I wouldn't lie to you, Alden. There's no point."

Leptune came over to stand in front of her, peering at her like she was an insect. "She seems to be under our control. The magic's working. I can feel it. Mom couldn't lie to Dad."

Alden sneered. "Then how did she get away from us last time? She must have lied to us at some point."

She blinked again, trying to remember what they were talking about. Her memories were a little fuzzy. "I think there was someone helping me," she said vaguely.

Alden's eyes sharpened on her. "Who?" His expression was hard, and Celestine knew it would be bad for whoever had helped her. "I don't remember." And she really didn't. But she also didn't want to remember. Her brothers would hurt the person who'd helped her escape last time. She knew that much.

Alden stepped closer and grabbed her by the arms, shaking her hard. "Tell me who, or so help me...." His words trailed off, but the violent expression in his eyes remained.

Leptune put his hand on their brother's arm. "Quit it, Alden. We need her whole for the show. A fortune-teller with bruises ain't gonna bring in the punters."

He gave her another shake, and Celestine's head snapped back and forth. "If what she's telling us is true, then she's useless to us anyway. All she's good for is a low-rent fortune-telling tent at the back of the Carnival. We need her for the high-end shows; that's where the money is."

Alden pushed her away, and Celestine took a step back. "I'm not lying to you. About anything." She was in a cocoon of warmth. There was no happy or sad, no worry or despair. She was just here with her brothers. Doing whatever they asked of her. That was her life.

"What if she can't do the show any more?" Alden shot a poisonous glare in Celestine's direction. She smiled back at him.

"We'll ask the witch doctor." Leptune pronounced the words like he'd come up with a cure for cancer.

"That old hack? What's he going to do?"

"Dad always used to go to him when he needed help with Mom. Remember?" Leptune remembered more about their mother than either Alden or Celestine. He was older by two years, despite Alden always taking the lead on their schemes and ideas.

Alden glanced from Leptune to Celestine. He looked at his watch. "We gotta catch him now, before he leaves. I told the boss she'd be ready for the next stop."

"Come on, then," said Leptune, grabbing Celestine's arm in a tight grip. She would have a bruise there later, but it would be all right. She could cover bruises on her arm.

She followed them quietly as they led her through the gaudy remains of the circus as it was being pulled down. She felt low-level visions flicker across her brain as if she was catching something out of the corner of her eye. She knew she needed to stay away from the other people if she wanted to keep her mind clear of the full-blown images.

They were at the end of the takedown process; trucks were being filled with equipment, the tents brought quickly to the ground, and the crew boss was yelling at the stragglers. The setup here was smaller, more of a travelling show than the full Jolly Knight Carnival. There was litter everywhere, and the signs were faded. The ground was all churned up and muddied underfoot. There was a dismal air about the place.

Celestine thought she might feel sad, if her emotions weren't completely numb.

They moved quickly through the commotion to another small trailer; this one painted in strange symbols and runes. Alden knocked. "Come on, old man. Open up," he said, looking around nervously. He was probably worried about the boss finding them slacking off instead of helping with the takedown.

The witch doctor opened the trailer door, peering out at them. "What do you want, Alden." He looked past her brother to where Leptune and Celestine waited. His eyes widened. "You found her?"

"We got her back, like I knew we would," said Alden roughly. "Can we come in?"

The witch doctor stepped back, welcoming them into his small place. Celestine followed Alden in, staring around at the bottles and containers on the shelves. They were filled with strange and disgusting creatures and body parts. The bottles were all attached to the shelves using an ingenious rubber band design.

"What can I do for you, boys?" asked the witch doctor, rubbing his hands together.

"She says she's lost her fortune-telling talent," said Alden.

The witch doctor looked sharply at Celestine. "Lost it? How?"

"She was part of some kind of ceremony, and now it's gone wrong."

The witch doctor walked over to where Celestine hovered just inside the entranceway. "You've lost your talent, eh?" he said.

As he came closer, images burned themselves into Celestine's head, multiple images of the witch doctor, going from wildly happy to dead on the ground. She scrunched her eyes shut and tried to block the images out. Her head started to pound, and she put her hands to her ears. "Stop. Don't come any closer," she said. "I can't think with all the images in my head."

"I thought she had to touch people to see their futures?" asked the witch doctor.

"Used to be. Now she's seeing them just by being close to people. They've done somethin' to her. Can you help us, Doc?" Alden peered anxiously at the strange man.

The witch doctor stepped away and the disturbing visions faded. Celestine opened her eyes.

"I think I can help. But we'll need to pull away from the main circus to do it. I can perform a ceremony, tonight, under the full moon."

"We have to get back to the main circus with her intact," said Alden. "I promised the boss."

"And the boss isn't someone you want to piss off."

"Right."

Something glinted in the witch doctor's eyes. "For this

kind of magic, there are special ways that things need be done. I don't make the rules. We need a full moon, we need moonlight." He placed one finger on the calendar attached to his wall. "You're just lucky that it's a full moon tonight."

Celestine shivered. It felt like a thousand tiny insects were running softly down her spine. She wished she were back in her brothers' trailer, curled up on the sofa.

A fist banged on the door. "Come on, old man. Get yourself on the road," shouted a voice on the other side. It was the crew boss.

"It was only a matter of time before he noticed," muttered the witch doctor. He raised his voice to answer the crew boss through the closed door: "Of course, Bartholomew. I'm just leaving now."

"Damn right you are," said the crew boss on the other side of the door. He stomped off to yell at some other poor soul.

"We'll meet at the clearing in two hours' time," the witch doctor whispered to Alden and Leptune. "There are things I need to prepare, and we need the full moon to be out for the ritual to work." He rifled through a box at one end of his trailer. He triumphantly pulled out a blood-red dress. "She needs to wear this. I'll bring everything else we'll need."

Celestine gazed blearily at the witch doctor. He came closer, handing the red dress to Leptune, and the images in her head returned.

There was something wrong.

He wasn't telling the truth. She could tell that much from the images she was getting. She opened her mouth to tell her brothers.

But from somewhere deep inside her head a small voice yelled at her to shut up. To keep quiet and see where this went. If the witch doctor was planning something against her brothers, then it might be a good thing for her.

So she closed her mouth and kept quiet.

If one of her brothers asked, she would tell them. Until then, she would stay silent.

CHAPTER 34

"I'm sorry, Sam." Jack's voice was grim. They were standing on the edge of the now-empty field where the circus had obviously been until recently. Churned up dirt and grass marked where the trucks and tents had been, and litter was scattered around the ground. Garth held a flash light and slowly shined it over the whole field.

"We have to follow them. Go to their next stop." Sam moved forward. "They can't have gone far."

"We'll go back to the Carnival and plan our next move," said Jack.

Sam shook his head. "We don't have time for that. They could go underground. They could take her anywhere. We need to catch them fast."

"I'm sorry, Sam. But I can't just go chasing off on the slimmest of notions. I have to protect everyone in the Carnival. We don't even know she's definitely with her brothers; this could be some kind of trap organised by Veronica. We have be sensible."

"She was here," said Garth from a few yards away. He was shining his flashlight at a section of the ground. "I can feel it."

"Can you tell where she is now?" asked Sam desperately. The darkness surrounding them made it feel like the world was pressing down on him, taking away his breath.

"She's still close by," said Garth in a strange voice. "This way." He started walking off to the far side of the field, and Sam and Jack rushed to catch up to him.

"Can you sense her?" asked Sam.

"She's this way," said Garth.

Sam glanced at Jack, who shrugged.

"The Carnival will help wherever it can," said Jack.

All three men strode across the field, and into the woods behind them. They followed a path only Garth could see, until the sound of voices ahead made them halt. Sam tried to make out if it was Celestine's brothers or not, but he hadn't heard them speak enough to know for certain.

"Who would be in the woods in the middle of the night?" whispered Sam.

"Hunters with big guns?" said Jack.

Garth shook his head. "I can feel magic swirling around them. And more forming. They're not hunters."

"We need to get closer, see who it is," said Sam.

Jack nodded and crept toward the sound of voices, with Sam right behind him.

Sam crouched down next to Jack and Garth and peered through the trees into a small clearing. It was lit by a small fire in the center and four candles placed at an equal distance around the edge of a circle marked by crystals. The full moon over their heads gave extra light, so the whole scene was laid out before them in ghostly colors. Four paths led off into different directions through the woods.

In the middle of the circle of crystals stood Celestine, dressed in a flowing red dress. Her hands were bound in front of her by red ribbon. She looked beautiful, but her eyes were glazed over, the violet light gone.

Her two brothers stood to one side of the circle. The bigger one stood with his eyes fixed like a hawk on an older man who was setting up a small altar in the middle of the circle. "You sure this is going to work, witch doctor?"

Sam clenched his fists and held in the urge to simply run and grab Celestine. He was no match for the two goon brothers. He glanced at Jack and Garth.

The third man, his face lined with age, white hair sticking out from under a top hat decorated with bones, glanced up impatiently at Celestine's brother. "Of course, Alden. I used to do this kind of thing for your father and mother all the time. Trust me." He smiled, and showed a gap-toothed mouth.

"He's lying," whispered Garth. "I recognize this ceremony. Full moon, crossroads, circle of crystals, red dress, red ribbon... He's trying to marry himself to her, and steal their powers. Put her under his power instead."

Sam's heart lurched in his chest. "No!" he said without thinking.

As one, Celestine's brothers turned to look in Sam's direction. "What was that?" said the smaller one.

The witch doctor looked up impatiently. "Go find out, will you? I need to make sure everything is exactly in order here."

The brothers strode around the edge of the crystal circle, clearly nervous about the old man's magic.

Sam glanced at Jack and Garth in apology. Garth shrugged and stood up. Jack and Sam were close behind him.

"Looking for us?" asked Sam. He moved out into the clearing and stood in front of the two brothers. Anger swirled around him, like a cloak. Jack and Garth were right behind him.

"It's those bastards from the Carnival where she's been

hiding," said the younger brother, his eyes wide. "How did you find us?"

"Thought you could just kidnap her, and we'd let you?" said Sam. "That's not how it works."

The bigger brother sneered. "Ask her what she wants to do." He turned to Celestine. "Celestine, tell them you want to stay with your brothers," he said.

Celestine turned to face them all. Sam felt like he was stuck in a painting tableau. They all waited for her to speak.

"I want to stay with my brothers," she said to Sam, her face blank of emotion.

Sam shook his head. "I know the power you have over her. She doesn't want to be here. I *know* it." He took a step toward the two younger men. Without warning, the big muscled brother took a swing at Sam and smacked his giant fist into Sam's face. Sam collapsed to the ground, his head spinning.

Garth and Jack surged forward, clearly more used to fighting. Garth took the larger brother and ducked fast under another powerful punch from the muscle-bound goon. Jack blocked a couple of rough punches from the smaller brother and then landed a heavy punch to the gut. Jack was taller by a good foot or so, and easily stronger. It was the bigger brother they had to worry about.

Sam crawled away from the fighting, shaking his head to clear it. He glanced up and saw the witch doctor pulling on Celestine's bound hands. She was shaking her head and trying to pull away from him. The witch doctor's face was no longer disinterested—he was snarling at her in the manner of a dog about to lose his bone. Sam struggled to clear his head. If the witch doctor managed to marry himself to Celestine, she'd be doomed a second time. He had to get her away from him.

Sam pushed himself to his feet and stumbled into the

crystal circle, still woozy from the punch. The witch doctor stuck out a leg, and tripped him up. Sam went flying again and only just managed to get his hands out to break his fall. He shook his head and pushed himself to his feet. He had to save Celestine. He couldn't fail. Turning he saw the witch doctor grab at Celestine, trying to pull her away from the fighting by one arm.

She was still resisting, pushing at the old man's hands, her face strangely expressionless.

Sam backed up a couple of steps and then ran at them. He yelled at the top of his voice, and tried to look crazy. The witch doctor saw him coming, and his eyes widened. Sam didn't slow down, he just kept coming, trying not to be obvious about what he was planning to do. The witch doctor attempted to pull Celestine out of the way, but she refused to budge. She watched Sam with her blank stare. It almost made him stumble, seeing her like that. She was normally so wild and sweet and emotional.

He gritted his teeth and kept going.

Sam reached them at top speed, and instead of tackling the witch doctor, who had stepped out of Sam's range, he grabbed Celestine around the waist. She tried to resist, but Sam had momentum on his side and he leaped with her, clutching her hands together at her waist, carrying her over the fire and away from the witch doctor.

As they soared over the flames, time seemed to slow. The moment stretched out, elongating until they came to a complete standstill, hovering in the air above the flames. Rainbow mists streaked and sparkled around them.

Celestine's dress flowed out behind her, the skirt touching the flames. Where their hands touched, light shone like a glowing beacon in the night, shimmering up their arms until it covered their bodies. Sam gazed down at their linked hands and then at Celestine. She stared back at him, her wide eyes shining a beautiful shade of violet. He wanted to ask what was happening, but he couldn't speak or move.

And then it was over; time sped up and they collapsed together onto the ground on the other side of the fire. The base of Celestine's long red dress was smoking. Sam sat up and smacked it out with his hand, before turning back to Celestine and helping her to stand.

"Are you okay?" he asked, still holding her hands. He tried to undo the ribbon tying her hands together, but it was too slippery.

"I'm fine," she said, her voice soft. She gazed up at him, her violet eyes filling with tears.

Behind him he heard the bigger brother roar. "He's taken her."

CHAPTER 35

*A*lden charged toward them, his arms reaching out like a massive bear. Celestine had never seen him so angry; shivers ran down her body, but she refused to give ground. It was only when Sam grabbed her hand and dragged her behind him that she moved, without really understanding why at first.

As they watched, Jack rammed Alden from the side, and they fell to the ground, struggling fiercely.

Celestine glanced between her brothers and Sam. She couldn't figure out what had happened. One minute she was completely under her brothers' control, and the next she was free. She felt clear-headed for the first time since she'd gone into the Carnival dreamscape—the multiple visions that had been plaguing her had disappeared as well.

Time dipped strangely, and Celestine felt herself disappear into the future for a second, joined by the Carnival and a bright new entity she didn't recognize at first.

And then she did.

Before she could say anything, Sam grabbed her again, lifting her up into his arms and carrying her to the edge of the clearing, out of the circle of crystals and away from the fighting.

Irritation rose in Celestine's chest. "Let me down," she said firmly to Sam, one hand on his chest.

"But—"

She eyed him fiercely. "I said, let me down."

He eased her onto her own two feet and stood beside her, watching her cautiously.

"Stop it," she yelled, turning to the others. "I said, stop it!"

Alden and Leptune glanced up at Celestine in surprise, pausing in their attack. Jack and Garth stared at her more warily.

"What are you doing, Celestine?" asked Leptune. His face was crinkled with confusion.

"I need all of you to stop it right now. No more fighting. It's over." And it was. The link that had kept her at her brothers' side all those years was gone. In its place was something different, a bright spark that connected her to Sam. Celestine tried to control the rising panic that was threatening to overwhelm her.

Something had happened as they'd jumped the fire. She turned to the witch doctor. "What did you do?" she asked fiercely.

"I think I might be able to help," said Garth. He gestured at the crystal ring and the four candles. "I think the witch doctor was trying to trick your brothers. He was going to marry you himself and steal the connection."

Alden growled and took a step toward the witch doctor. The old man whimpered and held his hands over his head, cowering away from Alden.

"Is that true?" Alden asked.

The old man didn't answer, simply trembled where he stood.

"It worked," said Celestine, the explanation making sense

of what she'd experienced. "Except not in the way he planned. When Sam and I jumped the fire, something happened. I think we just got married." She made a face. "At least according to my magic."

Beside her, Sam stiffened, and let go of her hand. She glanced at him; his expression was bleak.

She took a couple of shaky breaths. Was it so bad to be married to her? She was the one who had the most to lose—Sam could now order her about like a maid, and she would do everything he asked without question.

"Married?" said Alden incredulously.

"Doesn't that mean...?" Leptune trailed off. They all knew what it meant.

Jack stepped forward. "So there's no need for you to keep chasing Celestine. She's under the protection of the Jolly Knight Carnival now, and you can't do anything to force her back with you."

"Scuttle back off to the rock you came out from under," added Sam.

Alden looked over at Celestine in panic. "Tiny. We need you. How're we gonna to make a living without you?"

Celestine gazed back at him calmly. "Try, Alden. You're smart. You don't need me to earn your living."

Alden moved forward as if to grab her, but Jack and Garth stepped into his path. "Don't even think about it," said Garth.

"Good-bye, Alden, Leptune," said Celestine softly.

Sam put his arm around her shoulders, and they walked back out through the forest.

It was hard to know what to think.

"Sam...," said Celestine carefully.

"Don't worry about anything, Celestine. We'll figure this out," said Sam.

Their connection hummed, and Celestine found herself being layered with a well-meaning sense of comfort.

"Stop that," she said sharply. "I'm not a child."

"What?"

"We're connected now; you have a measure of control over me. But I couldn't bear it if you tried to force me to feel one way or another. You have to leave me to feel my own thoughts."

"But I didn't...."

"You did. Just stop it."

They'd reached the car by then, and Celestine climbed gratefully into the back seat next to Sam. The red dress was light and flimsy and didn't keep out the cool night air. Jack and Garth climbed into the front.

They drove in silence, each of them thinking their own thoughts. Celestine nudged at the link to Sam. Did he feel it in the same way she did? Did he feel anything when she touched it?

Celestine let out a long breath. She no longer needed to fear her brothers. The connection was gone; the little kernel of her soul that had been chained to theirs had disappeared. The thought was both energizing and terrifying.

There was a part of her that was happy, glad this had happened. But another part of her cried out. Sam hadn't wanted to marry her; they'd unwittingly finished off the ceremony without realising what they were doing. He'd been forced into it.

And so had she. Would Sam be any better than her brothers? What guarantee did she have that he wouldn't one day decide to make her do something against her will, for her own good?

There was no guarantee.

And so here she was, sitting in the back seat of Jack's car, wondering what was going to happen now. Wondering if she'd gone from one bad situation to another.

They'd left her brothers in the clearing. She wasn't sad about that. Alden and Leptune had never looked after her, never been the kind of brothers she'd needed. But Celestine had a hard time being angry with them. She wasn't radiating the same kind of anger that shimmered off Sam. They had been raised in the same environment she had. They'd been taught by their father to look upon the women in their family as the meal ticket.

She didn't want to be around them, or see them, but she couldn't bring herself to blame them.

Sam's hand slid over her leg and grasped her hand, and she looked down at their entwined fingers.

"Are you okay?" he asked.

Celestine gave him a look.

"You know what I mean."

"I'm better now you've rescued me," she said.

"For a while there, I thought we'd lost you. That your brothers had disappeared with you."

"I'm sorry, Sam."

"For what? It's not your fault they kidnapped you."

"No, I'm sorry I got you into this. You're married to me now."

He let out a breath. "It's not ideal. But we'll work through it."

Celestine's heart contracted. He really didn't want to be married to her. "We can get a divorce," she whispered.

Sam's hand clenched around hers. "I'm not leaving you prey to people like your brothers and that witch doctor."

"And I don't want to be married to someone who doesn't want to be married to me."

"Of course I want to be married to you. It's just a shock, that's all."

Celestine nodded and let him put his arms around her. But she'd seen the hesitation. This was all against his will, and that was as bad as being under someone else's control.

She heard a soft shattering noise somewhere deep inside her body and knew exactly what it was: her heart breaking into millions of tiny little pieces.

CHAPTER 36

"Do you want to come back to the clinic with me?" asked Sam. "Or shall we go to your trailer?"

Celestine shook her head. "You don't have to worry about me," she said.

He frowned at her. "I'm going with you. I need to make sure you're okay."

She shrugged. "My place then."

Sam felt a ping along their connection and suddenly felt guilty. Had he forced her to do what he wanted? It was one thing to convince her, it was another to force her through their link.

He gritted his teeth. At the moment, it didn't matter. He would have forced her to accept him through whatever means possible. So the end result was the same.

But he didn't know how long he could last in this situation. He didn't want to be connected to Celestine like this. It was the opposite of everything he'd hoped for. She didn't deserve to have someone who could take away her free choice. He knew what that was like and had no intention of forcing that on her.

"Come on, let's go," he said.

The walked in silence back to her trailer, and he opened the door, letting her go in first.

Artemis meowed and then leaped from the bed into Celestine's arms. She staggered slightly but otherwise caught the enormous cat and snuggled into her soft fur.

Sam just watched, emotion swirling around him.

"Stop it," said Celestine.

"What?"

"I can feel it through the link. All that emotion, the fear and anger."

"It's not directed at you."

"Isn't it?"

Sam took a step toward her. "No. Of course not. It's to do with this situation. I don't want to be able to force you to do things. I don't want that power over another person. It's my worst nightmare."

Celestine sighed and put Artemis back on the bed. "It's not exactly what I want either," she said.

Unable to help himself, Sam stepped closer and put his hands on her arms, rubbing them softly up and down. He waited for her to tell him to stop. She didn't.

"How come I can touch you now?" he asked. "Without the visions?"

Celestine blinked owlishly, hesitating over an answer. "I think it's because we're married. Your other powers don't affect me anymore, not the way they used to. And I can't tell your future. I never saw my brothers' futures either. Instead you can tell me what to do."

He felt rather than saw the tremors running over her skin.

He gazed into her violet-blue eyes, wishing things were different. "I've had enough of people controlling other people. I don't want to be able to tell you what to do all the time. I'd always win the fights and that would be no fun." He tried to smile at his own joke, but he couldn't force his mouth to move.

Celestine nodded, tears in her eyes. "This is almost worse than being in my brothers' power. You would always make me do what you thought was best for me, even if I didn't want it. I can't live like that. I can't be smothered like that."

Sam nodded, leaning his forehead softly on hers. "Then we're agreed?" he said, taking a ragged breath. "I'm going to leave the Carnival. I can't stay here and see you everyday and not want to be around you."

She pulled back sharply. "I didn't mean…." But her words trailed off, and Sam saw the realization on her face. If he didn't leave, she'd never be free.

Tears formed in her violet eyes and dripped down her face. He reached up one hand to wipe away the moisture. "How does your power feel?" he said softly. "Are you still having multiple visions?"

She hesitated. "I don't know. I haven't felt it since we… jumped the fire. I think it might be gone."

"Gone?" Sam didn't know whether to be happy or sad for her.

She nodded. "The multiple images disappeared as soon as we jumped, and I haven't felt anything since." She paused, thinking. "I can't read yours anymore because you're my husband now. But I was reading everyone around me before, and that shouldn't have changed. Unless it was your amplifying ability that was giving me the multiple images. Now that your powers don't affect me…." She shrugged. "But I don't understand why I don't feel anything at all."

Sam reached up and ran one finger down her cheek. "Aren't you upset?"

"That it's gone?" Celestine hesitated. "It's been part of me my whole life, made me who I was. But these last few years...."

"You're good at helping people, the ones who visit your tent," he said softly. "You have a way with people."

She sniffed again and nodded. "I'll miss telling fortunes in the tent."

"Or course you'll miss it."

"But I'll miss you more," she whispered.

Sam leaned in and pressed his lips to hers. There was one benefit to being connected to her.

She wrapped her arms around him and leaned in closer, their bodies touching along their whole length.

He deepened the kiss, trying to tell her without words everything he felt for her. He curved his arms around her body and drew her closer, as close as it was possible to be. Running his fingers softly along the skin of her neck, he followed with his lips; her skin trembled beneath his mouth.

Their link burst into life inside him, sparkling and bright. It was a reminder that he didn't want or need. He pulled back. "I think I should go," he said, leaning his forehead on hers again, his hands cupping her face.

She gazed up at him, anguish plain on her face. "Okay," she whispered.

He gave her one last hard and fast kiss, then strode out the door.

He didn't want to leave, but he couldn't stay.

CHAPTER 37

*C*elestine couldn't control the hiccuping sobs that escaped her body. Her face was wet with tears, and she was huddled against Artemis's warm body on her bed. He was gone, and she knew he wouldn't be back.

He'd been scarred by his experience with Veronica; she knew that. He wanted to be in control of her will as little as she wanted him to be. And he was willing to give up everything they had because of that.

She understood it, admired him for it, loved him for it. And wished he could find a way to change his own mind.

Even worse, she seemed to have lost her powers. She couldn't feel it bubbling inside her the way she always had. All she could feel was the connection to Sam, bright and strong, covering over everything else. She hiccuped.

Here she was, a *real* fake psychic. Would they still want her at the Carnival? Everyone else was so talented. She'd always felt so secure in her powers; *pretending* to be fake hadn't made her feel helpless. But she wasn't pretending any more.

Now she didn't know what to do.

Everything at the Jolly Knight Carnival reminded her of Sam. She was going to have to leave the Carnival and find somewhere new as well. But all she knew was fortune-telling, reading people's faces, drawing out their stories. She was good at it. How would she do it if she couldn't use her ability to read the emotions of the people in her tent to help her along? What if she couldn't do it without that?

A knock on the door interrupted her thoughts. "Coming," she said. Standing, she splashed cold water from the sink over her face. She'd stopped crying, but the blotchy red spots on her face would give her away.

She opened the door to find Indigo standing below, her face shadowed in the dark moonlit night.

"Uh. Come in," she said. She felt awkward. She didn't know the other woman very well and couldn't imagine why Indigo was visiting. She hadn't even realized she was here in the Carnival.

"Jack asked me to come see you. He told me what happened tonight." Indigo was so poised and elegant, even this late at night and in such strange circumstances. Her black pencil skirt and silky white shirt were paired with high-heeled black shoes—a touch higher than was practical in the Carnival, but very stylish. How had someone like Indigo emerged from a childhood in the Carnival?

Celestine's toes curled into her fluffy slippers. "Garth said it was a wedding ceremony."

Indigo sighed. "That's what it sounds like. An old form of the Carny wedding ceremony. The crystals, the candles, the red dress and ribbon. The ribbon must have somehow flicked over onto Sam when you jumped the fire together. It's part of the ceremony. Even Garth being there helped—he's a marriage celebrant these days."

Celestine gestured for Indigo to sit at the small table in

her kitchen area. "Can I get you something to drink?" she asked when the silence stretched out.

"No thanks," smiled Indigo gently. "I won't stay long."

Sitting down across from Indigo, Celestine widened her hands. "How can I help you?"

"Tell me about this new link with Sam," Indigo said.

"We can both feel the link," Celestine replied slowly.

"Has it changed anything else? Jack said you were seeing multiple visions?"

Celestine hesitated.

"What is it?"

"I think I've lost my ability to see the future."

Indigo's eyes widened. "What makes you think that?"

"I'm not seeing the future of everyone around me anymore. I can't feel it like I used to. I touched Sam and didn't see anything." Celestine marked off each point by holding up a finger.

Indigo seemed to think it through for a moment. "It's a pity. We could have used your help with seeing possible futures for us with Veronica."

Celestine sighed. "I'm sorry. But I really think it's gone." She spread her hands wide over the tabletop, and accidentally brushed Indigo's hand. Celestine stiffened, waiting for the usual involuntary reaction. For a moment, nothing happened, and she smiled. It was an old paranoia she could now let go of. She—

Time went still, and the familiar rainbow lights brushed across her vision, filling her sight with the otherworld she was so familiar with. It felt like everything was holding its breath, the whole world, the Carnival, and everyone in it.

And then her world exploded into color. The most specific and detailed color she'd ever had in a vision.

Indigo was standing next to a river. She was wearing old sweat pants and a sweat shirt. Her hair was ruffled and it looked like she'd been crying. Behind her, hundreds of Carnival folk were busily setting up a camp in the small clearing beside the river.

There were kids running around, screaming and laughing at the adventure of it all, but fear and apprehension hung in the air around the adults. There was something very, very wrong.

Two figures approached Indigo. Jack and Rilla.

Rilla put one hand on Indigo's shoulder. "Indy, you couldn't have known."

Indigo shook it off and took a step away. "I should have known better than to trust him."

"We all trusted him," said Jack.

"But I...." Indigo shook her head, unable to go on. Celestine could feel the heartache radiating off Indigo. Someone close to her had really hurt her. "And now...," She looked around them. "And now we're here. We've lost everything. The Compound, the Carnival. Everything. Because of *me*."

Rilla stepped forward again. "We haven't lost everything, Indy. We have each other. That's what's important. The people. That's what the Jolly Knight Carnival is really about. As long as we have each other, we'll be fine."

"Will we?" asked Indigo, her voice brittle.

The image started to fade out.

Celestine fought to stay. She needed to know who had done this to them. They needed the name of the person who had crushed the Carnival so badly they were camped out by a river. But she didn't have that kind of control, and the vision disappeared.

She opened her eyes. Her head was lying on a pillow on the tabletop.

"I didn't know what else to do. You were shaking rather badly," said Indigo awkwardly, a faint flush on her face.

Celestine sat up. "Thanks. It's fine. I don't even notice it."

"Can I get you something?"

"No, thanks. I'm fine."

"So I take it your powers haven't disappeared," said Indigo drily.

"I guess not." Celestine found it hard to look in Indigo's eyes. She'd seen the woman completely undone by someone who'd betrayed her. It seemed too personal.

"What did you see?" asked Indigo. "Does it relate to me? Isn't that the way it works?"

Celestine nodded.

"What did you see?" Indigo repeated. Her eyes were a dark blue, like midnight on a lake. She seemed mysterious and distant. Nothing like the broken woman by the river.

"I saw you... and the Carnival. But it wasn't the Carnival. We'd somehow lost the Compound and the tents and the rest of the equipment. Everything but the people."

Indigo's face went white. "How?"

"Someone close to you is going to betray you. I saw Rilla and Jack trying to console you, but you said... You said you should have known better."

Indigo shook her head. "There's no one who could betray me like that."

Celestine shrugged. "It's what I saw. You were... Not dressed as perfectly as usual."

Indigo's eyes sharpened on Celestine. "What do you mean?"

"You were wearing... sweats."

Indigo shuddered delicately. "Now I know it's not true. I would never do that."

"It's true, and it's going to happen unless we do something about it. We have to talk to Jack." Celestine leaned forward, suddenly overcome with the urgent need to tell the Ringmasters.

Indigo stood. "We can talk to him in the morning. He's

gone to bed. And you need to rest as well. You've had a long night."

Celestine felt her own face flush. "What I saw was a real vision, Indigo. I felt it. It will come to pass. It was stronger than any vision I've ever seen. I'm not making this up."

"I never thought you were making it up," soothed Indigo. But she clearly didn't believe Celestine. She stood. "We can talk to Jack in the morning." Indigo nodded at Celestine and then closed the door behind her.

Celestine let out a frustrated breath and leaned back in her chair. She couldn't force someone to believe her words, especially given everything she'd done to set up her reputation as a fake.

But she *would* talk to Jack tomorrow, and they would solve this mystery.

CHAPTER 38

*S*am had been on his way back to his own trailer when he realized he didn't want to be alone. He'd detoured and knocked on Frankie's door instead.

Frankie opened the door with his usual dour expression. "What do you want? I thought you'd be enjoying the spoils of marriage."

"How can you possibly know about that?" said Sam, taken aback. "Are you sure you never leave your place?"

Frankie shrugged. "Jack came by." He gestured for Sam to follow him inside.

"I can't stay married to her. I... just can't," said Sam, his voice breaking in the middle.

"Is this about that mad woman?"

Sam nodded. "I can't have that power over another person. I know what it did to me. I can't do it to Celestine."

"You're not that old witch. It wouldn't be the same."

"But it would, don't you see? I would always feel I was doing it for the best, for her. But what if there was something I really didn't want her to do? That she really wanted to do? I wouldn't be able to help myself. I'd force her to listen to me.

I'd be her keeper." Sam paced the small room, willing Frankie to understand him.

"That old hag Veronica, she really did a number on you, didn't she?"

"Ten years is a long time, Frankie. You don't leave unscathed."

"No, I guess not." Frankie looked around the small trailer where he was trapped.

"So you understand?"

"No. You've got this amazing woman who's married you —accidentally or not—and you're already talking about leaving her. I think you're crazy."

Sam turned away from Frankie. "I just can't do it. I don't trust myself. I don't trust the desire to overpower her choices."

Frankie sighed. "I'm sure you'd be able to work it out."

Sam shook his head. "You don't understand. That kind of power corrupts. Veronica never asked me to do anything bad in the beginning. It was only later that she started making me do terrible things."

"You're different—"

"No I'm not. None of us are." Sam paced up and down the small space. "Have you found out anything new about Veronica?"

Frankie shook his head. "Nothing useful. You're welcome to look through a few of the documents if you like."

Sam nodded. "I was hoping you'd say that."

Frankie shrugged and gestured toward a computer. Sam sat down, started looking through the documents up on the screen.

The next hour went past in silence except for the tapping of computer keys. Sam appreciated Frankie's ability to be silent. It soothed his bruised soul and enabled him to focus on what he really needed to be doing. Now that he knew Celestine was safe, he could go back to his mission.

Finding Veronica.

He searched the online documents, sometimes shocked at the kind of information Frankie been able to unearth. Bank statements, Veronica's birth certificate, old photos from before Marco was injured. It was all collected together, filed according to date.

The more recent documents were sparse; Veronica had been focused on The Experiment. There hadn't been much else happening in her life. Sam clicked the mouse and went back to the beginning again. He would find something useful. It was all he had to focus on now.

He looked again at a photo of Veronica and her brother Marco. They were leaning against a car, smiling at each other in perfect sibling symmetry. He'd never seen Marco looking so whole and healthy before. He'd known him as a pale and lifeless invalid in Veronica's back room.

Sam leaned closer to look at Marco, trying to understand what he might have been like all those years ago. His arm was protectively around his younger sister's shoulders, and she was gazing up at him in total hero worship. In the background was an old warehouse building with only part of the signage visible.

Something clicked in the corner of his brain. The words on the sign were the last three letters of the next city over from Nampa: Boise. Could that warehouse still have something to do with Veronica? Could it be that easy? They had been certain that she was nearby and Celestine had said that Veronica had been holding him in a warehouse in one of her visions. "Frankie. I think I'm onto something," he whispered hoarsely.

He turned, only to find that Frankie had gone to bed and was gently snoring from across the room. Shrugging to himself, he pulled up a map, looking for industrial areas nearby. Then he clicked on street view.

He would find that damn warehouse if it took him all night.

Three hours later he stared down at the computer screen like it was showing him a picture of a poisonous snake. But instead it depicted the same warehouse from the old photo. Newer, with a few updates, but the same building.

He stood and looked over at Frankie again. He was still sleeping soundly on his bed. He would have to wait until morning to get the computer genius's help confirming his suspicions.

Sam paced a couple of lengths up and down, then stopped. A sense of urgency was thrumming through his body. He couldn't wait. He had to find out if this really was Veronica's hide out.

He scribbled a quick note to Frankie and crept out. Everything was deserted; it was the middle of the night. Only idiots like him were up.

He headed to the parking lot, looking over the rows of vehicles. There were a couple of trucks for general Carnival-related errands. Jack had showed him where the keys were hidden, and he made quick work of getting inside the first beat-up old truck. He started the engine and winced when the engine roared across the silent lot.

He quickly backed out before anyone decided to come check on the noise.

It wasn't a long drive to Boise, and he soon located the street. He pulled the truck into a spot outside the building, staring up through the dusty windshield. It was mostly dark outside, the early morning light only just starting to creep across the sky.

The warehouse looked different from the photo, but something had pinged inside him when he pulled up. It was like an old muscle memory; something inside him could tell Veronica was close by. He shuddered. The thought that he was even a little bit connected to her made him feel dirty.

If part of him was still connected to Veronica, then part of Celestine was also connected to her now. The thought made his hands clench around the wheel. He was going to destroy Veronica, so she could never harm other people again.

He put the truck into gear and pulled away again, driving off down the street. He turned down a side street and parked the truck, pocketing the keys. Then he ran back to the warehouse, using the shadows as cover. He stood in the lee of the building next door for a long time, staring at the warehouse, trying to figure out what the best way in might be.

He was no good at this kind of thing. He knew it. If he'd really been thinking about this little trip, he would have found a gun on his way out. Then he would have gone in, guns blazing, shooting everything in sight. The thought cheered him until he remembered that he didn't have a gun and wouldn't know how to use one if he did.

But he could find out more information. He could get in and see what she was doing. It was unlikely that she was sleeping there, and it was still early morning. He could break in and confirm it was Veronica's lair without her ever knowing.

Creeping around the back of the warehouse building, he tried the main door, but it had a shiny new lock on some older chains through the handle.

No getting in that way.

There was a window higher up that might work, so Sam ferreted around and found an old drum; he rolled it over, placed it under the window and then clambered up. Cupping his hands around his face, he peered inside, but the window was too dirty and it was too dark for him to see anything useful.

He climbed down and crept around to the other side of the building. There was another side door, this one just as carefully locked and bolted as the last one.

He really had come on this mission completely unprepared. He didn't think of himself as being impetuous or spur of the moment, but that really was the only way to describe it.

Like he was trying to get himself killed.

For the first time, it occurred to him to wonder what would happen to Celestine if he died. Would the power revert to her brothers? Or would it revert to her? It was a tantalising thought. What if he could set her free simply by leaving this world? A bright light seemed to glow inside his head for a moment. If he took Veronica with him while he did it, he would be saving two people's lives.

But he didn't know if that was what would truly happen. He could be simply sending her back into slavery with her brothers.

He resisted the temptation to rattle at the chains on the door and crept back around to the back. He climbed up on his oil drum and peered inside again, just in case something had changed.

It hadn't. His hands clenched into fists.

The desire to do something, to change the lack of momentum in his explorations overwhelmed him. His skin felt as if he had a thousand ants crawling over it. A wave of frustrated emotion hit him, impetuous and sudden, and he didn't know what to do about it.

Without thinking, Sam lifted his arm and smashed his elbow through the window. Glass shattered all around him and inside the building. The noise of hundreds of pieces of glass breaking and then hitting the concrete floors inside the warehouse seemed to echo across the still night air, and Sam regretted it immediately.

But something urged him on and he kept going, pushing the rest of the old glass out of the sill, and onto the floor below. He peered inside, careful to keep his head away from the sharp glass edges. He couldn't see much more than he'd been able to see through the glass.

But now she was going to know that someone had been searching her warehouse property. Veronica was smart. She wouldn't stick around here once she knew this location had been compromised.

Sam swore.

His spur of the moment action had probably just cost them the best lead they'd had on Veronica since she disappeared.

Behind him, someone cleared their throat; the noise was loud in the quiet of the early morning. Sam jerked around, almost slipping off the drum in his haste. Below him stood a large man with short hair and tiny eyes, wearing a security uniform and holding a gun directed at Sam's chest.

"Slowly climb down off the barrel," he said, his voice low and rough.

Sam lifted his hands palm up. "Are you allowed to have a weapon like that?" he asked without thinking.

"Are you going to get down? Or do you want me to shoot you to check if I have real bullets?" The man sneered, showing large white teeth.

"Hold your horses," said Sam. He made a show of climbing down the oil drum and came to stand in front of the guard, putting a contrite expression on his face. "I'm really sorry, I got a little carried away. I didn't mean to break the window. I can replace it, if you'll tell me who owns the building." He smiled up at the guard, hoping against hope that the man wouldn't take this any further.

"Come with me." The guard gestured with the gun for Sam to lead around the side of the building.

Sam didn't move. "Are you going to call the police?"

"No need for the police. We can handle this ourselves," said the guard.

"What are you talking about?"

"You break something of ours, we break something of yours," said the guard with obvious relish.

Sam's heart was pounding hard in his chest. He had been so sure it was Veronica in there, it had never occurred to him it could be something worse. This man seemed like he might be part of some kind of organised crime network. "There's no need to go overboard. I'm sure we can come to some kind of arrangement."

"The only arrangements that we'll be making is how to get your body out of the river," said the guard.

"What river? There's no river around here."

The guard shrugged. "It's more of a saying. The boss'll decide what to do with you."

Sam shuffled slowly up the alley, trying to think of a way out of this situation. He kept glancing back at the guard, trying to find a moment when he wasn't paying attention. But the man never took his eyes off Sam, and his finger seemed to be trained on the trigger of the small handgun he still had focused on Sam's head. At least he was conscientious, whoever he was.

"In here," he said, gesturing with the gun. A small side door stood near to the front facade of the old warehouse.

The door opened before he could even touch the handle.

A woman stood in the doorway, her blonde hair shining in the glow from a nearby street light. Her eyes sparkled unnaturally in the darkness. "Hello, Sam," she said, lifting one hand in his direction.

Sam's breath stuck in his lungs. "Hello, Veronica," he said before blackness took over.

CHAPTER 39

*C*elestine opened her eyes. Something was wrong. She looked around the dark interior of her bedroom. It was still early morning. Artemis was stretched out along her side in her bed.

She'd been pulled out of her deep sleep, but she didn't know why. All she knew was that she had an overwhelming sense that something was very, very wrong.

Scrambling out of bed, she pulled on some clothes. "What do you think it is, Artemis?" she asked her sleepy cat. Artemis meowed and rolled over the other way, ignoring her. "I think so too. Something is wrong with Sam."

She'd woken earlier in the night with a nagging feeling that Sam was upset and worried. Their new connection might mean she couldn't see his future any more, but she could feel him.

Like a damn extra limb.

A limb that didn't want to be around her and was trying to leave.

But a limb nonetheless.

"What should I do?" she asked the sleeping cat. She sighed. She knew what she was going to do.

A few minutes later, she was knocking quietly on Jack and Rilla's door.

Jack answered, looking ruffled and half asleep, wearing only PJ bottoms. "Celestine? What's the matter?" He glanced around behind her. "Are your brothers here?"

Celestine shook her head. "Something's wrong with Sam."

Jack frowned. "He's sick? Where is he?"

"No, no. I don't know where he is. He couldn't... He didn't like being married to me, so he took off. But now something is wrong. Our... marriage bond... is telling me that something is wrong."

Jack rubbed one hand over his face, as if trying to wake himself up. "We need Garth and Frankie. Wait here for a minute. I'll be back shortly." He shut the door.

Celestine sat on the small wooden steps, holding her hands tightly in her lap. The feeling of foreboding was growing inside her, but she couldn't tell precisely what was wrong. She didn't even know where Sam was.

After the detail and precision of the vision she'd had with Indigo, this vague feeling was frustrating. Wouldn't it make more sense to have clearer visions of the people closest to you? So you could protect them? She gave a snort. Apparently not.

Jack yanked open the door, this time fully dressed in jeans and a T-shirt. Rilla followed right behind him. Celestine nodded at them both. "What do we do?" she asked.

"I called Garth, told him to meet us at Frankie's place. We start there."

Celestine nodded and followed them through the maze of campers. Frankie's trailer was close to the action of the Carnival and one of the farthest away from Jack and Rilla's in the center. Even then, they were there in moments.

Jack banged on Frankie's door. "Open up, Frankie. I know you're awake."

Frankie opened the door, rubbing his eyes blearily. "Actually, I was asleep, dude." He frowned down at them.

"Celestine thinks Sam's in trouble," said Jack without preamble.

Frankie glanced back into his living room. "He was here not that long ago," he said, pulling his door wider. "Come on in."

Celestine followed the others up the steps. She'd never actually been inside in all the time she'd been with the Carnival, but she'd heard about it from other people. She looked around at all the computers and the eerie blue light that coated everything. It lived up to the hype.

Frankie looked over at her, and Celestine swallowed. "Something's wrong. I can feel it through the bond we have. I woke up and just knew it."

"But you don't know what?" asked Rilla sharply.

Celestine shook her head. "This connection isn't the same as my visions. I can't tell you anything more. But it's getting worse." The feeling was intensifying, making her heart race, and leaving her breathless. She was having a hard time concentrating on what was going on around her.

"He was working on Veronica's information. Going over the records, trying to find something that might lead us to her," said Frankie. He moved over to a computer station near the kitchen. He pressed a couple of buttons and pulled up a Google map on street view and an old photo. "This was what he was looking at."

Celestine looked closer at the picture. She recognized Veronica, looking young and beautiful, and a man who looked similar enough to be family.

Frankie was concentrating on the computer screen, so Rilla saw Sam's note first. "What's this?" she asked Frankie.

He shrugged. "What does it say?"

"*Frankie, I've gone to check out a lead. Will be back soon. Don't worry.*"

"Turns out we do need to worry. Damn fool's gone and found her, hasn't he?" said Frankie, looking at Celestine.

Just at that moment, bright light burst into Celestine's head, like an explosion going off. It flared bright and unpleasant, and she cried out. And then it was gone. Along with the feeling of fear.

She could no longer feel the connection to Sam.

CHAPTER 40

*S*am groaned and rolled over. His hands were numb from the extratight ropes, and his shoulder was sore where he'd fallen on it.

He'd done it this time. He knew that now.

"No use crying over spilt milk, Sammy," said Veronica, her voice smug. They were in a large open space inside the warehouse. A bunch of chairs were stacked on one end, and nearby a young woman in an oversized knitted hat was sitting at a table and chair, typing furiously.

Veronica was glowing, and Sam blinked, trying to make sense of what he was seeing. Behind her, morning light shone through the high banks of windows.

The only thing that was missing from one of Celestine's visions was Jack and Rilla being dead beside him. At least he'd spared them all that horror. "Go screw yourself, Veronica," he spat out through his bloodied mouth. She'd let her goon punch him a few times before she'd started to work her own personal brand of magic on him.

"I always knew you'd come back to me," purred Veronica

as if Sam hadn't spoken. "Our powers mesh so nicely together. You bring me greater power than I've ever known."

"Everything you're doing is against my will. You're stealing from me."

"You're confusing me with someone who cares," she replied with a smirk. "You're mine again. The block I put on you today is ten times stronger than the one I had on you previously. There's no way the Carnival's paltry little Indigo —that's her name, isn't it?—will be able to get it off."

Sam gasped for breath, like a fish that's just landed in the bottom of a fishing boat. It felt like a thousand pound weight had settled on his chest. "You've put another block on me?" he said.

"Of course. How else am I going to be able to use you?"

Sam started struggling, desperate to undo his bindings so he could reach Veronica and strangle her with his bare hands. Every single fibre of his being was focused on doing her harm.

Veronica frowned. "I know you can't act on any of those urges you're currently feeling toward me. But as punishment for trying, you're going to stay tied up a while longer. You've done your part anyway."

It was Sam's turn to frown. "What are you talking about?"

"You've given me the extra power I needed to help Lacey here hack into a certain very secure server. A particular bank I wanted access to." Veronica smiled. "And you've also drawn the Ringmasters here. They're outside, trying to get in. There's something about this warehouse that makes people think I don't have any security." She glanced over at the large television screen behind her that showed a bank of small cameras. "When in fact I have a huge amount of security here, and I know precisely when someone is snooping around."

Up on the screen, Sam saw movement in a couple of the

cameras. He recognized Jack's tall frame and Rilla's dark head. Then his breath stopped. He saw Celestine's long curly hair, and he wished he could die right there.

"No," he said. "I'll do whatever you want of me. Just leave them out of it."

"Oh, are you concerned because your girlfriend is out there?" asked Veronica with a sneer. "Don't worry, she won't be around much longer."

Sam burst into action—he pushed and pulled against the ropes binding him, but they didn't budge. He kicked his legs —also tied up—and his muscled bulged. But nothing came undone. Tears coursed down his face. He couldn't do anything. This was his worst nightmare, the future he'd least wanted, and he'd led them all storming toward it from the beginning. He may as well have pulled the trigger himself.

He'd rather be dead than lead the Ringmasters and Celestine to their certain death. The thought calmed him and made him think properly for the first time since he'd seen Veronica. It gave him something to work toward.

"How did you override my connection to the Carnival?" he asked quietly.

"It was easy. I'm surprised the Carnival is still going. So much for their superior strength." Veronica shrugged and kept watching over the shoulder of her young companion. The young hacker hadn't looked up from the screen even once the whole time Sam had been there. She had long, dark, scraggly hair and dark brown eyes that seemed to absorb the light from the computer. He could feel the indifference rolling off her from across the room.

No help there.

He thought through her answer. The Carnival *was* strong. He knew that. So if she thought it wasn't, perhaps that was on purpose? Perhaps the Carnival had somehow managed to trick Veronica into thinking she had control of him, when she didn't? He poked around inside his head, trying to feel where the block was situated. He found it straight away, a stinging bright light that hurt his eyes.

He tried to access it at different points. Each time a jolt of pain shuddered its way through his body. She'd protected it much more this time. If he'd been the same young guy she'd first trapped into working with her, he might have stopped. If he didn't feel the weight of the Carnival somewhere behind him, the knowledge that Jack, Rilla, and Celestine would do everything they could to help him get out of here, he might have given up.

But he had people on his side now. He wasn't going to let it go, and he wasn't going to lie back and let Veronica win.

He pushed at the block, hard. It stung, but a crack appeared. She was relying on the pain to hide the fact that her block wasn't actually that powerful after all.

He glanced over at Veronica. She was the master manipulator. Her talent was persuasion, at least it had been in the beginning. Her power had expanded out so far that she'd been able to use the magic of The Experiment for more than just her original talent.

But she knew how to get people to do what she wanted. And for the years that he'd been with The Experiment, Sam had always given in. He'd waited for something to happen, for someone else to get him out of there. He'd thought he couldn't do it by himself. And perhaps he couldn't. But he'd never really *tried*.

He shoved again at the block. Stinging pain ricocheted through his body and he gasped. But the crack grew bigger. Veronica was lying. This block wasn't bigger or stronger than the last one. It was an illusion, designed to keep him within her power while she tried to finish whatever she was doing with the hacker.

Veronica was whispering to the young girl who nodded

without ever stopping the movement of her fingers on the keys. Veronica glanced over at Sam, who was careful to look beaten, and then she walked to where two large security guards stood bristling with guns. "I want you to bring the intruders inside. Tell them Sam will be killed if they give you any trouble. It should make them more docile."

"Yes, ma'am," said the second guard he'd met when he'd been pushed inside. The man had dark hair, a moustache, and a dead expression in his eyes that said he was under Veronica's control.

Panic surged through his body, and Sam wasted a few precious moments trying to pull his hands out of the ropes. He couldn't let the others be caught because of him. He wouldn't. He tried rolling over but just crashed into a chair that skidded on metal legs across the concrete floor. The noise made Sam wince.

He heard the sound of Veronica's laughter across the room. She was watching him, amused by his efforts. She was so sure of herself, so confident that she would succeed. He gritted his teeth. He could turn that into her downfall. There must be some way he could use her arrogance to his advantage.

She was all show, he knew that.

And the Carnival had overcome her once. They could do it again. She wasn't all powerful, especially not now.

At least he didn't think so. Did she have full access to his amplifying powers? Or was she simply siphoning off enough to use for whatever evil she was creating with her hacker? Surely the connection to the Carnival couldn't have been lost so easily? And what about his connection to Celestine?

Sam glanced over as the doors opened again, and Jack, Rilla, and Celestine walked in. Their grim faces said it all. They hadn't been expecting to get caught so easily. He wished he'd slowed down, woken Frankie. Talked to the others. Made a plan. Everything Jack had been telling him they needed to do.

He would have done anything in that moment to avoid the situation he'd gotten them into.

"Welcome to my abode," said Veronica. "Try not to burn this one down." Even from this distance, Sam could feel the anger emanating from his former boss. This was not going to end well.

He had to act fast.

While Veronica was distracted, Sam slammed into the block again, this time trying to use any spare ounce of power he had lying around inside him. The crack widened. He searched again through his consciousness. The connection to Celestine was there, but it was muted, as if something was covering it. When he searched for it, he realized the Carnival connection that Garth had forced into place floated every-where inside him, mimicking his own presence so well, that it was like it wasn't there. The Carnival had hidden in plain sight, allowing Veronica to put the block on him and think she had him back in her control. Sam clenched his fists and gathered the energy from the Carnival and his link to Celes-tine—apologizing silently to Celestine in case she felt some-thing—and hit the block with everything he had.

Sizzling light flowed out like a starburst and made him jerk in surprise. It burned his eyes and pain crackled through his body. More powerful than anything he'd ever experi-enced, it left the taste of cotton candy on his lips and the dizzy feeling of being on a roller coaster. When he looked again inside his head, the block was gone.

Sam opened his eyes and glanced up. Veronica was still talking to Jack and Rilla, her tense shoulders saying every-thing about how much she loathed the Ringmasters. Somehow she hadn't noticed the block being destroyed;

perhaps with help from the Carnival. It didn't matter, as long as it helped them escape.

His gaze caught and held Celestine's where she was standing to one side, watching Sam. He nodded slowly.

She nodded back.

He pushed at his ropes; something to do with the Carnival's burning help had loosened them off. He pulled his hands free, but discovered that the knots at his feet were too tight. He needed a knife.

But before that, he had to stop whatever it was that Veronica was planning. Checking to make sure she was still preoccupied with the others, he managed to crawl toward the young girl who was apparently some kind of hacking savant.

He was almost there when the young girl looked up at him. Her eyes were burning bright, like flames at the center of a forest fire.

"Don't bother," she said. "It's done." She slammed the laptop shut, put it under her arm, and moved silently out of Sam's reach. She was gone almost before he realized it, slipping into the shadows at the edge of the building. He didn't think she was coming back.

"No! Don't!" the words were ripped from Rilla's throat.

A gunshot echoed loud and clear through the entire warehouse.

CHAPTER 41

*C*elestine froze.

Even though it was all part of the plan, she couldn't help the feeling of dread crawling up her spine. The gunshot had been too loud, too real.

Jack collapsed to the ground, with Rilla next to him. Celestine concentrated on what she could see of the tableau in front of her. It was the same as in her vision. Rilla would be next.

She stepped up to Veronica, putting herself in front of the Ringmasters. "Where's Sam? Is he okay?" Her hands twisted in front of her as she tried to calm her pounding heart.

Veronica turned her attention to Celestine, allowing Rilla and Jack to make their next move. They were all wearing superthin bulletproof vests designed by Henry and Viktor, and throughout the entire car ride, they'd been planning what they'd do if Veronica decided to get trigger-happy. They had a certain amount of protection because of the Carnival, and the vests added to that. But they needed to control her and keep her contained somehow.

"Ah, yes. The girlfriend. I'm not surprised you're here. I'm just taking back what's mine." She lifted the gun and pointed it at Celestine's heart.

"He's not yours," said Celestine fiercely. "He belongs to no one."

Veronica laughed. "You're wrong. He was mine for *ten years*. I ordered him to do anything I wanted. He did it all, you know. Never said a word. *Never* complained." Veronica turned and spat in Jack's direction. "And then someone from the Jolly Knight Carnival comes along and destroys my world. Kills my brother. Leaves me with nothing. Less than nothing." She pulled the trigger again, and this time Celestine couldn't help herself, she screamed. She looked down over her body, and at first she couldn't see if she'd been hit. She let out a relieved breath—then the pain burst from just below her shoulder and she saw a spreading circle of red. This was what they'd not been able to plan for. Bullets that went wide or were aimed outside the vest range.

"You hurt him so badly, he may never be able to recover. But he doesn't belong to you anymore," said Celestine through gritted teeth, forcing the words out. She felt herself sway, but stood her ground. She had to keep Veronica occupied while the others forged ahead with the plan. "You don't own him." She would save Sam, no matter what it took. Even if it took her life.

At least he'd be free of her.

"I made him who he is," said Veronica, her whole attention focused on Celestine. "You are nothing, a speck, compared to me and my influence." She took a step toward Celestine.

Celestine opened her mouth to reply, but Sam spoke first.

"You have done nothing but torment and destroy," he said, appearing directly behind Veronica. He grabbed her around the neck and pulled his arm tight. "You are the worst thing that *ever* happened to me, and I will spend the rest of my life trying to atone for the terrible things you made me do." He jerked her neck tighter. "And I will never forgive you for that."

Celestine raced forward and yanked the handgun out of Veronica's hand with her good arm, before the older woman could think to use it on Sam.

"Let me go, Sam," said Veronica calmly, her words slightly garbled because of the choking hold Sam had on her.

"No. This is nothing more than you deserve," he said, his eyes dark orbs behind Veronica's head.

Veronica started struggling. "This is not possible. You have another block on you. You must obey me."

"You and your games. You're not powerful enough to put a full block on me anymore."

Veronica's face went purple, the veins standing out on her neck. And then she visibly calmed down. She stopped struggling. Her face returned to its normal color. She smiled. "Sam. You know you don't want to hurt me. You're a doctor. You must let me go."

Sam shook his head. "Never. You have no power over me now."

Behind her Celestine heard a scuffle, and turned. Jack was wrestling with one of the guards, their tall frames evenly matched.

But Rilla was on the back of the other guard, who was twice her size. Celestine hesitated, looking back at Sam, but he seemed to have Veronica under control. She stumbled over to Rilla and the guard. Her strength was leaking out of her, as well as blood, but she managed to slam the butt of Veronica's gun into the side of the guard's head. The guard simply grunted and kept trying to shake off Rilla.

When she tried to move in to hit him again, he reached out one arm, flicking at Celestine like she was a pesky fly. Leaping back out of reach, she gasped as a web of pain stretched out over her torso from her shoulder. She bit her lip and held up the gun with her good arm. Her finger hesitated over the trigger, but she couldn't pull it. She was a terrible shot and her vision was already becoming blurred. She was just as likely to hit Rilla as the guard.

They needed to end it quickly—the longer the fight went on, the more likely the guard was to win. He was bigger, stronger, and knew more about fighting.

Relying on the large man being distracted by Rilla, she rushed in close and jerked her knee up in one quick practiced gesture—her brothers had always fought dirty—and hit the guard squarely in the groin. He bent over into a groan, and she hit him again on the back of the head with the butt of the gun. This time he went down with Rilla on top of him.

Celestine stepped back quickly and her knees buckled. She fell to the floor as shudders wracked her whole body and landed heavily on her shoulder. Pain pulsed out from her wound and everything went blurry. She had to force her eyes to stay open. She looked up to see Veronica looming over her, a malicious sneer on her face. Celestine tried to lift herself back up, but her shoulder was a burning ball of fire, and she just groaned instead.

What had happened to the others? To Sam? Had she killed him? She couldn't even move her head to see.

Smiling, Veronica leaned down and took the gun from Celestine's nerveless hand.

"Goodbye, my dear," said Veronica, holding the gun loosely in her hand before bringing it up to point at Celestine's chest. Light from the overhead lamps created a halo around Veronica's face, and Celestine blinked rapidly, trying to clear the image of Veronica as an angel.

Time stood still, and rainbow colors appeared in the world around her. Celestine gasped, trying to pull herself back out of the vision. Her whole body was tensed for the bullet that was about to rip through her. But it didn't make any difference. The vision couldn't be stopped. Her body would be shaking with a seizure, but her mind was here, about to be a reluctant voyeur into Veronica's future.

Veronica was standing over a small grave. Around her were rolling hills and meadows full of sheep. She wore an immaculate suit, cream with intricately patterned gold buttons. Her hair fell gently around her shoulders, and she looked more relaxed than Celestine had ever seen her.

"I did it, Marco," she whispered, looking down at the gravestone.

Celestine could see Marco's name engraved into the marble. Underneath, the date of his birth and death were followed by the line: *Fly free, brother. I love you still.*

A breeze stole in across the meadow and blew gently across Veronica's face. She shivered. "I vowed to avenge your death, and I did it."

A bird screeched high in the sky, and Celestine looked up, watching it wander lazily across the sky.

Veronica leaned down and placed a single red rose across the tombstone. She placed her hand softly next to the rose, as if touching her brother's face. "I love you, Marco."

Then Veronica stood and walked carefully back out of the small graveyard, past a tiny stone church with a single tower and bell. Celestine looked around, trying to find a landmark or a name, perhaps an address that would mark where they were. Nothing seemed familiar or extraordinary enough that she might be able to find it again.

Veronica climbed into a large cream car. As she drove away, the vision faded, and Celestine returned to her body, her whole being tensed for the pain of being shot.

Veronica had won.

CHAPTER 42

*S*am rolled to his feet, searching the warehouse for Veronica. His heart lurched when he saw her standing over Celestine, who was lying prone on the floor, her whole body shaking in a seizure. He roared, sprinting toward Veronica.

She wasn't going to hurt Celestine again.

Veronica looked up and saw Sam running toward her. Her eyes widened, and she held up her arm, pointing the gun directly at his heart. "Stay back, or I'll shoot you too," she said loudly.

He kept running—he didn't care about a bullet, he would keep going through anything she sent his way, just to save Celestine.

She hesitated, watching his progress toward her as if she didn't understand what was happening.

He was almost on her, when she seemed to make a decision. She sneered at Sam, then turned and ran. Sam got to Celestine seconds after Veronica left her, skidding to a halt beside her.

He glanced up at Veronica as she escaped through the

metal door at the side of the warehouse, but he didn't chase her. His hand slid into Celestine's, fitting perfectly. He ran his other hand across her forehead, pushing strands of red-blonde curls out of her eyes. "It's okay, Celestine. You're going to be okay," he whispered to her as her seizure ended.

The link between them brightened and glowed. He leaned down and kissed her cheek, feeling the magic of the Carnival working through both of them. Celestine opened her eyes and looked up at him. "Are you okay?" she asked.

Sam let out a breath. "You're the only person I know who would wake up after being shot and having a seizure, and ask if *I'm* okay," he said on a laugh.

"I know how I feel," she said.

"How do you feel?"

"Rotten." She made a face.

Sam looked around for the other two. Jack and Rilla were tying the guards to a couple of old heating pipes not far away. The door burst open and Frankie and Garth came running in. They both had guns.

"Are we too late?" said Garth.

Jack shook his head. "She didn't do as much talking as we expected. Just went straight to the shooting." He fingered the hole in his shirt.

Garth noticed the blood on Celestine's shoulder. "Do we need the hospital?" he asked Sam.

Sam blinked and realized that he'd been so busy holding her hand, that he hadn't properly checked Celestine's wound. "I'm so sorry, Celestine. I wasn't thinking." He ripped the shirt around the wound, and leaned in for a closer look. The bleeding had already stopped, and he found an entry and exit wound, so the bullet has gone through cleanly. There was also a humming inside him that he recognized. The Carnival was helping heal Celestine as well.

"I think we can leave it for today. I have all the supplies I need in the clinic. But we need to get back to the Carnival so I can dress this wound as soon as possible."

Frankie looked around. "Where's Veronica?"

"You didn't see her on the way in?" asked Jack.

"No."

"Then she escaped."

Frankie looked around and hesitated. "You don't think...?" he said quietly. He glanced at Celestine. "Didn't she see...?"

Jack looked at him and then Rilla. "Everyone out! Right now!" he yelled.

Sam glanced up at Jack in confusion, but the expression on the Ringmaster's face said it all. He thought Veronica had something more planned for them. It wasn't like her to just slip away in the night. She liked to leave a big impression.

He scrambled to his feet and dragged Celestine with him. She groaned, but let him do it. He put her good arm around his shoulder and helped her to half walk across the floor to the exit. To one side Rilla and Jack were untying the same guards they'd just tied up. Frankie held a gun on them and kept glancing at his watch.

Sam emerged into the outside world. Everything was covered in pinks and oranges, the shades of a beautiful early morning sunrise. He kept moving, dragging Celestine as far away from the warehouse as he possibly could. He didn't know where their car was, but he still had the keys to the truck jangling in his pocket, so that's where he headed.

He'd only taken a dozen or so steps when a deafening explosion filled the air around them. A wall of heat and air hit Sam, knocking his feet out from under him. Sam clung tight to Celestine as the detonation inside the warehouse ricocheted along the whole street, pulsing outwards and striking everything in its path.

As they were flung through the air, Sam managed to twist his body so that he landed first, pulling Celestine down on top of him. She cried out as they landed heavily on the ground, and then went limp.

He curled onto his side, trying to protect her from whatever debris might find them. Moments later wood, bricks, metal piping—the whole damn lot—started raining down from the sky. Sam held himself still over Celestine's body, taking the brunt of the explosion fallout, clenching his teeth against the pain each time something smashed against his back.

After what seemed like hours, but was probably only minutes, Sam looked up. His body was battered and torn. Dust and debris was everywhere. Nothing big had fallen on them, but it was pure luck. A massive brick block was embedded into the concrete less than five yards from where they'd fallen.

"Jack! Rilla!" His voice was rough and he cleared his throat. "Garth! Frankie! Anyone!" The thought that Veronica might have won after all flitted through his head. Perhaps this had always been her plan. Destroy the Carnival by taking out four of the main leaders. And he'd led them all straight to her.

"Don't," said a soft voice below him.

He looked down into Celestine's gentle eyes. "What?"

"I can feel you trying to blame yourself. Just don't."

"But I led you all here...."

Celestine shook her head. "Veronica would have crossed their paths whatever happened. She's been on a collision course with the Carnival for a very long time. You gave us the opportunity to take her on."

Sam looked up at the destruction around them. "They're dead. All of them."

Celestine shook her head. "No, they're not. Look through your Carnival link. You should at least be able to pick up Rilla and Jack."

Sam took a breath. She was right. Of course she was. If the Ringmasters were actually dead, the whole Carnival would know it. Grief would ripple across the whole structure.

"We need to find the others, though," she said.

Sam shook his head. "I'm not leaving you. You're hurt."

"Go find them," she said gently. "I'll stay right here."

He leaned in and gave her a hard kiss. "I love you," he said, for the first time realizing he really meant it.

She nodded and smiled back at him, the future in her eyes.

Sam stood, turning in a small circle next to her. "Jack!" he yelled. "Anyone?"

Groans from behind a large metal container led him to Jack and Rilla, a small distance away.

"Jack's leg is stuck under the container," said Rilla. She was trying to push the metal contain over, but it didn't even budge.

Sam looked around quickly, trying to find something to help. He spotted a broken piece of metal piping just as Frankie and Garth limped up to them.

"Help me with this," said Sam, gesturing to the other two. He grabbed the piping, shoved it under the container to form a lever and heaved. Between them, the metal container swung into the air. Rilla dragged Jack out, tears running down her face.

Sam crouched down beside Jack's mangled leg. "I think this might be a little beyond my skills," he said. "I think you might need surgery."

Jack looked up at Rilla. "Get us back to the same town as the rest of the Carnival. We'll go to the hospital there."

"Where's the car?" asked Sam.

"I'll go get it," said Garth straight away. He ran off to the other side of the building.

"We need to hurry," said Frankie.

"Because he's badly hurt?" asked Sam. "He'll be fine, I just don't have the tools."

Frankie shook his head. "No, because the only reason I can be outside the Carnival is because Jack's been blocking me. If he loses consciousness, then we're all in big trouble. Me being here is going to disrupt the Carnival more than anything that old battle ax could do."

Sam felt it then, little lines of distress coming from the Carnival link inside his head. "I'll carry Celestine. Frankie, you help Rilla with Jack. Let's go."

CHAPTER 43

*C*elestine came back to consciousness just as the truck was driving back into the Carnival parking lot. On one side of her, Sam was edgily tapping the steering wheel as he turned into a spot. On the other side, Frankie was tapping his foot.

"What's the matter?" she asked blearily.

"Everything's fine," said Sam, turning to smile down at her.

"Then why are you both so...?"

Frankie's lips tightened. "Jack refused to go to the hospital until I made it back into my trailer. He's worried about what might happen."

"He's still conscious?"

"He was last time we checked in with Rilla and Garth." Frankie managed a small tight smile. "It's all okay so far, right?"

Celestine tried to check, but she was so weak it all felt the same to her. "I don't know," she said.

"Are you sure she doesn't need to go to the hospital?" said Frankie, over Celestine's head.

Sam glanced down at her. "I think she's okay. Unless you *want* to go in, Celestine?"

She shook her head. "Just give me a little time to get over the vision. I'll be fine."

A figure was running toward them down the trailer alleyway. Sam opened his door and stepped down. Frankie opened his side and followed suit. Celestine squinted until she recognized Joey, the runner.

"What's the matter, Joey?" asked Frankie with concern.

"Something's wrong with Viktor. He's been acting strange. I have to tell Jack and Rilla."

Celestine's stomach dropped. She thought of the vision where Viktor reprogrammed the animals to fly off the carousel. "We need to stop the carousel immediately," she said. "This is another of my visions. It's coming true."

"We need the Ringmasters. Viktor's too strong for anyone else," said Joey.

"They're not available. We have to do this ourselves," said Frankie. "Come on, show me where he is." Frankie strode after Joey.

"Keep Viktor away from the carousel," called Celestine after them, levering herself up on the seat. The pain had dulled to an ache, but it was spread across her entire body now, making it difficult to move quickly. She edged her way over to the door. "Sam, get me down from here."

Sam helped her down and then put his arms under her knees and shoulders.

"What are you doing?" she asked, weakly batting at his arms.

"I'm carrying you to your trailer," he said, his voice rough. "No arguments."

Celestine briefly considered making a stand, but her shoulder was hurting and she wasn't sure she could actually make it to her place on her own two legs. "What are we going to do about Viktor?" she said instead.

"*You're* going to do nothing," said Sam. "*You've* been shot. I'm going to get you settled, and then I'll go try to help where I can."

"Your power is why Viktor is strong enough to tinker with the carousel and make the animals fly off," said Celestine carefully.

"I know that," bit out Sam. "Don't you think I know that?"

Celestine winced. She hadn't said that very well. "What I meant was that perhaps we can do something to turn off your power? So that it doesn't work anymore?"

"Like what?"

"We go to Jack. Instead of going to my trailer, we head to his place. We get him to absorb your powers."

Sam shook his head. "Jack's about to lose consciousness at any moment. He's not strong enough to absorb anything right now. I'm surprised he managed to stay conscious long enough to get Frankie here."

Just then, a car came screaming into the parking lot behind them, a big, dark-purple Lincoln that looked like it had come straight out of the seventies. It sprayed stones as it came to a halt nearby. A tall elegant woman climbed out, her long legs encased in fashionable skin-tight jeans and a red silk shirt. She had long dark hair, and dark glasses that hid half her face. "I'm looking for Jack Knight," she said. "I heard he was here."

Sam glanced from her to Celestine. "We're... uh... in the middle of a crisis at the moment... Jack's not available."

The woman huffed out an exasperated breath and pulled off her glasses. "Look, I'm tired and pissed off. I've just spent the last twenty-four hours on a goddamned plane getting here to see him, so he can bloody well stop what he's doing and see me." She glanced at Celestine and blinked, seeing her properly for the first time. "Is that blood?" she said.

Celestine nodded apologetically. "You better come with us. Jack's been hurt. You really won't be able to see him right away, I'm afraid."

"Hurt? Where is he?" the woman looked around as if she was going to run and find him.

"*Rilla's* with him," said Celestine gently. "He'll be okay with her there." She needed to make this woman understand that she wasn't going to be able to just come back into Jack's life and insert herself where she didn't belong.

"Rilla?"

"His wife."

"He has a *wife*? I go away for a little while, and suddenly he's in a Carnival and he's shacked up?" The woman spared a scornful glance at the big top in the distance.

Sam let out an exasperated breath. "Come with us. I have to get Celestine back to her trailer. You can stay with her until Jack's ready to see you. In the meantime... We do actually have a real emergency," said Sam.

Celestine gestured for the woman to follow them.

"I'm Celestine and this is Sam, by the way." She gave a small smile. It was getting hard to hold her head up, but she felt compelled to try in the face of this graceful creature.

"I'm Hannah. Jack's sister."

Celestine managed to hold in her small gasp. Sam stumbled, stopped and then righted himself. She hung on tighter around his neck.

"I... ah... didn't know he had a sister," said Sam.

Hannah shook her head impatiently. "He probably doesn't talk about me much. I'm a disappointment to my staid older brother." She glanced around. "Although I have to say I would never have thought he'd stick around somewhere like this. More our father's scene than Jack's."

"Jack's found a new home here since he met Rilla," said Celestine. Her shoulder was starting to throb, and she was thinking about her bed in the same way a person lost in the desert might think about water.

"Apparently so," murmured Hannah.

She followed in silence until they reached Celestine's trailer and opened the door when Sam gestured at it.

Celestine closed her eyes, tears of relief edged under her lashes. She grasped Sam's hand when he placed her gently on the bed. "You need to find Frankie. Go help him. This is part of my vision. Veronica has been here. Tell him to keep Viktor away from the carousel."

Sam shook his head. "No. Your shoulder needs to be looked at first. I need to wash out the wound, get it all patched up."

Celestine shook her head. "My shoulder is the least of our worries right now. If you don't help Frankie, Veronica could win. Then we all lose."

Sam hesitated and then turned to Hannah. "Do you know anything about first aid?"

Hannah shook her head once. "Nope."

If the circumstances had been any different, Celestine would have laughed at Sam's torn expression as he hovered next to Hannah. As it was, she just watched him and tried not to think about the vision of Alfie lying dead next to the carousel.

Sam didn't take long to decide. "Just wash out the wound," he said. "Get it clean and then put something over it to keep it uncontaminated until I can get back."

Hannah nodded uncertainly. "That doesn't sound too hard."

Sam turned to Celestine. "I'll be back as soon as I can. Sooner." He leaned in and gave her a kiss.

She gave him a small half smile and then he headed for

the door.

Celestine watched him race back out into the Carnival with fear in her heart. Viktor's vision with the carousel had been particularly disturbing.

If Jack wasn't wounded he could have absorbed Veronica's magic and everything would have been fine. Sam's amplifying ability could even have helped them, making Jack far stronger for battling her.

But Jack was badly hurt and the Carnival just wasn't as strong. Not only had they lost his ability to absorb the magic, they'd also lost one half of their Ringmaster duo.

She could also feel the Carnival pulling on the magic to help him heal, in the same way it was helping her. All of that was sucking energy that should have been used against their nemesis.

Celestine shifted restlessly on the bed. How were they going to beat Veronica? What if all her predictions were about to become true?

They'd beaten Veronica this afternoon, but the explosion, and now this threat from Viktor made Celestine wonder if that hadn't been Veronica's plan all along. Make them think they'd won, just so she could really sink them properly.

Hannah moved over to stand next to the bed. "I guess I better take a look at your shoulder," she said.

Celestine blinked and her focus returned to the tiny bedroom. Hannah leaned down and, before Celestine could stop her, touched Celestine's arm. Fear surged up through her body—she wasn't strong enough to survive this right now. Celestine tried to pull back, to tell her mind to stop. But as always, there was nothing she could do.

Time stood still. Sparkling lights the color of a rainbow fluttered across Celestine's vision. But instead of going into a future vision, Celestine found herself in the Carnival dreamscape. Misty clouds covered the landscape and two bright lights stood in front of her.

One of the lights moved forward and crossed his light over hers. As soon as it touched her, she recognized Jack.

The Carnival needs our help.

Celestine nodded. That much she already knew.

I think I can push my blocking power through the Carnival landscape into Hannah. I know she's there with you. I can feel her. The Carnival thinks she might have a similar ability to mine.

"What will that do?"

If we can break the magical hold that Veronica has over Viktor, we can stop what's about to happen. What you saw happen.

"How do you know all this?"

I can feel it through everyone at the Carnival. Sam being part of the Carnival has truly expanded what we can do. But I'm unconscious. I can't move or come to you any other way. Believe me, I would if I could.

Celestine could feel the desperate longing in Jack's voice; he meant what he said. It was up to her.

Bring Hannah here, to the dreamscape.

Celestine blinked open her eyes. Hannah stared back down at her, fear in her eyes. "Oh, thank God. I thought you were going to die or something," she said.

Celestine reached up and grasped Hannah's hand. "I know this is going to sound crazy. I know you don't know me, but I know your brother. And he needs you. We all need you. You need to close your eyes and follow me."

Hannah pulled back. She held up her hands as if to fend off Celestine. "Look, no offence, but you're starting to sound crazy. I think your fits might be affecting your brain." Hannah backed up again. "I'm really sorry that you're injured, but I think I better leave now."

She grabbed her handbag off the side table, then ran out the door.

CHAPTER 44

"*H*e's holed up in there and we can't get him out," said Frankie, talking over his shoulder at Sam. In front of them was the old inventing van Viktor tracked around the circuit with them. It had all his tools, devices, ideas, and plain old junk stored inside it. Luckily it was two doors down from Frankie's own trailer, so the Chancemaster was managing to stay nearby.

"Have you got someone around the other side just in case?"

Frankie nodded. "He's surrounded. But he's acting crazy. I've never seen him like this before." He hesitated. "When he puts his mind to it, Viktor is a cunning old bastard. He'll find a way to escape if he really wants to."

"Veronica's managed to get her claws into him somehow."

"We have to figure out what she's done to him."

Sam nodded, wracking his brains to remember the details of the visions Celestine had told them about. "I'm going to ask Celestine if she can remember anything that would help," he said.

As he turned, Sam saw a flash of red going past and

looked up. Jack's sister Hannah was running awkwardly along the alleyway in her high-heeled shoes. "Just a minute," he said to Frankie, and strode over to intercept her.

"You okay?" he said. "You look scared."

Hannah looked up. Relief flooded her face. "You're the doctor, right? You need to get back to that woman. She's having some kind of delusional fit."

Sam froze. "She had a seizure?"

Hannah nodded, her expression relieved. "Yeah, a seizure. It's finished, but now she's talking like it hurt her brain or something."

Sam grabbed Hannah's arm. "I might need your help, if it's as serious as you're saying."

Hannah glanced back the way she'd come. "I don't...," she said.

But Sam wasn't in the mood for no. He grabbed Hannah's arm and dragged her back to Celestine's caravan.

When he opened the door, Celestine was getting herself dressed.

At least she was trying to.

Blood was dripping down her arm, and her hands were shaking as she held a clean shirt against her body. She looked up with relief when the door swung open, and tears welled when she saw it was Sam.

"We have to find Hannah," she said. "She's the only one who can save us."

Sam looked back to where Hannah was hovering behind him in the doorway. Hannah shrugged and wiggled her finger in circles by her forehead. *Crazy.*

"Come on in," he said to Hannah.

She shook her head. "No. Look, I'm sorry for your friend, but she's freaking me out. If you'll just point me toward my brother, I'll get out of your hair."

Sam glanced back at Celestine.

"We need her," she whispered at him.

He turned back to Hannah. "Jack was badly hurt by the same woman who's currently trying to hurt us here at the Carnival."

Hannah glanced up and down the alleyway. "Seriously, just point me in the direction of his place... trailer... whatever." She gestured at the row of trailers with one arm.

Celestine came to stand beside Sam. She put her good hand into his, and squeezed. She was trembling and pale, but otherwise composed. "Jack is in trouble. He needs your help. Desperately," she said.

"Jack's never in trouble. He doesn't take risks."

Sam smiled ruefully. "He does now. This Carnival, the people in it, are worth taking risks for."

Hannah looked at Sam curiously. But then she shook her head. "You all sound just as crazy as each other."

"Look, Hannah, we need you. *Jack* needs you. Can you please try to trust us?" said Celestine beside him. She swayed, and Sam put his arms around her.

"You should be in bed," he said to her.

She shrugged. "No point being in bed if everything is going to be destroyed around me," she said hoarsely.

Hannah let out a huff of breath. "You're both serious, aren't you?"

Sam glanced back at her. "Of course we are. Are you going to help or not?"

Hannah held his gaze for a moment, as if she could tell by just looking at him that he was lying. Then she shrugged. "I've got nothing better to do while I wait for Jack, I suppose."

Sam grinned and stepped back into the living room. He helped Celestine to sit on the bench seat in the kitchen and then turned to Hannah, who'd followed them inside. "Make yourself at home," he said. "Do you want something to drink?"

She shook her head. "Let's just do whatever it is you want me to do. Get it over with."

Sam gestured to the other side of the kitchen table and Hannah sat down. Sam grabbed the spare stool and sat next to Celestine. "Are you okay to start, Celestine? Or do you want to get changed first?"

She shook her head. "We have to get this done as soon as we can. Every second we waste, Veronica has a chance to beat us."

Celestine grasped Hannah's hands across the table. The other woman held herself stiffly, but allowed Celestine to do what she needed. Sam put one hand on Celestine's arm, unsure if he was supposed to be part of this or not.

Before he could even think to ask anything more, the trailer around them disappeared. Instead they were in a white, misty landscape he recognized from when he'd been forcibly joined to the Carnival bond. Sam saw bright lights; he didn't know how, but he knew they were Jack and Rilla. Beside him, he felt Celestine's softly glowing light, and next to her was a buzzing light that was changing fitfully from purple to yellow to white and back again.

Hannah.

The two lights moved forward. One, a brightly glowing light that was definitely Jack, glided over to Hannah and crossed light with her. Immediately her changing colors stopped, and she glowed a warm golden color.

Without knowing how, Sam knew that Jack wanted them all to gather closer together, overlapping their light and helping to push the energy from Jack to Hannah. He settled close to Celestine, and they both moved forward. As soon as he touched her light, Sam felt Celestine's energy. She was weaker than she'd let on. Her arm hadn't even been properly bound since the explosion.

He hesitated and tried to draw back. He needed to tend to Celestine before they went any further.

What are you doing? asked Celestine in his head.

"You shouldn't be here. You're too weak. We should leave," he said.

They need us. This has to be done, or the whole Carnival will die.

"But—"

Sam. We must do this for the Carnival.

The tantalising thought that he could make her leave this place flitted through his head. He pushed it away. This was her decision, not his; it always would be.

He stayed in position next to her, waiting for Jack's next move.

In this place, emotion was easier to understand than words. Sam found himself "knowing" things he hadn't been told, like what Jack was saying to Hannah to convince her to help them. She gave way under his presence and soon they became one large glowing ball, rather than five separate entities. There was no hot and cold in this place, but the light was so bright he felt like he should be sweating. He closed his eyes and saw the same scene. There were no eyes in this place, it was inside their heads.

Then it was over. Jack and Rilla moved backward, away from Hannah. She was glowing brighter with her borrowed powers.

Jack had given them the plan inside their heads; there was no need to talk about it. They just knew.

Sam blinked and opened his eyes back in Celestine's kitchen. He watched as Celestine and Hannah came around.

Hannah seemed different, less cocky, more unsure. "How do we do this?" she asked.

Sam stood up. "Celestine, you need to stay here. You

aren't strong enough to walk all the way there. Hannah, you come with me."

Celestine shook her head. "Jack was really clear. I need to be there. It won't work unless you and I are there, providing the link for Hannah. Together we're strong enough to make this happen."

Sam looked down at Celestine again, images of her lying next to Veronica going through his head. "What if—"

She shook her head. "You can't protect me from everything. You have to let me make these decisions on my own."

Hannah stood. "Come on. Jack said we had to hurry to get this done. I need to get him out of my head as fast as I damn well can." Her expression was a mixture of distaste and frustration.

Sam helped Celestine to her feet and they all headed out the trailer and down the alley. Hannah strode along with her long legs, like she couldn't handle walking any slower. She broke into a run every few paces, and glanced back impatiently at Sam and Celestine as they stumbled together, Sam's arm around Celestine's waist.

"When this is over, you need to rest," said Sam. "For several weeks."

She grimace up at him. "Thank you." Little beads of sweat on her forehead were the only indication that she wasn't as calm as she looked.

"For what?"

"Not forcing me…to do what you wanted…me to do." Her breath was coming in gasps, and Sam just wanted to bundle her into his arms and take her back to her trailer.

Instead he just gazed down at her. "I would never do that. As much as I might want to, I would never do it."

And he meant it.

CHAPTER 45

*H*er whole body was burning up in the flames emanating out from her shoulder. Every time she took a step, it felt like someone was sticking a hot poker into her shoulder. Sweat dripped from her face, her back —everywhere.

But they were going to save the Carnival from Veronica, so it didn't matter. Beside her, Sam's comforting presence helped her focus on what was important. He kept her moving one foot in front of the other.

Viktor's inventing van, when they arrived, was surrounded. Frankie had called in reinforcements, trying to make sure Viktor stayed inside.

"What took you so long?" asked Frankie, the lines on his face deeper than she'd ever seen them. Garth stood to his right, black eyes focused on Celestine.

"You've been waiting for us?" asked Sam.

"Of course. Garth said the Carnival was doing something through Celestine and you."

Celestine stumbled, and Sam grabbed her tighter against him. "We've got Jack's sister with us. She's going to block the magic around us, so whatever Veronica's done to him won't work. Then we can try to get Viktor away from her."

Celestine swallowed hard. "She's got his grandchild. At least... In my vision, she did."

Frankie flicked a startled glance at Celestine. "Are you sure?"

She shook her head. "No. But we need to check on his family. Make sure."

Frankie called over Joey and whispered in his ear. Joey took off at a run, grabbing two other young runners with him as he went.

"Let's do this. We don't have time to waste," said Frankie. "The longer we leave it, the worse the odds become." He finally glanced over at Hannah and stopped. "You're Jack's sister?" he asked in surprise.

She scowled at him. "Yeah. So what?"

Frankie shook his head. "Nothing. Just not what I was expecting."

"What were you expecting?"

"Some one... older."

She put her hands on her hips. "I'm plenty old enough," she said, scowling at Frankie and suddenly seeming much younger.

Frankie shrugged and turned back to Sam and Celestine. "How do we do it? What did Jack say?"

Celestine took a deep breath. She felt the smooth energy of Sam's power curling around her, building her up and making her stronger. "On her own, Hannah isn't strong enough to absorb anyone's magic. But with the rest of us helping, including Jack, we have a shot at it."

"But if she's absorbing magic, won't it absorb all our magic too?" asked Frankie, frowning at Hannah like it was her fault. She scowled back.

Celestine shook her head and tried to ignore the waves of

nausea lapping over her stomach. "Hannah's going to absorb Veronica's magic through one of my visions. She'll be doing it in the future, and we'll be back here in the present, protecting and supporting her, so it shouldn't affect us. While she's doing that, we have to get Viktor out of that trailer, and bring him physically close to us. We're all going to be linked together, you, me, Sam, Garth, and Hannah."

"How?"

"Through the Carnival dreamscape. The Carnival and I are going to try to control what I see in my vision, then I'll link with Hannah and draw her in. She'll absorb the magic in the future, leaving the present alone. By the time we catch up to the point where she's absorbing, when all our magic will be absorbed as well, it should be over. Theoretically." Celestine winced as a wave of pain rolled across her body.

"Is that even possible?" asked Frankie.

"The Carnival believes it is."

"What if it's not enough? What if Veronica's stronger than us?"

"She's not as strong as she'd like us to think." Celestine licked her dry lips. Frankie's face blurred in front of her for a moment and then cleared. The Carnival's magic was weaving itself around her, holding her close, and helping with the pain.

"But where *is* Veronica?" Frankie asked with a frown.

"Jack says she has to be close by," said Sam, tightening his arms around Celestine's body. She slumped against him gratefully.

Frankie nodded. He gestured to another of his young runners, and spoke in an undertone near the boy's ear. He ran off.

It was time to begin. Celestine took a breath, trying to gather courage around her like a cloak. "Hannah, can you hold my hand? Gently." Celestine couldn't move her wounded arm, but Hannah slipped her hand into Celestine's fingers without incident.

Time stood still, but with the faintest smell of cotton candy on the breeze. Everything hung in midair for a miraculous moment in time. Celestine glanced down—even the drops of blood seeping out from her wound seemed to sparkle with an incandescent magic. She breathed in, and as she exhaled the rainbow lights burst around her. But they were different this time; they moved faster, with more purpose than they ever had before. The presence of the Carnival lay heavy over everything.

The vision came into focus. This wasn't a far-distant future; this was only minutes ahead. Everything was almost the same as it had been, except Celestine saw herself lying on the ground, midseizure. Sam had her in his lap, and Hannah sat on her other side, still holding her hand for all she was worth. She'd never seen it from this perspective before, and for the first time understood why it was so disconcerting for the others to see her jerking and moving uncontrollably.

Through the physical link between their hands, Celestine drew Hannah into the Carnival dreamscape again. This time it was made up of many more lights than Celestine had ever seen there. They were surrounded on all sides by the glowing balls that represented the souls of the Carnival folk in this alternate landscape.

For Hannah to be able to use the absorbing talent from Jack, she had to have a cushion around her, people to protect her from the punishing waters that almost overwhelmed Jack when he fought the magician Hugo Blue. The Carnival had brought everyone to help her.

Celestine saw Hannah's light, then felt her presence inside her vision. They wouldn't have long, seconds really, before the real absorbing talent of Jack and Hannah would catch up with Celestine's future seeing, and render all of their abilities useless. It would have to be enough to allow them to create a layer of protection around Viktor.

Inside her vision, Frankie and two other men were using a crow bar to open the door to the invention van. They went inside and pulled a dazed looking Viktor out of the small space, dragging him over to Celestine and the others. Garth put his hands up to Viktor's head, and his all-black eyes glowed with the power of the universe for a single second.

Viktor cried out, then the whole vision disappeared.

CHAPTER 46

*C*elestine felt a wooshing sensation all around her, like she was being sucked down a pipe. It was as if all her magic was being forced out of her, leaving her small and weak. She struggled to open her eyes, her own body fighting against her desire to wake. A part of her half expected to find that she was somewhere she didn't recognise.

She let out a small relieved breath when she saw Sam above her, holding her tight in his lap. "Did it work?" she asked softly. Hannah clenched her fingers around Celestine's hand, sending painful shockwaves up her arm.

Sam nodded, his eyes never leaving her face. "Viktor seems okay, but we haven't heard back about Veronica or his grandchild. We don't even know which one it might be."

"Has Hannah stopped absorbing?" Celestine had to force the words from her mouth; they felt sloppy and slurred.

Sam glanced at Hannah. "I think so. As soon as Viktor's block was destroyed, the Carnival turned the flow of energy from Jack off."

Celestine tried to lift her heavy head to peer around

them. The area that had been buzzing with activity only moments before was almost empty.

"Just keep still, Celestine. Don't try to move," said Sam sternly. He brushed one hand along the side of her face to push back her wayward hair. "We'll rest here a moment, let you recover, then go back to the trailer."

"Where is everyone?"

"Frankie and Garth are with Viktor, everyone else is searching for Veronica. Jack is determined to get her this time." Sam leaned closer and searched her face. "Your eyes are full violet. The strongest I've ever seen," he said.

Celestine blinked and tried to focus on Sam. He wavered in front of her for a moment, like a shimmering optical illusion. "I…" She swallowed against the dryness in her throat and tried again. "I think I need to go home," she whispered.

"Of course," said Sam, scrambling awkwardly to his feet. He gently gathered her into his arms, and cradled her against his chest.

Hannah stood next to them, glancing uneasily around at the now-empty trailer alley.

"Come with us," said Celestine softly to her. "Jack won't be able to see you for a while now. We're all a bit wiped out." She gave a half smile. "Thanks to you, we saved Viktor, and the Carnival."

Hannah shook her head. "Oh no. I didn't do anything. I'm not even one hundred percent sure what we just did. I just stood there while everyone else sorted it out."

"Well, however it worked, we're all very grateful you're here."

Sam started walking, and Celestine couldn't stop the small moan of pain that escaped her mouth.

"What is it? Did I hurt you?" Sam said, pausing.

Celestine shook her head. "Just get me home." Once she was there, she'd be able to handle anything. The pain radiating out from her shoulder wouldn't feel so bad. The headache that was forming inside her skull wouldn't hurt so much.

Sam strode swiftly through the alleyways and Celestine half closed her eyes, letting the motion soothe her battered body. He would take care of her. It would be fine. The agony would go away and she'd be able to curl up on her bed, with Artemis against her side, the cat's purrs vibrating along her body.

It was going to be fine.

Celestine kept repeating the words in her head, even though she didn't believe them. She felt like she was slipping away, leaving pieces of herself littered along the grassy alley.

Moments later, just as she was slipping gratefully into sleep, Sam stopped abruptly. His hands slipped in his hold of her, and Celestine cried out as a bolt of fire burned its way down her body. Her eyes were forced fully open, and she immediately understood what had happened.

Veronica stood in front of them, hands on her hips and a smile on her face, looking like the cat who'd got the cream. "If it isn't my doctor and his new girlfriend," she said in her most charming voice. "I've been looking for you." The words flowed over them like liquid honey. Celestine shook her head, trying to get rid of the pungent charm magic Veronica was coating them in.

Sam's grip tightened on Celestine, but it didn't matter anymore. The pain was secondary. Celestine's whole focus was on trying to remember if she'd seen this scenario in one of Sam's futures. Veronica had been wearing the same cream suit, her hair perfectly styled in the same manner. But had she seen it here? In this place with these people?

Was it one of the times Sam had died?

Her breath hitched. What if it was? There was nothing she could do. She was just a pathetic bundle in Sam's arms.

Through their link, she could feel Sam's desire for revenge flare up, a bright light in an otherwise calm landscape. In all of her future visions it had been his downfall; his unrelenting desire to see Veronica pay for what she'd done to him.

Celestine felt like she was breaking into a thousand pieces. She longed to step between them, to tell Sam he didn't need vengeance. That Veronica wasn't worth his life. But her body wouldn't move. She could barely hold her head up.

She couldn't do anything to protect Sam.

"What are you still doing here, Veronica?" said Sam. "Haven't you learned that you can't beat the Jolly Knight Carnival?"

"Can't beat them? I already have. They just don't know it yet." Veronica's eyes glinted with a hint of madness and she smiled slowly, like she was picturing their downfall in her mind's eye. "The only way for you to survive is to come with me now."

Celestine shivered. She felt every muscle in Sam's body tensed to strike. He was staring at Veronica like she was a mouse and he was a particularly hungry hawk.

Except Veronica was more like a snake than a mouse, and even if Sam was a hawk, she just had to bite him in the right place, and he would fall. "She's just playing with your emotions, Sam. That's what she's good at, remember?" she said, her voice croaky and low. "Don't let her get to you."

Sam glanced down at her, his expression unreadable. "She has no power over me anymore."

Veronica laughed. "Yes I do. I'll always have power over you. We're linked together forever—no matter that your new friends destroyed my block. I can still feel your emotions through our bond. I know what you're thinking before you think it."

Sam's whole body shuddered, and his hands clenched involuntarily against Celestine.

"It's not true," said Celestine urgently. "Our bond is stronger. We blocked her out, remember?"

"She's never going to stop. She'll keep coming after us."

"We're stronger than her, all of us together."

Veronica laughed again, a strange unnatural sound. "You're not stronger than me. I already have your defeat orchestrated. This is just a skirmish."

Sam took a step forward. "You've hurt too many people already. I won't let you hurt anyone else."

"These people you're with have hurt people too. They killed Marco. They stole Kitten from her mother." Veronica's voice softened and her words danced around Sam like they could seduce him just by being there. They probably could.

He shook his head. "You're twisting the truth."

Veronica held out her hand. "Come with me now, Sam. Together we could be more influential than you could ever imagine. Put the girl down, and come with me." Her persuasive tone slid over them, curling into their minds, making her words seem the only logical option.

Celestine's eyes fluttered closed as she tried to resist the pull of Veronica's magic. Part of her wanted to tell Sam to dump her on the grass and go with Veronica. For a moment, it made perfect sense.

But Sam gave a defiant shake of his head. "I'm not going anywhere. And neither are you." He took a breath, and yelled at the top of his lungs, "Help! She's over here!"

Celestine's eyes flicked open in surprise. Sam yelled again, and they heard answering calls from around the Carnival.

Veronica froze, her eyes darkening. "You're going to regret doing that," she said, her tone low and sharp, like a knife. "I'll make you watch as I kill your girlfriend and all your friends. And then I'll keep you around as my pet doctor, doing my bidding." Her words seemed to cut into their skin.

Sam let out his breath in a whoosh. The tension in his body faded. "Thank you for reminding me what you're really like," he said. "I'm not your whipping boy. I don't have to do your bidding. And I won't be manipulated by you."

Beside Sam, Hannah stepped forward. "Is this the woman who hurt Jack?" she asked.

Celestine blinked. She'd forgotten Hannah was even there.

Sam nodded. "This is the woman everyone in the Carnival is searching for right now."

Hannah pulled a small gun out of her handbag and aimed it squarely at Veronica's chest. "Then you better start talking, lady, and tell me why I shouldn't just shoot you now."

Sam glanced at Hannah in surprise. "Where did you get that?"

Hannah shrugged. "A girl's gotta protect herself."

Veronica held up her hands, palms showing. "Now, now, calm down. I don't know who you are, but I have no problem with you," she said, her voice returning to its previous smooth charm. "I think both of you had better look to the psychic. She's about to lose consciousness. If you're not careful, she'll die in your arms, Sam."

Sam's grip on Celestine tightened as he looked down at her, his expression panicked. Celestine smiled woozily up at him. As much as she hated to admit it, Veronica was right. She could feel herself getting weaker and weaker.

Everything started to blur, and time stood still around her. The rainbow lights from her pre-vision landscape closed in on her, and Celestine's heart thumped in a staccato beat. Was she about to have a vision? Whose would it be? Or was this what happened to fortune tellers when they were about to die?

For several seconds she wavered in that halfway land, dreading the next step, knowing she wasn't strong enough to survive the after effects.

But moments later she emerged back into the real world, Sam still clutching her to his chest, and Hannah watching over her with a concerned expression.

Celestine frowned, trying to understand what had just happened. Glancing to where Veronica had been standing, she inhaled a tiny breath. "She's gone," she whispered.

Hannah glanced back, and immediately swore. "How the hell did she get away?"

"She did something to us. It was like she put us on pause for a moment," said Celestine.

"She's a persuasion talent. She can get you to do almost anything without realizing you're doing it," said Sam softly.

"I'm sorry," whispered Celestine. Tears welled in her eyes.

"For what?"

"For being the reason Veronica got away."

Sam shook his head. "She didn't get away. I let her go. You're more important to me than some stupid vendetta." A glow of emotion pulsed down their bond, encasing Celestine in the love he was sending her way. He pushed energy down their bond too, and her head cleared a little.

Just then Frankie ran around the edge of the closest trailer. "Did you see her?" he said in a rush. "Which way did she go?"

"She was here. But she got away," said Hannah.

"Is that a *gun*?" he said, staring at the tiny handgun in Hannah's hand.

"What of it?" asked Hannah waspishly.

"Why do you have a gun?"

"None of your business," she snapped. "You're worse than my brother."

Frankie shook his head as if to clear it, then glanced at

Celestine and Sam and frowned. "You guys look terrible. What're you doing out here?"

Celestine felt hysterical laughter bubbling up in her chest, but it hurt too much to let it out.

At that moment, Joey ran around the edge of a camper and went barreling straight up to Frankie. "She got away. Davos had her holed up near the ticketing booths for a minute or two, but she got away."

"She didn't get to any of the children?"

Joey shook his head. "Didn't have a chance. Not with everyone looking for her."

Celestine let out a sigh. They'd stopped it. They'd changed the future she'd seen for them all.

She leaned back into Sam's arms. "Can you take me home now?" she said.

"Always," said Sam.

CHAPTER 47

Sam wrapped the bandage around Celestine's shoulder, carefully tying up and tucking the end section. "No moving," he said sternly. She was sitting in her small kitchen, the morning sun streaming in through the window.

"Yes, sir," replied Celestine with a silly smile.

He paused in midair. "That wasn't a demand, was it? One you can't disagree with?" he asked. It was less than a day after their run-in with Veronica, and they were still trying to figure out their new situation.

All he really knew was that he was enjoying being married to Celestine. He searched her gaze. He hoped she felt the same way.

Celestine put her head to one side. "Everything you say could potentially be an order. But I've realised that it's the intention behind it, the belief you have as you say the words."

"Meaning?"

"You never want me to just do what you say without agreeing to it. I feel that now. I know it. So even when you *are* telling me what to do, it's not an order that I can't talk to you about. It was never like that with my brothers. They'd been taught by my father that obedience was the only thing to ask for from me."

Sam sat down on the chair beside her. "I was Veronica's slave for all those years. I'd never ask anyone to be the same for me."

"I know that." Celestine lifted her hand to Sam's cheek, her soft palm rubbing the rough stubble.

He caught her hand in his, and turned his head so he could plant a kiss on her palm. "I want us to stay married, Celestine," he whispered.

"I do too," she said, tears in her eyes.

He leaned in and was about to kiss her, when a sharp knock sounded on the door. He ignored it and touched his lips to hers.

"I know you're in there, Sam. We have a problem." It was Garth, in full Giftmaster mode. "Alfie's dogs have escaped. We need all hands on deck to help him round them up."

Celestine gasped and put one hand over her mouth. "Oh no, I forgot," she said.

"Forgot what?" Sam said.

"I saw George, the great Dane, escaping from his kennel in one of my visions. It's too small for him. I meant to tell Alfie, but with everything that's been going on…" She put her hand on Sam's arm. "Tell Alfie what the problem is. He needs to get George a bigger kennel."

Garth banged on the door again. "Come on, Sam. No more time wasting with your new wife."

Sam sighed and leaned his forehead against Celestine's. "There's always something around here, huh?"

He reluctantly stood up. "Coming, Garth," he called through the door. He kept Celestine's hand in his for a moment longer, gazing down into her beautiful violet eyes.

"Promise me you'll talk to Alfie," she said.

He nodded. He was also going to have to talk to the Carnival leaders about the hacker he'd seen with Veronica and what she'd said just before she disappeared.

They needed to start making plans and checking all their possible weaknesses. There was a lot to do. This wasn't over by a long shot.

Celestine smiled. "As long as we have each other, we'll be fine."

"I love you," he whispered.

"I love you, too," she said.

Thanks for reading *The Shadow Prophecy*!

There are two more books to be written in the Dark Carnival series.

The next features Indigo, the shy librarian, and Baxter the banker who's about to foreclose on the Carnival. And then Frankie's story is the finale to the whole series...

But while those two books are being written, perhaps you'd like to keep reading another of my series...

Turn the page to read an excerpt from the first book in the Dragon Rising series, Hidden Dragon.

EXCERPT FROM HIDDEN DRAGON

Si's muscles flex as he swings his long fighting stick at me. He looks like an avenging angel; his short black hair is slicked back off his face, and his dark, almond-shaped eyes give nothing away. Mostly those same eyes are wreathed in smiles, lines crinkling around the edges, but in a fight, he's hard and unforgiving. To him there is nothing more than to win or lose, to live or die. Perhaps he's right. I know he's only trying to save me from my enemies.

I block his next attack with my own fighting stick then leap back out of range, taking a quick swipe to his side as I go. Si's expression doesn't change. I'm sure it hurt like hell—there wasn't enough time to pull up his supernatural defenses—but he's a pro at hiding his emotions.

Sweat's dripping off me, and my legs and arms feel like jelly. We've been at this for a couple hours now. Fight and retreat. Smash and return. I'm tempted to call time, but I know I have to fight on. If I give up, Si will make it ten times worse. He's big on lessons that will make me stronger.

Life doesn't just stop because you want it to. If this was a real fight, do you think your enemies would let you take a break?

Si shifts his fighting stick to the other side, his loose cotton trousers swishing as he moves gracefully into a different fighting stance and attacks again—this time slamming his stick toward my midsection. I block, then attack, kicking one leg high toward his face. He evades and steps back. "You're not concentrating, Mei. You're going to get yourself killed," he says, frowning. His voice is rough—some long-ago fight messed with his vocal chords. Probably defending me, for all I know.

But with his smooth olive skin and thick dark hair he could pass for any age between twenty-five and forty. It's his chameleon genes, I guess. He could be two hundred, for all I know.

A shiver runs along the spell web clinging to my skin, alerting me to another presence nearby; Jeff has stepped into the training ring alongside Si. The older man might have slowed down with age, but he's a dangerous opponent, and uses whatever tricks he can.

Like surprise, for example.

Luckily I have a secret weapon—my link to the spell web makes it impossible for anyone to sneak up on me at close quarters. I turn, pushing out a back kick, attempting to put Jeff off and give myself a few seconds to prepare for fighting the two of them at once.

Jeff avoids my kick and I feel the movement behind me as Si attacks again. Sidestepping, I manage to avoid a stick to the head. I strike out at Si with my stick, landing it against his side, even as I avoid another attack from him. I twist in midair, landing with a thump, and roll into a low fighting position.

Jeff can't quite keep up with my movements, and I turn fast behind Si to land a kick on Jeff's stomach. He grunts and moves backward. I take no satisfaction from scoring a point over Jeff. It's like hurting an old faithful dog—a Rottweiler with big teeth, and a nasty streak—but an old dog nonetheless.

Even worse, today he's wearing a lurid Hawaiian shirt instead of his usual dark shirt and tie. He's even got a bit of salt-and-pepper stubble on his face. He looks like a damn tourist instead of a wily SIG agent.

"You're scared of the new agent," says Jeff, his breath puffing as he tries to recover from my kick. "Maybe he'll be a stickler for the rules. Won't let you go off on your own like I do." He smirks at me, his bright blue eyes perceptive. That's how Jeff wins his fights these days—through mind-fucking his opponent. He's not fast or particularly fit anymore, he's just tough and smart. And it works.

Despite the fact I *know* it's an attempt to make my emotions take over and put me off, I feel anger and resentment rising up. Who the hell does he think he is? He doesn't know what I'm feeling. I take a deep breath and let it out, trying to release my animosity. I narrowly sidestep a punch from Jeff, only to have Si land a solid hit to my leg.

My resistance crumbles along with my leg. I stagger to one side, barely escaping another slam from Si's stick.

Who am I kidding? I don't want Jeff to go. He's the one who figured out how to keep me safe. He's been around a long time; he watched me grow up, which is more than my own father did. And maybe he's a little on target. What if the new guy *is* a total jerk? I try to imagine the replacement SIG agent. All I can picture is some starched-up dude in a suit.

And just like that, Jeff lands a punch to my side and I spin backward. I only just manage to stay on my feet.

"I heard he goes by the rules," Jeff taunts. "Talked to an old friend at the cadet academy. He's fresh out of training and won't want to ruin his chances of promotion."

The words make my hands clench tighter around my fighting stick. Another ripple goes through the spell web and

I finally use it in my defense. I reach out along the glowing grid and push a pulse of energy toward Si. He blinks and shakes his head, stepping back out of my range. I can't do the same to Jeff, because he's human, but I hit out at him with my stick—I'm too distracted to even get close.

Desperately, I try to find my focus. I know I won't get any points for taking on the two of them at once. Si barely counts Jeff as an opponent these days. The spell web ripples in warning, and Si's weapon slams into my side, knocking the breath out of my lungs with his precise positioning. Where Jeff is all brute strength and trickery, Si is precision and accuracy. I stumble backward.

Jeff takes the opportunity offered and kicks my legs out from under me. I land on my back; stars fill my vision, and for a millisecond, I wonder what I'm supposed to do. They've got me on the ground, two against one. Si and Jeff loom over me, both waiting for my next move. They're not stupid enough to think I'll stay down.

There's really no question what I'll do next.

Magic.

I seldom use it. Si says it's a crutch and has banned it in the ring. But desperate times...

And Jeff started it.

Water from the nearby fishpond slams into the two men towering over me before either of them knows what's happening. It knocks them both down, pushing them away so I can scramble to my feet. Seconds later, I use my stick to strike three precise hits to both Si and Jeff.

This time Si knows it's coming and has already pulled his protective chameleon scales over his skin, and probably doesn't feel it. Jeff rolls away with a grin, and I can see he's enjoying my response.

I strike again with my stick, directly at his smug expression.

But Jeff's been doing this too long to be caught by a cheeky sideswipe to the head and he ducks back out of range.

"I'm thinking I might not come back, like I planned. I might take a long cruise. Maybe meet someone," he says.

Even though I know it's a lie designed to knock me off balance, I still let his words affect me. I stumble and glance toward Jeff. He knows I'm strung out by his impending retirement, and he's using it against me.

Jeff just raises his eyebrows at me. "You better keep an eye on both opponents, Mei. You never know when the other will strike."

Again, a ripple along the spell web alerts me seconds before Si slams his stick into my left thigh. I crumble to the ground, but manage to turn it into a roll at the last minute, and come back to my feet, a little bit away from Si. I turn toward him, ready to take him down once and for all.

Behind me, Jeff speaks again. "I came out to let you know your father's coming tomorrow. He's going to do the debrief himself."

I drop my guard in surprise. My *father*? I haven't seen him since I was four years old. An emotion I can't name grabs hold of my heart. I turn to Jeff again. "What?"

An arm snakes around my neck from behind and pulls me into a lock position, slamming me into the ground and holding my face to the floor. I struggle, but can't break the hold. My concentration is shot; I can't access my magic. Even the spell web feels like it's smothering me. It tingles along my skin, making my magic short circuit.

I'm done.

"Enough," I mutter. "You win." They're cheating, not letting me fight Si properly. They've been doing more and more dirty fighting in the last year. I don't know why I'm surprised every time it happens.

"You can't give up like that," Si says. His voice is inches

from my ear. He speaks softly, with only the barest trace of an accent. "You'll die."

"It's not a fair fight. Jeff knows all the buttons to press. I won't be fighting someone who knows that much about me."

"You don't know that. You have to train for all eventualities. It's the only way to survive," Si replies, before letting me go.

"Is he really coming?" I uncurl from my prone position on the ground, but remain seated, my legs crossed.

Jeff hesitates, then nods. "He is. Said he wants to meet this new agent personally."

"He didn't do that when *you* started." I don't remember much about it, but I'm certain my father didn't come out twelve years ago when Jeff first came on the job.

"Maybe he didn't think you'd make it to twenty at that point," Si says. "There's less than two months to go now. There's more at stake."

I try not to let the words hurt. Si isn't trying to sting me, not like Jeff would have in the ring. He's just stating a fact.

What I am means more to my father than who I am. He's not coming to visit with his daughter; he's coming to protect an asset.

Want to keep reading? Check out **Hidden Dragon** at your favorite retailer!

Want to find out how the Carnival *really* started? Or learn more about where the wishes and curses came from?

Apply to join Trudi Jaye's Secret Society to get free access to the highly classified **Shadow Archives** to find out *more…*

You'll also get the top secret, highly hush-hush weekly Trudi Jaye Secret Society bulletin with inside information on characters, ongoing stories, and early notification about sales and new releases.

Head to the website to apply to join the secret society today! www.trudijayewrites.com/shadow-archives

Other Books by Trudi Jaye

Dragon Rising Series
Lost Dragon (Prequel Novella available via the Trudi Jaye Secret Society)
Hidden Dragon
Searching Dragon
Fighting Dragon
Cursed Dragon
Warrior Dragon (coming soon)

Demon Hunter in Hiding Series
Dreams & Demons (Prequel Novella available via the Trudi Jaye Secret Society)
Secrets & Demons
Agents & Demons
Magic & Demons
Dragons & Demons
Spells & Demons

Elemental Witch Series (with Tania Hutley)
The Trouble with Magic
The Problem with Witches
The Danger with Demons

Firecaller Series
Salt (Prequel Novella available via the Trudi Jaye Secret Society)
Subtle Knife (Prequel Novella available via the Trudi Jaye Secret Society)
Fire Mage
Royal Mage (due out soon)

Dark Carnival Series

The First Wish (Prequel Novella available via the Trudi Jaye Secret Society)

If Magic Were Wishes

The Gift

Magic for Lost Souls (available via the Trudi Jaye Secret Society)

High Flyer

Hidden Magic

The Shadow Prophecy

ABOUT THE AUTHOR

Hi! I'm Trudi Jaye, and I'm the author of this book. I live on a rural property in New Zealand, surrounded by horses (not mine!) with my lovely husband and cheeky tween (not quite a teenager, but thinks she's a teenager) daughter.

For a long time I was a magazine writer and editor, and wrote articles on everything from cruise ships and movie stars to chainsaws and architecture. Now I write novels full time.

I enjoy yoga, although I'm not very bendy, and karate, although I don't like the idea of hitting anyone.

www.trudijayewrites.com